AN UNCLEAR FUTURE

AN UNCLEAR FUTURE

UNPLANNED PRINCESS™ BOOK 7

MICHAEL ANDERLE

This book is a work of fiction. All of the characters, organizations, and events portrayed in this novel are either products of the author's imagination or are used fictitiously. Sometimes both.

Cover by Mihaela Voicu http://www.mihaelavoicu.com/

A Michael Anderle Production

LMBPN Publishing
PMB 196, 2540 South Maryland Pkwy
Las Vegas, NV 89109

Version 1.00, September 2021
ebook ISBN: 978-1-64971-965-2
Print ISBN: 978-1-64971-966-9

THE AN UNCLEAR FUTURE TEAM

Thanks to our JIT Readers

Veronica Stephan-Miller
Deb Mader
Zacc Pelter
Jeff Goode
Paul Westman
Dave Hicks
Dorothy Lloyd

Editor

SkyHunter Editing Team

CHAPTER ONE

The colorful banner that stretched across the back wall of the living room declared HAPPY BIRTHDAY, ZAENA. Bouncy pop music filled the room. Men and women munched on cake and sipped drinks. Everyone smiled and chatted happily.

Zaena hadn't gotten what she wanted, but it had been a good week, and the party pleased her. Her patrol had gone well the day before, and there was no reason to expect violence in her living room during her birthday party. It had taken her longer than expected to mentally readjust to living with Grace again after giving Saelli her apartment, but the advantages of the shift in living location were made clear that night despite the lack of one key party element.

She'd asked for a piñata. The whole idea of violently smashing open a fake animal to receive treats was the kind of delightfully strange custom only humans could have come up with. She almost wanted to slice one open with an air blade.

Grace suggested that the other guests to the party

would find it odd. It was a late-enough party that they decided to keep it an adult affair, despite the lack of anything more salacious than free alcohol.

"Perhaps beating a fake animal open is darker than would be appropriate," Zaena mused. "Even without children around."

"What's that, boss?" asked Tony from nearby. He held a glass of champagne. "Something about animals?"

Zaena herself eschewed alcohol, but Grace had supplied plenty of sparkling grape juice for her and the other teetotalers. The sheer amount of alcohol humans drank continued to surprise her, despite her time on the surface and the warnings of her tutors.

Grace, Karl, Tony, and a good chunk of the restaurant staff huddled and chatted. Karl had suggested keeping the guest list small. It cut down on the chance that Zaena might accidentally expose her elven nature. She always disguised her ears when she was outside her home, and the restaurant staff was comfortable with her unusual behavior, or at least they were willing to humor her since they believed she was a foreigner who represented a powerful group of investors that funded the White Ruby Corporation and the restaurant.

"It's nothing," Zaena replied to Tony. "I was thinking about American birthday rituals. They are interesting in many ways. Reading about something and experiencing it are different things."

"Things are different back home in Switzerland, huh?" Tony looked curious. "It isn't all *Midsommar,* is it?"

She hoped it wasn't. The gangland violence she'd been dealing with in America was trying, but there was a certain logic to it. She had no doubt strange cults existed in the pockets of humanity, but she now understood how much human entertainment exaggerated things.

It'd taken a while for her to adjust to that reality. Royal Elf stories were not as focused on entertaining lies.

"That's Sweden," Zaena corrected. "Not Switzerland, and I rather doubt the film is an accurate representation of rural Sweden."

Tony laughed. "I'm just messing with you. My cousin went to Sweden, and no one tried to sacrifice him the entire time he was there."

"Good, and yes, things being different? That's an accurate summary of my entire time in San Francisco. To be clear, I'm thoroughly enjoying my birthday."

Tony smiled. "I tried to get Grace to tell me how old you are, but she wouldn't budge. Come on. Give me a hint. I'm sure the mountain air back home did wonders for your skin since I can't figure it out. You look so young, but you come off so mature. There's being an old soul, but sometimes when you talk, you remind me of my great-grandma."

"I'm older than I look," Zaena said with a smile, "but I won't give you any more hints than that."

"Older than you look, huh? Hey, you're hotter…uh, or you're exactly as hot…" Tony gulped some champagne. "I think I'll go grab some cake before I embarrass myself more, boss."

Zaena laughed. She'd not thought much about her birthday until Grace brought it up. Elves didn't celebrate their birthdays. She wasn't sure why humans placed such emphasis on it. Perhaps having fewer years to live made each that much more precious and a reminder of their birth that much more glorious. Grace had insisted on knowing the date, and now here they were, celebrating the joyous mid-May occasion.

Zaena saw no problem with allowing the human birthday ritual. Fun didn't hurt anyone except piñatas. They had it coming anyway. They shouldn't be filled with delicious treats.

Grace finished her conversation with one of the servers from the restaurant and made her way toward Zaena in the corner. "Is it everything you hoped?" She held up a hand. "I acknowledge you wanted the piñata. I'll get you one some other time."

"Yes. It's lovely." Zaena smiled. "I'm glad you suggested it. I sometimes get so focused on the darker side of human culture I forget all the wonderful things you have besides reality TV."

"Reality TV belongs in the dark side of the human culture column," Grace suggested.

Zaena's brows lifted. "I understand that point of view, but I won't stop watching my shows."

Grace leaned closer. "Did you want more people here? I felt like Karl and I railroaded you a little on that, but he did have a point about keeping it small and easier to control."

"You and Karl are my closest human friends. It was most important that you're here." Zaena motioned at her huge security chief across the room, where he sat sipping a beer. "I'll admit I'm disappointed but not surprised Vokasin and Saelli didn't want to come. Lae'yul would never come to such an event."

"I wish Saelli would have come," Grace whispered. "I

know it's only been a couple of months, but she's still so awkward around humans. She's been traveling among humans for a lot longer than you."

"She's an unusual elf even by the standards of Ice Elves," Zaena noted. "I still don't know what to make of her. She means well."

Grace gave a curious look. "She's on your side. That's what's important."

Zaena let that hang in the air without a response. For all the accusations of egotism thrown at her, the revelation that she stood at the center of a prophecy continued to challenge her. It would be easier if she could dismiss it as nonsense.

"I still don't see why we couldn't have invited Agents Lyle and Waves," Zaena complained, wanting to discuss something other than the prophecy.

"You wanted to invite two government agents to your birthday?" Grace asked in an incredulous tone. "Wow. You sure know how to party."

"They might not be my friends, but offering them a fun encounter might have endeared me to them." Zaena shook a finger. "Think of it as a social manipulation tactic."

Grace snickered. "I think you can survive one night without the government spying on your birthday party."

One of the dishwashers, a college girl named Clover, approached with a bright smile. "Happy birthday, Zaena. Thanks for having us over."

"Thank you for coming."

Clover looked around. "Nice party. This is a great place, but I always figured you lived in some huge mansion in a gated community. This is so normal."

She wasn't far from the truth. The palace back home *was* gated.

"I don't need luxurious accommodations." Zaena inclined her head at Grace. "I have her to thank for my party. I'm unfamiliar with American customs. I think it would have been embarrassing if I'd set up my party."

"Oh?" Clover tilted her head and stared at Zaena with open interest. "What kind of thing did you do back home?"

"Birthday parties weren't much of a thing, but in general, celebrations were grander and less entertaining. A lot of recitations of our ancestral lineage and their deeds."

"Your deeds? I thought you grew up in a small village." Clover looked confused. "Is this one of those, 'Oh, my great-great-great-great-great-grandpa saved the King of France in some medieval battle' kind of thing?"

Zaena hadn't realized she'd let her cover slip. She forced a smile. Her time among humans had taught her the value of feigned sarcasm.

"Yes, that sort of thing," she commented. "Helping kings and queens and princes and princesses." She laughed. "The occasional stopping of a magical threat or rebellion. Oh, and the hunting of the stray magical beasts who threatened innocents, back when such things still roamed the Earth openly."

Clover laughed. "You're such a riot. It must be all that neutrality that makes you funnier." She winked and leaned closer. "Okay, I have to ask because we've got a pool going. How old are you?"

"A pool?" Zaena stopped herself from turning over to Grace to ask the meaning. She'd found that her increasing experience in America often let her figure things from context if she waited long enough.

Clover rubbed her hands together. "Yep. It's a decent-sized pool. Everybody's in, including Tony. Whoever guesses right will earn a decent chunk of change."

Zaena smirked, understanding dawning. "I see. That's why he asked. I wonder if he's placed his bet yet. You can tell everyone I'm 251."

"251?" Clover rolled her eyes. "Come on, be serious. We all want to win that money."

"I'm completely serious," Zaena offered with stone-faced sincerity.

"I hope I look that good at 251."

Zaena's stomach tightened, but she wanted to experiment more with sarcasm. She kept her smile on her face. "I can only tell the truth, nothing more."

"Whatever," Clover replied. "Be that way. We'll find out later, or we all get our money back." She waved. "I need more champagne. Drinking good champagne is awesome when somebody else is paying for it."

Grace glanced between Zaena and the departing woman. "Look at you. I never thought I'd see the day when you could pull that off so naturally."

"You don't think I made a mistake?" Zaena asked. She brought up her hand and killed the background noise with a sound curtain. "You don't think I've revealed who I am?"

Grace laughed. "No one's going to believe you're 251. Even if she somehow believed you weren't joking, she would never convince herself you're an elf."

"What would she think?"

"I don't know." Grace shrugged. "That you're a vampire?"

"I go around during the day." She frowned. Calling her a vampire was as bad as calling her a Night Elf.

"You could be the sparkly kind that lives in rural Washington?" Grace chuckled and patted her on the shoulder. "The point is nobody's going to get near the truth. I think your secret is safe unless you use magic right in front of them. Even then, you've seen what happens. People rationalize things away. Everyone still believes the Crimson Wind is a woman using technology, not magic."

There was some relief in that. Humans did a good job of ignoring the obvious. But there was another worry.

Zaena watched as Karl polished off another beer. "He doesn't seem to be enjoying himself."

"Karl's not a social guy," Grace reminded her. "It's good to drag him out of that dungeon he calls his apartment. He needs to remember there's another side to life other than planning for bad guys and head-butting mobsters. I wish I knew someone who was his type to hook him up with, but the last thing he'd want is us messing with his love life."

"He's been doing much better," Zaena noted. "He's reaching out to old friends."

"I get that, but he's a lot like me. It's easy to get overwhelmed by all this elf and gangster stuff." Grace motioned around the room. "When we do, we forget the simple parts of life. It's kind of like being a workaholic. No, it's not 'kind of like.' It's *exactly* like being a workaholic."

"Judge Jorge suggests a balance of work and personal life," Zaena noted. "Though I'm far more accustomed to duty above all."

Across the room, Karl rose from his seat. He set his bottle on the table and moved through the crowd. People parted instinctively as the huge man headed across the room.

Karl stopped for a moment and looked over his shoulder with a frown. "You're blocking out the sound?"

"I've long since learned that it's easy to do when there's a lot of other noise around. No one expects to hear a conversation from across a crowded room."

"You should lighten up," Grace suggested to Karl. "It's a party."

"I'm not a party guy," Karl stated. "You did a good job."

"Thanks."

Karl searched the room. "You still having your little after-party with Saelli and Vokasin tomorrow, Zaena?"

"They've both agreed to it. Vokasin might claim that only whims motivate him, but I can't recall a time he didn't come to an agreed-upon meeting. He's far more reliable than I ever would have expected."

"Did you need to schedule it right after your birthday?" Grace asked.

"Why not?" Zaena replied. "Saelli will need to commune soon, so it is better to do it now than wait and waste her magic. Vokasin was planning to commune soon also." She sighed. "I didn't intend to demean your efforts or give any indication I don't value them. I appreciate your party, even if I would have preferred more penguins and piñatas."

She stopped herself from suggesting penguin piñatas. Whacking open a fake penguin was unacceptable.

"Why not?" Grace asked, "You've made so much progress so quickly." She wore an exasperated look. "I get how important your mission is, but you're well ahead of schedule, and you're still doing weekly patrols. Sometimes more than once a week. And meeting with that reporter, too, and that's when you're not letting the government point you at their problems." She sighed. "Forget it. I just don't think it hurts to relax now and again without any immediate plans to do something else. Birthdays are a convenient excuse for that."

Zaena surveyed the room. Her sound curtain blocked the joyful chatter and music, but the happiness on the faces of the gathered humans was visible.

A heaviness settled in her chest. Vokasin, Saelli, and Lae'yul weren't her people, even though they were allies. Karl and Grace weren't even her species.

She missed her family. Her father was overly cautious, but she understood his fear of the Creeping Azure. Her family deserved to be able to leave the enclave and experience the glories of the ocean and the true sun for themselves.

"You okay, Zaena?" Grace asked.

"Thank you for a lovely party and your continuing concern," Zaena replied with a soft smile, "but if I've accomplished as much as I have with the level of effort I'm putting in, that only motivates me to try harder."

Karl grunted. "You got yourself an Ice Elf, but it's not like the government isn't looking hard for elves. There's not much to worry about until you run into a Mountain Elf."

"No. That's why I want to have my after-party, as you called it, with the others. The more prepared we are for the future, the less trouble we'll have. The experience with

Amanda Morton showed that we need to be as independent as possible."

"I agree," Karl replied. He noticed Tony approaching. "Better drop the spell. That guy's too sharp for his own good."

Zaena released the magic. Music and conversation rushed back.

"Don't worry, Grace," Zaena offered. "I'll enjoy my party, but tomorrow it's back to work."

CHAPTER TWO

Clad in her armor, Zaena marched through the forest clearing. She held her sword up as she looked into the dense clouds above for the coming enemy. Knowing it was a training exercise didn't quell her excitement. She enjoyed testing her skills in battle.

"Are your headsets comfortable?" she asked.

Vokasin walked beside her, wearing his cloak and elven form. "This human toy has its uses, but when I change form, it won't change with me."

"There's little we can do about that," Zaena replied. "We don't have the necessary expertise to create such an artifact."

"I haven't needed one for centuries. I don't think I need one now."

Saelli trailed behind them in a tank top, shorts, and boots. Puffs of breath emerged from her mouth despite the modest temperature, proof of the cooling envelope she'd wrapped around herself. She wanted to practice maintaining cooling spells while fighting.

The modest mid-May temperatures were perfect for Zaena but uncomfortable for the Ice Elf. Her homeland was a frigid enclave below a cold country. It was hotter in late spring in San Francisco than at the height of summer in Iceland.

The irony of Zaena being from a forested kingdom beneath Antarctica wasn't lost on her. The Ice Elves tried to make things easier for themselves by finding the perfect environment. Arguably, the myths concerning hidden creatures living in Iceland proved that the Royal Elves' strategy might have been superior. There hadn't been humans to hide from in Antarctica for most of human history.

Zaena kept watching the clouds for the enemy while she pondered Saelli and the absent Lae'yul. Knowing other elves had reformed their bodies over the eons was different when she was dealing with them directly.

The Ice Elves and the Sea Elves had gone through their changes long before Zaena was born. She'd been taught how they'd altered their fundamental essences to the point where they might be considered a different species, but in the back of her mind, she continued to think of them as elves who happened to live somewhere else. It had taken her a while to understand what a challenge it was for them to survive in a different environment than the arboreal paradises she preferred.

Zaena glanced at Vokasin. He'd not complained much about San Francisco being too cold, but she'd not thought to ask until recently when he'd admitted he occasionally used warmth spells. In general, he experienced less discomfort than Saelli. His shapeshifting ability also granted him better temperature tolerance in both directions, a useful trait for an elf who traveled the world outside his enclave.

To her chagrin, Zaena realized the Royal Elves' bodies remained closest to those of the Mountain Elves. Both types of elves had preferred environments for communing but lacked the extreme differences of the other tribes. That made her encounter with Mark Wong less one of destiny than simple statistics.

"Even when we cure the Creeping Azure, there will be limited mixing," Zaena declared in a glum tone.

Saelli looked her way. "What are you talking about, Princess?"

"There will be no grand city for all tribes," Zaena explained. "It'd forever be uncomfortable for at least some of its inhabitants."

Vokasin scoffed. "Did you think that was ever happening, Fourth Born? I'm aiding you to give my people more freedom, not to rejoin the tribes into an elven kingdom."

"It wasn't about rejoining the tribes." Zaena sighed. "I didn't think that would happen, although it's a lovely thought. The weight of the centuries grows more obvious the longer my mission continues. Sometimes it sets me to thinking in strange new ways. I never thought like this when I lived in the kingdom."

"This entire thing is weird if you think about it," Karl answered over her headset. "One woman is supposed to save an entire race?"

She'd almost forgotten he and Grace were involved in the exercise.

"No, not one woman." Zaena smiled at Vokasin and

Saelli. "I've only gotten this far because of my allies, human and elf. That will be my metaphorical city of all tribes."

Vokasin eyed her, then the corners of his mouth curled up in a borderline smirk. "Is that why you had Selene D'Arcy's people supply machines for us to fight? You wish to bind the human rulers closer to you?"

"It was technically my idea," chimed in Karl. "I figure if you're going to have to fight more than magic statues, it might help, and I don't think human Special Forces would enjoy getting tossed around. Zaena shouldn't have to spend all her money on gadgets when the government has her running around stopping terrorists."

Vokasin didn't look convinced. "Don't let yourself become dependent on any human organization, Fourth Born. That should be the lesson of the battle in Iceland. They might help you one day only and betray you the next."

"I haven't forgotten," Zaena replied, "but engaging with Miss D'Arcy and her people more directly will help us keep better track of their intentions and avoid more surprises."

Grace cleared her throat over the line. "I don't mean to be the paranoid one, but taking out one billionaire isn't the same thing as taking out the government of the most powerful country on the planet."

"We don't need to take out the government," Karl insisted, "and Selene's got this information locked down pretty tightly. But yeah, it'd be nice if we didn't have to fight a bunch of Marines who are convinced Zaena's a terrorist queen."

Vokasin motioned around. "Do you think they're

watching, beyond whatever they might be doing through toys?"

"They probably are," Karl noted. "Is that a problem? They're one of the reasons you guys can go all out without us worrying about reporters sniffing around."

"I don't fear your government," Vokasin replied. "I want to know what they know about us, but I don't worry much. All they can do is kill me."

"Most people think that's pretty bad, if not the worst. What do you think the worst thing they could do to you is?"

"Kill my people while I survive," Vokasin explained. "It doesn't matter. My people's freedom is protected by the secure enclave. Once the Creeping Azure is cured, it'll be impossible to eradicate the Desert Elves. Our freedom will live on."

"What about you, Saelli?" Zaena asked. "Do you worry about me growing closer to the American government? It's as Karl says. For now, beyond helpful equipment and information, they are doing a lot to keep things contained. People are aware of the Crimson Wind, but not that I'm an elf."

Saelli lifted her hand. Frost coated her clothes. "Their aid was invaluable before. I chose to follow you to your destiny. It's too late for me to climb out of the raging river."

Zaena smiled despite her unease. She couldn't dismiss the prophecy out of hand. The changes in other tribes proved how far elves had drifted from what they once were.

Vokasin said something, but Zaena wasn't listening. She was too focused on Saelli's use of the word "destiny." She wanted to believe she would succeed and that the prophecy pointed to her victory after challenges, but one line haunted her.

She will choose the fate of elves for good or for ill.

Zaena took a deep breath. A positive attitude didn't guarantee success, and that chilling line suggested that failure remained a possibility.

It didn't matter. All she needed to do was continue to recruit trustworthy allies and minimize her mistakes. The prophecy had swayed Saelli to her side, but it didn't change her plans.

The other lines suggesting horrors were unpleasant, but they also didn't change anything. Monsters didn't frighten Zaena. She knew she'd have to face them in the Night Elf enclave. A fanciful prediction about that wouldn't make the monsters stronger.

"Is there a problem, Princess?" Saelli asked.

Zaena jerked out of her reverie. "What? No. I was lost in thought."

"A poor choice in battle," Vokasin suggested.

"We're not in battle yet," Zaena noted. "Grace, Karl, are you close?"

"Yeah," Karl replied. "I've never controlled a fleet of drones carrying Taser darts before." He chuckled. "The government does have all the toys, but I can see where terrorists could light these up pretty easily."

Vokasin gestured at the sky. "I want it clear that I don't intend to practice restraint. I don't care about the survival of the flying toys."

Zaena lifted her sword in front of her face. "I have no expectation that the drones will survive the encounter. I doubt Miss D'Arcy's prepared to give us this many very often, but I thought it would be a good change of pace for you, and though this is only the second time Saelli has participated in sparring, it's also useful for her." She lowered her sword, enjoying the glint of light on the blade. "You could come with me on patrols. We could use masks to disguise your faces."

"I don't think that's a great idea," Karl offered. "The government probably doesn't want an entire super-team running around stirring things up. You just got done pointing out that they're keeping things quiet. I know we're running our own parallel media campaign, but you start doing too much stuff in public, and things might get messy, fast."

"True enough, though it would be wonderful PR for later."

Zaena wasn't sure how important secrecy was anymore. Now that she'd been among humans for almost a year, she was far less concerned about their ability to accept the existence of elves. Even the human villains she'd battled hadn't seemed inherently disturbed by the existence of her kind.

The problem as she saw it wasn't that people would become concerned about elves, but the opposite. She couldn't complete her mission if too many people showed up and became elf groupies or asked to be taken to the enclaves. She also anticipated far too many foolish questions about baking cookies in trees.

"I have no desire to spend my time stopping humans from preying on other humans," Vokasin replied. "Human violence is a problem for humans to solve."

"You helped me during the fire," Zaena pointed out. "A fire in a human building."

She'd come to question the truth of much of what Vokasin said. For all his declarations about his obsession with freedom over all other things, he could easily live a life of total freedom that didn't involve helping her or his tribe.

"Yes, I helped you," Vokasin clarified, "but that wasn't a matter of humans preying on humans. Helping a creature not die pitifully doesn't go against freedom."

Saelli's brows knitted. "I'd be happy to aid you if you thought it'd be helpful, Princess, but I can't fly. Your patrols go all over the Bay Area. The methods I have for traveling quickly might stand out in a way you don't want."

Karl laughed. "From what you told me about your little merc adventure in Iceland, I don't think any of you need much training in fighting humans."

"The American military forces helped us," Zaena recalled. "It would be inappropriate to ignore their contributions."

"Sure, but you weren't exactly in trouble when they showed up. A little exercise now and again is a good thing, but your team is tough. Lae'yul gave you a run for your money when you first met. Once you get five or six of you together, you'll be pretty damned deadly."

"I have tried to get her to train more with us." Zaena glanced back and forth. "Though I can understand how fighting in a forest wouldn't appeal to her nature."

A squadron of small dark shapes broke through the clouds in the distance. The Mountain Elves might have their stone soldiers and the Night Elves their monsters, but humans had mastered summoning and controlling minions without magic. Zaena would never stop being impressed by it.

"You ready?" Karl asked. "I'm not a hotshot DIA drone pilot, and I barely understood half the stuff the tech showed us with all these fancy formation options, but I'm going to go to town on you guys. How about you, Grace?"

"I'm ready," she replied. "I can't say I ever imagined trying to take down a bunch of elves with Taser drones."

"Every day is a new adventure!" Zaena shouted. She brought her sword back. "Now, let's prepare for combat."

Vokasin frowned at the closing drones. They were nothing more than black shapes at this distance, and they broke into two groups to circle the elves.

"This will be too easy," he insisted.

"What would you prefer?" Zaena asked.

Vokasin pointed into the air. "Join the drones, Fourth Born. The priestess and I will take you on, along with the human toys. That is a more worthwhile exercise." He looked at Saelli. "Don't use the diamond. In a real battle, you must do what is necessary to win, but the last time we sparred, you spent most of your time in your shell and not fighting. You were more impressive in Iceland without relying solely on the diamond. I'd like to see that elf who can both attack and defend again."

"As you wish," Saelli replied, bowing her head.

"You're fine with the change?" Zaena asked, frowning. She couldn't deny Vokasin's evaluation. Saelli had been far more timid in battles outside of her homeland.

"I'm happy with whatever you decide, Princess," Saelli noted. "I understand we need to be prepared for all manner of threats. I admit it's hard for me to get used to this climate, but that will come with time."

"We should move forward with this." Zaena lifted into the air and moved backward. "Let's minimize the damage to the forest."

"I'll do my best."

Vokasin laughed. "Selene D'Arcy is making sure no one sees this, right?"

"That doesn't mean you get to burn half the forest," Zaena insisted.

"Half?" Vokasin stepped back with a grin. "I'll make sure not to burn half."

Zaena sighed and continued flying up. "I can't easily adjust frequencies with my armor on. I didn't think about that when I agreed to the change."

"It's fine." Vokasin nodded to Saelli. "Remove the headset. Let Zaena bring an army against us, and we won't rely on the human devices."

Saelli lifted her arm. Clumps of earth and rock ripped from the ground and circled her. "I'll do my best." She pulled off the headset and tossed it to the ground.

Vokasin did the same before shouting, "Take us down, Princess. Show us your Tarilan might!"

CHAPTER THREE

Karl snickered over the radio. "We're about to waste a lot of taxpayers' money."

"The more we practice," Zaena began, "the more ready we'll be for anything. I've had to face gangsters, UFOs, and werewolves since beginning my quest. A dragon wouldn't be surprising. I'm sure Judge Jorge would say prepare for the unexpected, and you'll never be surprised."

"You don't intend to go full-out," Grace noted. "You're the one who said you didn't want to burn half the forest."

"This is sparring, not a battle to the death." Zaena stopped rising. Vokasin and Saelli spread out beneath her, their features barely recognizable from her altitude. "I think given the change in environment and teams, different tactics are in order."

"What do you have in mind?" Karl asked.

"I'll fly in and distract them with rapid fire," Zaena explained. "Once their attention is focused on me, you can come in with the drones and attack."

"Roger that," Karl and Grace replied in unison.

Zaena circled the elves below. She hoped Vokasin would waste magic trying to hit her with fireballs. He remained on the ground in his normal humanoid form, which meant he wasn't worried. Dealing with a battle-trained elf was frustrating.

She accelerated and adopted a twisting figure-eight flight pattern above them. There was no reason to make things easy for her elven allies.

Magic pulsed from below. Rocks shot into the sky and exploded into a cloud of sharp chunks. Their fragments bounced off Zaena's armor. Another nearby rock shattered. The impacts stung and left scratches.

"Drone status?" Zaena asked. "Saelli is filling my flight path with rock shrapnel. It won't get through my armor, but I don't think a drone could survive it."

"We're staying away until you give us the call," Karl noted. "All drone feeds are green for me."

"Same here," Grace reported. "Uh, over? Do I need to say that?"

"I can recognize your voice," Zaena noted. "Should I say over?"

"You're way easier to recognize over the radio than either of us," Karl replied. "Just talk normally. No reason to change things up now."

Saelli's anti-aircraft barrage continued. Dirt continued to fill the air, followed by shrapnel and a hard rain of rocks.

Zaena twisted and dove toward her tormentor. Vokasin had been right earlier. Battles couldn't be won on pure defense. Her plan required an active attack.

Her spiraling path threw off Saelli's aim. The scratches

and stinging decreased.

Zaena had dropped halfway to the ground when Vokasin joined his comrade. Now shrapnel and fiery explosions filled the air. She jerked back and forth, spinning to dodge and avoid direct hits. Even if she could survive such an attack, one lesson she'd learned was that she relied too much on overwhelming power.

That had worked out when she'd dealt with human criminals, but battles in an enclave against monsters might need a more careful technique.

The Mojave incident had provided further proof. She needed practice fighting without using up huge portions of her power right away.

"Come on," Karl encouraged. "From what I can tell, you aren't taking any shots."

"True. That ends now."

Zaena pointed her sword in front of her and fired an air blade at Saelli. One of the Ice Elf's floating dirt shields took the blow and was blasted into a cloud of blinding dust. Saelli stumbled back and flung away the dirt, which gave Zaena the opening she needed to fire a couple more air blades to destroy Saelli's defenses and close the distance.

Zaena's aggressive charge sent her to the forest floor. She was feeling smug about her strategy until Saelli launched the cloud of dust toward Zaena, coating her helmet and blinding her.

She shot up on instinct. A fireball exploded against her leg. She hissed in pain but kept flying up. It was better to take a hit or two in the air than slam into the ground.

A crash wouldn't injure her, but she'd be a sitting target.

Saelli and Vokasin would pound her and trap her. Escape would cost her.

With that fate avoided but still blind, Zaena swept her sword in front of her. An air gust wiped away the dirt in time for a fireball to strike her in the chest and a decent-sized boulder to blow apart in front of her.

The combined blasts knocked Zaena backward. She dropped toward the ground, dazed, with gouges all over her armor. Another boulder flew toward her.

Zaena spun in the air and conjured an air gust that sent her screaming toward the ground. She righted herself at the last moment, crashing through a couple of low-hanging branches before shooting air blades toward Saelli.

Saelli hadn't bothered with her preferred element of water, but Zaena understood. There weren't as many easy sources of water here, and concentrating humidity into usable water wasn't as effective as utilizing the rocks and dirt that were all around them. It was the same reason Zaena tended to rely on her air magic more than her water magic.

It was also obvious that unlike Zaena's balanced skill with air and water magic, Saelli was better at using water magic than earth magic in battle. Given her living conditions in the enclave, that wasn't shocking.

Saelli had been hesitant and slow in their last sparring session. Despite having control over two magical elements, she was far too dependent on large masses of ice being around and had never anticipated having to wander far from her enclave.

Zaena didn't mind. Training would help with that. Every weakness could be fixed with time and effort.

She brought her feet down and hit the ground, transitioning into a sprint. Freeing up concentration and lowering magic usage were necessary for her next tactic. She flung her sword back and forth to produce a near-constant stream of air blades targeted at the other elves.

Vokasin grunted as a blade tore into his chest. Saelli gave up on her moving defense and brought up a thick dirt wall to protect her. The blades crashed into the wall and left deep cuts. Dirt and small pebbles shot out.

Zaena charged Vokasin. She'd sparred with him enough to understand he knew his limits. She launched into the air and gripped her blade tightly.

Vokasin shifted into his dinosaur form to meet her and roared. Flames filled his mouth, and a bright fireball blasted at her.

Zaena spun to dodge the attack, and Vokasin's armored and clawed arm raked her side. The claws dug deep into the armor, and the sheer force of the blow sent her flying in a different direction.

"Damn, Dino Boy," muttered Karl over the line.

The drone swarm circled closer. Their plan had worked. With all the attention on Zaena, the skies were free of magical anti-aircraft activity.

Saelli rolled out from behind her wall and thrust her hands forward. Rapid-fire pebbles pelted the injured Zaena as the Ice Elf returned to cover.

She landed in a roll and hopped back up to her feet. Vokasin was already charging. She pointed her sword in his direction and concentrated on a more powerful air blade. At the last second, she jerked the blade to the side to release the spell.

The magic shot off and sliced through a tree, and the collapsing trunk nailed the charging dinosaur. He roared in defiance.

Saelli ran from behind her dirt wall again, and a large rock smashed into Zaena and sent her into the brush.

A group of three drones closed on Saelli. One fired its wired dart, but Saelli knocked it out of the way with a rock. She ignored the first drone to blast small rocks at them. There was no explosion of shrapnel, only rocks accelerated to high speeds by earth magic.

The first rock ripped into the center of its target. The drone careened to the side. The second rock knocked off a propeller from the second, which collided with the third. Both drones smashed into the ground and produced a surprisingly large cloud of debris.

Vokasin growled and managed to push off the tree pinning him. He swayed.

Black drones filled the sky. They broke into small groups and dove toward Vokasin and Saelli.

The elves tore their attention away from Zaena and sent exploding rocks and fireballs upward. Drone after drone was blown apart or crashed.

Her chest and abdomen throbbing, Zaena flung herself forward with a loud gust that echoed amongst the nearby trees. She zoomed toward Saelli and ended her approach with a spinning kick to the other elf's chest.

Saelli flew back and slammed into a tree, gasping. Zaena jumped on her, pinned her with her knee, and put her blade to the Ice Elf's exposed throat. Saelli sucked in air.

Vokasin ran toward the pair. Drones swept low and

fired their darts, but they bounced off his thick hide. That proved the drones would have never been anything more than expensive options for target practice.

Zaena jumped back and placed her sword on her hip. She offered a hand to Saelli. "Are you okay?"

Saelli managed to sit up and took deep breaths. She averted her gaze. "I apologize for my performance, Princess. In a real battle, I would have been killed."

Vokasin slowed. His emotions were impossible to read in his reptilian eyes. The surviving drones retracted their darts and increased altitude.

"We done already?" Karl asked, sounding disappointed. "I was just getting the hang of these things."

Zaena sighed. She glanced at her side and saw blood leaking out. "We never set down victory conditions. I don't wish to brawl until we're all seriously injured."

Vokasin reverted to his elf form and smirked. "A tie, then? You could have killed one of my team, and we destroyed much of yours."

Saelli stood. "I'm ashamed. My performance was even worse than last time."

"There's no reason to feel that way," Zaena insisted. "I've seen you fight humans carrying guns and grenades and do well. You just need more training in this unfamiliar environment."

"I can't be useless just because there's no snow and ice." Saelli curled her hands into her fists. "I won't be able to help you. And Vokasin was correct; I can't always depend on the Diamond of Protection, and if we have to take on an enemy away from the nexus, I won't have creations to help me."

"You've done a lot of impressive things at the White Ruby Building," Zaena replied, placing her hand on Saelli's shoulder. "We all have our specialties and styles. With more time together, we'll learn to operate better as a unit."

Vokasin inclined his head toward the retreating drones. "You did destroy a lot of those toys. These only have stun darts, but if they had guns or something bigger, your air-burst attacks would have been crucial in letting Zaena and me attack more aggressively."

Zaena retracted her helmet. "It's interesting to explore the limits of the technology. Karl and I want to avoid having too much human security, and I've been curious how well we can make up for it with this kind of technology. I see it has limits, especially when it's controlled by a small number of people who are inexperienced in its use."

"Hey, I heard that," Karl replied.

Grace laughed. "She's not wrong. I never studied mass tactical experimental drone control in college. Did they teach you that at the police academy?"

"Must have been sick that day."

"I'm not blaming you," Zaena noted, "and I'm also no longer worried. We have Saelli and me either near or close to the nexus at all times and a third elf who's there often enough." She smiled at Vokasin. "We continue to shore up our defenses, and now that we have access to the nexus, it's only a matter of convincing the Sea Elves to loan us one more of their brethren for the attuning ritual. Once that is in place, we'll be able to secure the nexus, and Saelli can start producing a small army for us. The nexus will be safe."

"The sparring today?" Vokasin asked with eagerness in

his voice. "Will that continue? We can set down more rules, and we don't need to brutally injure each other, but Karl is right. It's only been minutes of battle."

Saelli gave a firm nod. "I insist we continue, Princess. The only way I'll become better at fighting here is by practicing."

Zaena watched her for a moment. Pushing past one's limits was important, but it'd become clear that not everyone had the same level of warrior training Zaena had received.

"Let's take a moment to catch our breath and try again." Zaena pointed her sword at the retreating drones. "How about this isn't over until we've gone through them all?"

Vokasin shifted back into his dinosaur form. "Good," he growled. "I need more entertainment."

CHAPTER FOUR

Zaena stared at the crimson sphere floating in the heart of the massive chamber. A stone cage surrounded it. Holes in the cage left the sphere visible, but they were too small for anything more than a finger to poke through.

The sparks coming off the sphere were almost hypnotic, combined with the massive amount of power emanating from the heart of the nexus. Even though the thought disgusted her, she understood how Mark Wong had become intoxicated with this power.

"You've done an excellent job, Saelli," Zaena declared, motioning around the stone chamber at tunnels leading in every direction, "and in only two months with no aid."

Saelli had created ground-level and higher exits, easily accessible with the help of magic. Rather than a simple cavern connected to the basement by a tunnel, she had carved an elaborate multi-level mazelike warren with its tunnels and dead ends marked with special symbols only understandable to Team Princess.

Key points of the tunnels and the main nexus chamber

were protected by metal plates. It wouldn't stop a powerful user of earth magic from trying a direct approach, but it would slow them down. Human invaders wouldn't have a chance. It was more than sufficient to stop a serious disruption of the nexus.

Vokasin frowned at a bare patch of wall. "You're sure about that? About him?"

Zaena walked over to the wall and motioned to Saelli. The Ice Elf raised her hands. A slab of stone slid open to reveal a sealed stone coffin.

"What would you have me do with Mark Wong's remains?" Zaena asked, staring at the coffin. "After everything that happened with Amanda Morton, I don't feel comfortable turning over elven bodies to anyone other than elves."

Vokasin raised an eyebrow. "Even Selene D'Arcy?"

"She has us helping her," Zaena replied. "She doesn't need more samples to develop anti-elven defenses, and they don't know much, considering they were depending on an outside source for their pills, if not Mark Wong."

"What if she demands it?"

Zaena scoffed. "I will not be bullied into anything of the sort. My relationship with the American government must be equitable, or all my diplomatic efforts are for nothing. The only thing she's suggested that I'm reluctant about but could be convinced of is the necessity for direct cross-training with American Special Forces."

Vokasin agreed. "Their help in Iceland was appreciated, if unnecessary."

"I've not yet made up my mind about that," Zaena noted. "I don't want to tighten our relationship with the government until we've fully attuned the nexus." She waved at Saelli. "Her passive defense efforts are excellent, but they're only a stopgap until we have the power of the nexus. Then she'll be our general of stone soldiers. Having several elves and an army defending it will make this place impregnable."

Saelli looked uncertain. "You're placing a lot of faith in me, Princess."

"Because I know you can do it."

"What did she have in mind?" Vokasin asked. "The human woman? Just training, or does she want to send us against the enemies of this land?"

"It's more complicated than that. From what she told me at our last meeting, the US government desires a rapid-response force composed of both human and elven assets to deal with hostile magical incidents. They want us to form the core of that team."

Vokasin snorted. "I don't like them trying to put us on a leash. Don't be fooled, Fourth Born. That's what this is—a way of watching and controlling us."

"Perhaps, but I can't claim it's a terrible idea," Zaena countered. "We have great power, but we don't have access to fast airplanes and other such vehicles. If Iceland proves anything beyond the potential existence of prophecy, it proves that we can no longer rely on everyone coming to San Francisco, even with my bold public displays. It also proves there are elves so taken by madness that they'd risk anything, including the Creeping Azure, for their goals."

"I'm not averse to training with humans," Vokasin replied, "but I refuse to take orders from them, no matter what position they have in their government."

Zaena chuckled. "You're a Desert Elf. You don't even take orders from an elven princess. Why would you listen to an American official?" She smiled at Saelli. "How about you?"

"I intend to follow your lead," Saelli replied, her eyes downcast.

Zaena wasn't surprised by the response since she'd heard it countless times since she'd brought the apprentice priestess back from Iceland. It was convenient, though she would have preferred a choice less dependent on something as difficult to pin down as prophecy.

"For now, I've demurred," Zaena explained, "and Miss D'Arcy has given little indication of taking offense at that."

"Keep in mind why she's helping you," Vokasin suggested with a shrug. "On some level as a threat, she sees friendly elves as a defense against that threat. She's helping us for the moment, but that doesn't mean she'll not betray us if she doesn't think it'd benefit her country or people."

"I would never expect someone to place their homeland in danger," Zaena replied. "I want to trust her, but I agree with you. I've long since learned that not every human is Karl or Grace, but that doesn't mean every human is Amanda Morton either."

"Trust goes both ways," Vokasin noted. "I'll believe in her more when she feels comfortable enough to share a room with you. It's like she's afraid you'll harm her or take control of her if she's too close."

Zaena had noticed the same thing but hadn't brought it up with Selene. She didn't want to risk harming the burgeoning relationship.

It was hard to blame the woman for her paranoia. Mark

Wong had proven that some elves possessed dangerous mental abilities. Given what Selene had said about pills, it was obvious she was deeply worried about less obvious manipulation of humans by elves.

Zaena's jaw clenched. Mark Wong's selfish plans had poisoned everything before she'd even left the kingdom. She stepped away from the coffin.

Maybe he had been the one who'd made the pills. She hoped his death had ended their existence.

A loud rumble echoed as Saelli closed the coffin chamber.

"The prophecy has been weighing on me," Zaena admitted.

"You believe it?" Saelli asked, sounding surprised. "You often speak of it with barely concealed disdain."

Zaena shook her head. "I'm unsure, but I can't ignore it. That might prove to be a mistake."

"If this is about leading us to good or ill, that's not worth worrying about," Vokasin replied. "You could say that about anyone on any day. It's not prophecy; it's a simple truism."

Saelli averted her eyes. "The prophecy is real. Disbelieving it doesn't change that."

"That's not what I'm..." Zaena began before stopping. "That is to say, it does bother me, but there's something more specific worrying me." She took a deep breath. "*The last of the great beasts will awaken.*"

Vokasin's face hardened. "If that's true, it might be a problem. Even if we could gather every immune elf on the planet, it might not be enough to take down a kraken or an elder dragon by ourselves. Even if we *could* pull it off, they'd have enough time to cause major damage."

"That's my fear," Zaena replied. "I tell myself those beasts are nothing but dust and bones, but after what I saw in the Mojave, it's foolish to assume it's impossible for such a creature to be sleeping and kept alive by residual magic. On some level, I've already been expecting that from the Night Elf enclave, or otherwise, I would have gone there first."

"A wise precaution."

"It doesn't matter even if it doesn't have long to live after waking up," Zaena noted, "and we don't have jaegers. It'll be the opening of *Pacific Rim*."

"Hunters?" Saelli asked, looking confused. "What's *Pacific Rim?*"

"Jaegers are giant robots that hunt giant monsters," Zaena clarified. "*Pacific Rim* is a movie featuring them."

"Human movies confuse me. Why do they spend so much time purposely consuming lies?"

"Because they're entertaining," Zaena explained. She hesitated before asking her next question. "You're sure you have no idea what this beast could be, Saelli? I know I've asked before, but I was hoping maybe you had a new prophetic dream or remembered something you didn't before. That might help me be more accepting of it."

Saelli's shoulders slumped. "I'm sorry, Princess. I've nothing else to share."

"Given the preceding line about past sins being unearthed," Zaena mused, "the most likely explanation is our raid of the Night Elf enclave will unleash the great beast. As I noted, I've always expected a handful of monsters, but nothing on that scale. That's another reason I'm considering taking Selene D'Arcy up on her offer."

Vokasin looked surprised. "You want humans to fight monsters?"

"Tanks and missiles might be nice against great beasts," Zaena insisted. "A surprise dragon attack against a town might kill thousands, but if the humans are ready, they could demonstrate their terrible power and save those lives."

"That would mean telling the humans where a nexus is," Vokasin replied, his jaw tight. "You're afraid of giving them Mark Wong's body, but you want to give them access to a nexus? The centuries might have passed, but there are undoubtedly the bones of at least some elves there."

Zaena stared at the entrancing nexus. "I know. It's a consideration, but it's as you said: there's an issue of available forces. We need to protect this nexus, so there's a limit to how much power we can draw from it when away, and the Night Elf enclave is thousands of miles away. We can't transport even the largest army in creation without human help, and we won't be able to make an army away from the nexus."

Vokasin frowned. "We can somehow destroy the enclave on the way out."

"That would be an impressive feat, but again, we won't have enough power."

"If we bring enough elves, we could attune ourselves to the nexus and use its power."

Zaena shuddered at the thought. "I honestly don't know, but we'll have to think about it more. I don't intend to go to the Night Elf enclave until we've secured the

Mountain Elf artifact. I think there's important symbolism in that."

"Good," Vokasin agreed. "Let the monsters sleep for longer."

Saelli walked over to the nexus heart and brushed her fingers over the stone cage. "You're right. I'll need this power before I can produce any armies for you, Princess."

"I'm well aware," Zaena replied. "I'm hoping that even though the Sea Elves were reluctant to offer more aid until we'd secured the help of all tribes, Lae'yul has been able to convince them now that we have you. We'll know soon enough. She promised an early return regardless of success or failure, so we won't have to wait until June to plan more."

"The Sea Elf Council is stubborn," Vokasin observed with a sneer. "That is the problem with dealing with governments instead of individuals."

"It is what it is." Zaena shrugged. "They're not going to change. We can only pray for her success."

"What if she's failed?"

"I'll try to think of a better argument and send her back." Zaena narrowed her eyes on the heart of the nexus. "I'm not going to worry about the Mountain Elves until this nexus is attuned. We can't keep worrying about defending this place while looking for other elves."

Her words sounded confident, but she didn't feel that way. It didn't matter. She needed to be more than a powerful warrior; she needed to be a leader.

Saelli offered Zaena a contented smile. "Trust in fate, Princess."

"Fate sometimes needs a little grease to move it along,"

Zaena countered, "but there's nothing much else we can do until Lae'yul gets back. You should both go and commune while you have time. If she comes back with a Sea Elf, we're all going to need to prepare for the ritual."

Vokasin chuckled. "Fine, Fourth Born. Try not to get swallowed by a great beast before then."

"I'll try." Zaena looked at Saelli. "You're comfortable with Grace taking you without me? There's a couple of things she needs to finish before she can get away. I apologize for the delay."

"I trust our human allies." Saelli bowed her head. "I trust your faith in them. I'll refrain from using much magic until we go. It's my deficiencies that require me to be taken to the glacier so often."

"I brought you to California when you spent your entire life living under the ice. It's not your fault. I didn't think certain things through." Zaena grimaced. "Oh, no."

Saelli looked concerned. "What is it, Princess?"

"Great beasts swallowing! That reminded me of an appointment." Zaena turned toward an exit. "I've got to get going. I almost forgot about my lunch date with Grace."

CHAPTER FIVE

Zaena finished swallowing a bite of her spinach artichoke flatbread and smiled at Grace from across the table. "I'm glad you encouraged me to join you today."

"It's good to just hang out sometimes." Grace inclined her head toward the window. People and cars hurried past. "Everything can't always be training and planning, especially when you're waiting for Lae'yul anyway. You've been running yourself ragged, including increasing the number of patrols, which I don't approve of, by the way."

"So you've said."

Zaena sometimes worried that her constant use of sound curtains in public would end up backfiring and exposing her. She'd learned to sit with her back to the wall when possible to spot approaching waitresses and avoid surprises. Despite that, during her time in San Francisco, no one had noticed.

Sometimes an elf needed to go out and discuss her secret magical plans while having delicious flatbread. There was nothing wrong with that.

"Everything you've said is true," Zaena offered. "Though with the others communing or about to, there's not much for me to do other than patrol."

"Patrols use up magic," Grace noted. "Shouldn't you be saving it up right now?"

"I suppose." Zaena sighed. "Without the nexus, we're at our limit of reward-for-effort with defensive spells. Starting too early on the attunement could affect the flow of power."

"You've not been watching much TV and movies lately." Grace looked concerned. "I know you're not always communing when you go to the forest. The thing I should be happy about, you slowing down, seems to mostly involve you staring out the window saying nothing. Creepy much?"

"I've been thinking when I'm not exploring the city or patrolling," Zaena explained. She went for another piece of flatbread, only to find nothing but crumbs. "And planning. Everything's coming together, but whether or not I accept the prophecy, there is another concern. Lae'yul and Vokasin are proof. Saelli is, too."

"Proof of what?" Grace took a careful sip of her tea and watched her friend over the rim. "Don't look for problems when you have enough already. It wasn't all that long ago a billionaire sent a super-heavily-armed team of paid killers to take you out. You should be relaxing more in my opinion, because we both know you have a lot more work coming up. I mean actual relaxing, not trying to work through a hundred different failure scenarios and coming up with counter-measures."

"I'm aware of that, but it is as your great strategist

Sonny Bono said, 'Victorious warriors win first and then go to war, while defeated warriors go to war first and then seek to win.'"

Grace set her cup down. Her forehead wrinkled. "That's good advice, but I'm pretty sure that was Sun Tzu unless Sonny Bono was a lot more dangerous a guy than I realized."

"Oh." Zaena blinked. "The names sound so similar to me. No wonder I mixed them up."

"They do? How?" Grace waved a hand. "Never mind. Someday I'm going to ask you to teach me Elvish."

Zaena smiled. "I'd be happy to do that when we have more time. I don't know that a human has learned Elvish in the last few millennia, but I'm sure as someone with a command of a tonal language, it wouldn't seem alien to you."

"Not all of us get decades of dedicated time to learn our languages before needing them." Grace sighed. "Setting aside the strategic wisdom of Sonny Bono and the potential tactical genius of Taylor Swift, you're doing a great job. You do know that, right?"

"I know," Zaena replied. "That might be the problem."

"How is doing a good job a problem?"

"Because I've attracted attention," Zaena offered.

Grace managed to look even more confused. "I'm lost. You wanted attention. It brought the others, right?"

"Yes." Zaena patted the Ruby of Tarilan. "This artifact is associated with the royal family, and all the other elves I've encountered have been aware of that despite the separation of centuries. They either knew I was a member of the royal family immediately or thought I was a servant of the royal family."

"That's a bad thing? Doesn't it mean they understood right away that you speak for the kingdom?"

"I used to believe that, but now I don't know." Zaena frowned. "All the enclaves must now suspect or know the royal family is active again in the greater world. Before, it was as you say; I considered that a good thing, but it's hard to ignore how there's been more obvious magical activity since I emerged, and not all of it is centered on San Francisco."

Grace said, "Saelli might be right. I don't know how much I believe in fate, but I still read my horoscope most days, so I'd be a hypocrite to act like I think the idea is stupid."

"Ancient magics are hidden all over," Zaena noted. "That's what the Mojave event proved. I might be frightening elves into seeking dangerous and forbidden magics. I might be creating a self-fulfilling prophecy of doom."

"You've got no indication that's happening," Grace replied in an exasperated tone. "Mark Wong was an asshole before you left your kingdom. For all you know, he might have been an asshole for longer than you've been alive." She gestured at a stream of people crossing the street. "All the stuff leading to those Ice Elves going after Saelli goes back longer than you've been alive." She grinned. "I hate to tell you this, Princess, but even though you're going to save all elves, you're not the center of the world."

Zaena narrowed her eyes and looked past Grace. A man had settled in across the restaurant and was staring at her table. His ill-fitting white pinstriped suit made him stand out, as did his size and the scars running across his face. She couldn't say gangsters and criminals always dressed like their stereotypes from shows and movies, with the noticeable exception of a fondness for tracksuits she'd noticed in the last year, but it was hard to spot a man like that and not think "mobster."

"We are being watched," Zaena whispered in Cantonese. Her sound curtain kept her words in but did not do anything about her lips. It never paid to underestimate the enemy.

Grace's eyes widened. "Watched?" she replied in Cantonese.

Zaena nodded. "A gangster."

Grace scrubbed a hand down her face. "I'm glad I'm finished," she continued, switching back to English. "I hate it when people ruin the mood."

"There are too many people here," Zaena noted. After dropping the sound curtain, she reached into her purse to pull out a couple of fifties and tossed them on the table. "This should be enough."

"More than enough."

Zaena headed out without further discussion. Grace grabbed her clutch and followed, offering an apologetic look to their confused waitress, who emerged from the back.

The waitress smiled when she spotted the bills. "Thank you for your generosity."

The pinstriped man rose and headed toward the exit. He didn't bother to hide his intent. With his size and outfit, that might have been difficult.

Zaena stepped into the parking lot with a frown. Being in bright daylight in front of a crowded lunchtime restaurant put her at a disadvantage.

Defeating a single gangster would be trivial, but the thin cover she'd been able to maintain might be lost. She had no chance to coordinate with the government to cover up the incident. Too many people would film it on their phones.

Zaena headed deeper into the parking lot. "You continue toward the car, and I'll go off to the side. It's more likely he's interested in me."

"If he's not?" Grace asked.

"I can hit him with an air blade from a good distance," Zaena advised her in a grim tone.

"Talk him down if you can," Grace suggested. "This might not be about what we think. It might be someone trying to put pressure on the restaurant but not the kind of guy who is going to try to murder a woman in broad daylight."

"I believe this is one case where you woefully overestimate the self-control and intelligence of professional criminals." Zaena waved and headed in the opposite direction. "I'll keep that in mind."

She turned toward a corner leading to an alley passing behind the restaurant. Because of her lunch date, she'd worn heels, which weren't good battle gear. It would be easy enough to discard them when the violence came. One gangster wouldn't require the power of her artifact.

"Hey, Miss," the man called as Zaena reached the corner. "Slow down there. You're going too fast, and I need to talk to you."

Zaena stopped and turned. Her gaze flicked to Grace, who was watching from beside her Fusion.

"I'm slowed to the point of stopping," Zaena replied in a cold tone. She slipped her purse off her shoulder and set it on the ground. "Do I have business with you, sir? I don't recognize your face?"

He reached into his jacket. Zaena brought back her arm. An air gust could knock him down with decent plausible deniability.

The pinstriped man pulled out a business card with a grin. He stepped toward Zaena and flipped the card in his hand to face her. "You might find this useful, baby. I'm going to make you a star."

Zaena took the card and read it aloud. "Larry Spring, Talent Scout?"

It'd been a while since she'd had this kind of encounter, but it wasn't her first.

The man grinned. "One of the best, baby."

Zaena's brow lifted. "Are you an actual talent scout, or is this a Mr. Soprano-claiming-garbage-collection-as-his-vocation ruse?"

Larry laughed and shook a finger. "Ah...beautiful, great style, and a sense of humor. You're going to be more than a triple threat. Quadruple threat. We're going to get you an EGOT and whatever thing they pass out for comedy."

"A triple threat? A quadruple threat?" Zaena dropped the card into her purse. "I'm already proficient and knowledgeable in battle tactics for land, sea, and air. Is that not already a triple threat, and isn't that enough? I don't intend to fight in outer space."

He guffawed and slapped his thigh. "Oh, and that

accent. It's perfect. I was thinking modeling, but you can be the exotic but funny rom-com lead. People will eat up the accent." He snapped his fingers. "Where are you from? France? Germany? I was going to say something more Scandinavian, but you don't have the look to me. Too many years in Minnesota before I moved to California not to recognize it."

"I'm from Switzerland," Zaena lied.

"Oh, it's obvious now that you say it." Larry rubbed his chin. His gaze roamed her body, starting at her legs. "Geeze. Wait. I didn't even think to ask. Do you already have representation? I don't care if you've already signed with a modeling agency. I've got a good lawyer, and we can cut through that like nothing. Movies? TV? Net? Singing career? I can get you whatever you want, baby. You're the total package."

"I don't have representation," Zaena admitted. "I'm not a model, or an actress or a singer. Nor do I practice professional comedy."

"That's insane." Larry's eyes widened. "I never thought I'd find someone like you up here. I was just visiting a friend for a couple of days. I'm ready to get you an apartment in LA today if you agree to sign with me. Baby, you don't even have to be *good*. When you look as hot as you do, you can have all the parts and chances you want."

Zaena folded her arms. "I'm adequately employed at this time."

"What?" Larry blinked. "Do you understand what you look like? Do you understand what you could achieve in the entertainment industry?"

Zaena stared at him. "Yes, I've been made aware I'm

attractive." She waved and walked toward Grace. "My appearance isn't a useful primary trait for my job."

"Hey. At least give me your number. Every woman wants to be a star at some point in their life."

Zaena waved. "I have your card. If I decide to pursue a career in entertainment, you'll be the first one I call."

Larry's shoulders slumped. "The best raw talent of my career, and you're not even interested." He stuck his hands in his pockets and headed back into the restaurant. "My horoscope was right about today. I'm glad I didn't buy that lotto ticket."

Grace waited by her car with a pensive look and her phone in her hand. Her eyes darted around until Larry stepped back into the restaurant.

"Was he trouble?" she asked.

"A predator, just not the kind we thought," Zaena replied.

Graces offered her an amused look. "Another talent scout?"

"Yes." Zaena rolled her eyes.

"Maybe we should start disguising you as a hundred-year-old whenever we go out," Grace suggested.

"I'm 251."

Grace chuckled and slid into the driver's seat. She waited until Zaena sat to continue speaking. "The last thing I want to do is give you more reasons to be gloomy, but your meeting with Lae'yul is tomorrow. What are you going to do if the Sea Elves refuse your request for more help right away?"

Zaena pondered the question and smiled. "What I've been doing: keep pressing ahead the best I can."

CHAPTER SIX

Saelli lifted her sunglasses and stared into the window of a small jewelry shop. This kind of place didn't feel so strange and foreign compared to so many of the other local neighborhood stores. So many left her disoriented and confused. The heavy fatigue oozing into every muscle in her body didn't help.

Everything about San Francisco was too big, too tall, too cramped. She could deal with the uncomfortably hot weather with magic, but every step outside of the White Ruby Building was a reminder she was far from home.

The humans looked and sounded different. Their buildings did as well.

When she had wandered among the humans back home, she tended to stick to small villages and towns rather than places like Reykjavik, but by her old standards, even that grand expanse of humanity was nothing compared to the tight and dense quarters of San Francisco.

She'd barely left Chinatown, and the rest of San Francisco was even more overwhelming. At least close to the

White Ruby Building, she always had a familiar place to catch her breath.

Saelli turned to leave and stopped when she caught her reflection in the mirror. She took a deep breath and slowly let it out. There was something unnerving about having round ears. It didn't matter that it was an illusion.

She wandered away from the shop. It wasn't far from the White Ruby Building, only a few blocks. It was rare she traveled farther than that except when going to the glacier to commune. She would be leaving in a couple of days with the help of Grace to go to her sanctuary.

Princess Zaena tried her best, but Saelli had to constantly use her magic to keep things comfortable. Combined with her excavation activities and battle practice, she'd had to make far more trips to the glacier than Zaena had anticipated when they'd met.

Saelli continued down the street, offering smiles to people she recognized in the neighborhood. That was the small comfort and advantage of rarely leaving the area. She was becoming acquainted with more of her neighbors. More familiar faces might ease her discomfort.

She passed a store selling sunglasses. Matt, the young man who worked there, looked up from his display and out the glass door at her. He hurried over and opened the door. They'd met a month ago when she'd stopped in to buy a pair.

"Hey, Saelli," he greeted her. "You doing good?"

"Yes, thank you for asking." She smiled. "I hope the day treats you well."

It'd been an adjustment learning to deal so directly with humans, but the people of Chinatown were warmhearted and accepting of her. Those small moments of interaction helped push away the homesickness.

"It's been okay. Business is a little slow, but I can't complain too much." Matt shrugged. "What about you? Everything okay at the White Ruby Building?"

"Yes, though I'm not working with the restaurant, so I can't speak to what's going on there. They are always so busy, so I'm grateful I don't have to worry about it."

Saelli had been cagey about what she exactly did for the White Ruby Corporation, and no one pressed her on it. She'd also had to adjust to the dreamy and stunned looks of many humans when first dealing with her. Humans, especially men, were far too willing to accept whatever she said once they saw her face.

Grace and Zaena had warned her to be prepared, but it remained unnerving. Helga had been the first human to see her unmasked, and at the time, Helga hadn't been in a situation where she had time to soak in true elven beauty.

Matt looked back and forth and leaned closer to whisper, "I'm not trying to freak you out, but have you ever seen anything weird in there? In the White Ruby Building?"

Curiosity mixed with fear colored his tone. Saelli tried her best to follow Princess Zaena's lead concerning sharing information with outsiders.

"Weird?" Saelli cocked her head to the side. "Please be more specific."

"You know, like ghosts?" Matt sighed. "You might think it's crazy, but a lot of people think that place is haunted. We're all glad the triad who used to control it is gone, but you can't have that much violence in one place without it making an impact. I figure it's got to have the ghosts of dead triad guys there."

"Everywhere there is life, there is death," Saelli replied. "Shouldn't ghosts be wandering around everywhere people have ever lived? This city is vast and filled with humanity. Death is ever-present, yet spirits don't overwhelm us."

Matt stared at her. "You don't believe in the supernatural?"

"I believe there's much we can't see easily," Saelli offered. "Call that what you will, but I don't believe there are ghosts in the White Ruby Building. I've not seen or heard any, and I'm sure the building is safe."

She knew that for a fact. Princess Zaena had gone out of her way to clean out any lingering influences of the wicked Mountain Elf who'd controlled the building before.

"The night it went down, there were all sorts of strange things." Matt looked uneasy. "This probably sounds crazy to you. The government said it was probably just gas making people seeing things and robots, but I swear I saw a statue moving on its own. There are plenty of people who think there's a coverup to hide some crazy stuff that went on because they don't want people freaking about ghost statues controlled by gangsters."

"Would that be such an awful thing?"

Matt blinked. "Huh? You want gangsters to have ghost statues?"

"No," Saelli said firmly, "If there was a great evil in the building and people rallied to defeat it, does it do anyone good now to know it was there in the past?" She smiled at him. "I've seen no ghosts there and no threats. I'm happy I moved from Iceland to help the White Ruby Corporation. I can assure you the building isn't haunted and will only be a source of positivity moving forward."

Matt's gaze ticked to the side until it fixed on her hand. He blushed. "If you say so. Just be careful. Hey, uh, can I ask you something?"

"Please do."

Matt stepped back and squared his shoulders. "So, you know, you've been living in the neighborhood for a while now. I see you around more often lately, too."

Saelli asked, "Am I doing something inappropriate? I'm from a very small village in Iceland. I know Americans have different customs. I'm trying to learn, and I apologize if I've caused any offense."

"No, no, no. Nothing like that." Matt let out a strained laugh. "Nobody's going to complain about another gorgeous woman in the neighborhood. It's like the White Ruby Company only hires goddess-level hot women. Zaena, you. Grace might not be at your level, but she's still pretty cute. Oh, crap." He scrubbed a hand down his face. "I can't believe I just said all that. I'm not a pig, I promise. I was about to ask you out, but I get that after delivering that line, it's probably a no-go, huh?"

"It's fine." Saelli smiled at him. "I find no offense in you finding me beautiful."

"I do," squeaked Matt. "I'm not going to say you don't look different, but it's not bad. It's kind of, uh, I don't know. Angelic?"

"I'm no angel." Saelli bowed her head. "I'm very busy with my dedication to my duties at the moment. I don't have time for an American courtship. I'm taking another business trip soon. If there comes a point where I'm seeking out companionship, I will remember your offer."

Matt rubbed the back of his neck. "Yeah, you do go on those a lot from what you mentioned. You can't blame a guy for trying." He shuffled toward the door. "See you around?"

"I will see you soon." Saelli waved and walked away.

She both pitied and envied him. He led a simple life focused on simple pleasures. He didn't worry about prophecy or helping a Forest Elf meet her destiny. He was even cute in his own strange, round-eared way, but she sought neither human nor elven companionship.

Saelli headed back toward the White Ruby Building, her gaze fixed on the sidewalk. She didn't hate San Francisco, but it wasn't home.

The prophecy had indicated she'd need to make a choice. It hadn't guaranteed she would be happy afterward.

A shiver of shame ran through her. She'd been too easily defeated during their sparring session.

Princess Zaena valued Saelli's earth magic, but it was clear Vokasin would be a greater aid in future battles. Saelli had let the glacier spoil her. There was no guarantee their next battle would be on one.

She needed to offer more to the princess. There had been a reason destiny drove them together, and it wasn't simply to reinforce the dangers involved with the great mission.

Saelli stopped at a traffic signal and waited for it to change. She didn't realize it had until the fourth person passed her.

Setting out across the road, she tried to focus on what the princess needed the most. The answer was obvious.

The nexus-attuning would be helpful, but Zaena's task also required all the tribal artifacts. Every artifact had been pledged except for the Mountain Elves' Thunder Opal, and the Night Elves couldn't complain about losing the Onyx of Shaping. What Princess Zaena needed was a Mountain Elf who could convince his people to hand over the opal.

Saelli continued to the other side of the crosswalk, barely aware of the jostle of people around her. None of the members of Team Princess knew where the Mountain Elf enclave was. They'd need to find a Mountain Elf.

She froze in the middle of the street. A man almost bumped into her.

"Hey, watch out!" He pinched the bridge of his nose, and his features softened. "Be careful, ma'am."

Zaena's human and elven allies couldn't provide a Mountain Elf. The mighty Selene D'Arcy and all the resources of the US government she claimed to wield hadn't led Zaena to a new Mountain Elf. Technology and humanity had failed. It was time to trust prophecy.

Saelli had spent her life half-ashamed of her ability and how it set her apart from other Ice Elves. She'd never been encouraged to try to invoke a prophecy, and her experiments over the decades had seen little success.

She stepped out of the flow of people and watched them in the hope of inspiration. The elements hadn't granted her this ability without reason.

A loud car horn sounded from a nearby intersection. Screeching tires followed. A Prius managed to stop inches from the back of a delivery truck. Both vehicles idled for a moment before the truck rolled away, the driver sticking his arm out the window with his middle finger extended. The Prius driver turned at the intersection and headed in the opposite direction.

"Damn," commented a passing man. "Did you see that? That could have been nasty."

"That idiot was looking at his phone," a woman answered.

"Doesn't mean he deserved to die."

Saelli stared at the receding Prius. Life ended with death. The greatest mountain was worn away by the water and air until it was nothing. Volcanoes would birth new land in the deepest ice or ocean, starting the cycle anew.

No one deserved death, but no one survived life. She'd come close to death many times, even before the assassination attempts.

Saelli gasped. An idea ripped from the depths of her mind like magma from an undersea vent.

Her prophetic dreams had seemed so random throughout her life. There was nothing special unifying their circumstances, or that was what she'd thought.

There had been one incident when she'd been injured in a magical training accident. An ice spear had almost killed her. She'd had a prophetic dream while she was asleep from the injury.

Other times had involved similar situations. They didn't explain all her dreams or even most of them, but there was a clear relationship between being injured and having a prophetic dream.

Saelli let out a dark chuckle. She'd suffered serious injuries in magical accidents and unexplained failures several times in her life. Before, she'd always assumed she was unlucky, but now she wondered if the Azure Knives had been after her far longer than she knew.

She narrowed her eyes. The humans spoke of their entire life flashing before their eyes before death. It was the opposite of prophecy, but she was not human.

"I know what I have to do," she whispered.

She knew where she needed to do it. She couldn't let Zaena know. Some risks were worth taking for others. Once she made it to the glacier, she'd be ready. The days of waiting felt like an eternity.

"Forgive me, Princess. What I do, I do to save us all."

CHAPTER SEVEN

Zaena stared at the basement wall. Saelli's magic had sealed the tunnel well enough that no one would ever suspect it led anywhere. Right now, they were at a disadvantage in that they needed Saelli to open the passage to the first tunnel, but once the nexus was attuned, she could set up a magical lock to solve that issue.

Though she had always known she'd be recruiting other elves as part of the mission, having access to them had proved more satisfying than she'd expected. Much of her life in the kingdom had been focused on training rather than doing anything real. She'd wanted to be a hero worthy of legend, not an elf who sat around reading about other heroes. Now, she was doing something no one in her family had done for millennia: leading a team of elves from different tribes in a greater cause.

Her phone rang, and she pulled it out of her pocket. She looked at the caller ID.

"What is it, Tony?" she asked cheerfully, basking in her self-evaluation.

"We've got major trouble," he replied in a tense voice. "Big damn trouble, boss. This might be the greatest threat to our place since we started."

Zaena furrowed her brow. "Calm down and explain what's going on. Whatever it is, I'm sure we can handle it."

She would not let wickedness infiltrate even the smallest part of her life. Whatever gangsters threatened the restaurant would be destroyed by her power.

"You don't understand!" Tony shouted. The following words came out in a breathless stream. "The Star Killer is coming to the restaurant tonight. I heard it from two different sources. He likes to surprise his victims, but we got lucky…or unlucky. I don't know if knowing he's coming is better. Oh, man! The Star Killer!"

She didn't expect that level of aggression. She wavered between seeking police aid and handling the problem as the Crimson Wind.

"Wait." Zaena hurried toward the stairs. "Who is this Star Killer? Why is he so dangerous?"

"He's the greatest assassin in the industry," Tony explained, "and he's coming for us. If he gets his hits in, there's no way we'll survive."

"Why would he come for us?" Zaena asked. "Do you think he has some sort of connection with the Azure Knives?"

She reached the first step before shooting herself up the stairs with a gust. She didn't land until she arrived at the top step. Tony was a valued employee and remained a useful informant, but he didn't know anything about magic or the truth about Saelli and the Azure Knives. He had no reason to be aware of the insane cult that had tried to kill the Ice Elf priestess.

"He's coming because he wants to take us down," Tony insisted. "That's the only reason I can figure out."

"We can't fear one man," Zaena suggested. "His strength and abilities have to be limited."

"He's the Star Killer, boss," Tony explained. "The one and only. Don't underestimate him 'cause he's freelance. I've read about people making that mistake. He has more power than any of the guys employed by the big boys. He could destroy the restaurant with one hand tied behind his back."

Zaena threw open the basement door and slammed it closed behind her. "He's that powerful?"

"Yeah." Tony swallowed. "He's brought down big places backed by big people before."

It didn't make sense. No individual humans were that powerful. Even Amanda Morton hadn't been that powerful.

"Why haven't you warned me about this man before? I didn't know this kind of threat existed."

"Because there was no reason a guy like him would come to a place like ours," Tony insisted. "We have not been around long enough, and we're not the kind of place he tends to care about."

"Despite our restaurant being built on the bones of the Demon Overlords?" Zaena asked. "A man of his background would of course be interested."

"I don't see why, but he doesn't care about that kind of thing. Not that I know of."

Zaena felt a grudging respect for the professionalism of

an elite killer who lacked any loyalty to any individual. That didn't mean she wouldn't destroy him if he threatened her restaurant.

"His capabilities?" she pressed. "His attitude? Can he be negotiated with? I don't wish to start a conflict that would harm the restaurant or any of the employees."

Tony let out a strangled laugh. "Negotiated with? The guy lives for his job. Once he sets his eyes on a target, he never gives up. He's immune to influence. If he even thinks you're trying, he'll not only take you down, he'll go after your friends and their places, too."

Zaena stopped. "This is just one man. If we hire additional security, he might be frightened off."

"What good would security do? He doesn't care about that kind of thing. It means nothing to him. He's not easily impressed. It won't slow him down or make him reconsider."

She could handle an individual human with ease. This mysterious assassin might be skilled, but even magic pills wouldn't make him strong enough to fight a Tarilan princess one on one.

Attacking him at his base was the best way to minimize innocent casualties and damage to the building. It was worth a shot.

"Where does he live?" Zaena asked.

"Huh? I don't know. I've heard he lives in Oakland, but even if we found it out, there's no way going to his house to talk to him would help. It'd only make things worse. He'd destroy us in revenge for showing up."

Zaena frowned. She couldn't be sure he didn't have magic. The terrorist incident proved that someone had managed to give humans magic-like abilities. Selene and the government had a poor handle on the source. Magic could explain the Star Killer's fearsome reputation.

"If he's that strong, it might be dangerous to get the police involved," Zaena mused. "We'd have to explain how we knew he was coming, and that could lead to questions we don't want to answer."

"The police?" Tony sounded confused. "How could they help?"

"A man that dangerous can't only be targeting us," Zaena explained. "I wonder if he was hired by those men who were trying to pressure our suppliers? I'm also surprised this man hasn't fled the city, given the Crimson Wind's activities. Whatever power he thinks he has must be inferior to hers."

"The Crimson Wind?" Tony asked. "Why would he be worried about her? I know she's mentioned food a couple of times in her interviews, but it doesn't seem like she's going to start touring Bay Area restaurants."

"His targeting our restaurant isn't only about food," Zaena insisted. "He's an underworld assassin. This must be somehow related to criminals."

"Huh? What?" Tony groaned. An audible slap sounded over the phone. "Damn it. I'm sorry, boss. I get what you're saying, and with the crap we've been dealing with since opening, I get why you thought it, but the Star Killer isn't a hitman or criminal."

"He isn't?" Zaena replied, her voice thick with confusion and her thoughts still swirling with planned defenses.

Tony laughed sheepishly. "He's a food critic. Gerald Right. He's to the Bay Area what Jonathan Gold was to LA, but unlike Gold, Right's a straight-up dick. He writes a food blog, *Right is Never Wrong,* but he also does a lot of freelance pieces for magazines, newspapers, and websites."

Zaena sighed. "Oh, that simplifies things. We can handle a food critic far easier than an assassin."

"No, we can't! This guy is called the Star Killer because his reviews led to more than one restaurant losing a Michelin Star."

"I continue to be puzzled that a publication started by a tire company has become synonymous with objective food evaluation," Zaena noted.

"Huh? Really? Never thought about it, but now that you say it…wait. We're getting off-track, boss." Tony groaned. "I'm kind of surprised you haven't heard of the guy."

"I'm not concerned about such things," Zaena noted. "If we continue to put quality into our efforts, the public will respond. Quality creates an impervious reputation."

"This guy is different than most critics," Tony explained. "He's kind of an asshole and a troll. While he hasn't ever outright screwed a place without some justification, he has a way of taking the smallest mistake and playing it up like it's the worst thing ever, and because he's a good writer, people tolerate it."

"A troll. Ah, yes, a hostile internet denizen. That one still confuses me. If we give him good food, there's only so much he can do. We've yet to earn any stars to take. He can't kill that which doesn't yet live."

Zaena strolled along the hallway, now calmer. Arrogant critics could annoy but not kill. There was little to worry about.

"We have a reputation," Tony insisted. "The Star Killer

does praise good places, but it's like his goal in life to find places he thinks are overhyped and tear them apart. It's weird; people don't care much about his positive reviews, but his negative reviews are so heavily followed there was even talk about making a show based on his life. I know you don't think he's a big deal, but the only reason he'd even be coming to a place like us is that he thinks we're overhyped. He could destroy our reputation. It could take us years to recover."

Zaena scoffed. "Then you should find your courage."

"My courage?"

"Yes." Zaena threw out her arm despite no one being in the room. "We reclaimed this space from gangsters and ensured that thugs would not take it from us. One killer, no many how many stars he's slain, will not take us down. We shall prepare for this man, and when he comes, we will destroy him with the glories of our food and force his surrender to our gourmet might."

Tony moaned. "Easy for you to say. You're not doing the cooking."

"I have faith in you, Tony," Zaena commented. "I have from the beginning. You've gone from a common criminal to my valued head chef, and you can't let this man intimidate you. Have faith in your skills, and you know that no matter what this man does, I will back you."

"Okay, okay, boss." Tony took a deep breath. "I can do this. *We* can do this. We will own the Star Killer. We'll make him cry."

"Yes, we will defeat him. He will weep tears enough to fill a lake."

"We're going to blow him away with our fusion menu."

"Yes!"

"We're going to make him wish he could live in our restaurant."

"Make him believe in the power of century eggs!" Zaena shouted.

"Yeah!" Tony shouted back. "We're going to kick the Star Killer's ass. He's going to come begging for more for the rest of life."

"Let the Sleeping Dragon awaken," Zaena replied, "and let our enemies tremble before us!"

CHAPTER EIGHT

Zaena sat in the corner of the restaurant, disguised by a wig and Grace's makeup skills. She sipped her tea and downed her soup at a slow pace while she watched and listened to Gerald Right in another corner with the help of a spell.

His arrival time might have been unknown, but internet research provided plenty of pictures to circulate among the staff. She knew the second he parked.

There was nothing distinguished about the food critic. He was on the skinny side, and his dining partner appeared to be a local businessman. They were working their way through different dishes, tasting but not finishing anything. Dedicated servers flocked to and from the table to ensure his comfort.

To his credit, Gerald was polite to the staff. That wasn't enough for Zaena to drop her guard.

She had faith in her staff and Tony. The restaurant had already earned rave reviews. Tony was a talented young man with a destiny of culinary glory. One critic wouldn't stop him. She'd make sure of that.

Zaena took another sip of tea. Despite her power and magic, there was little she could do. She was terrible at cooking human food, let alone the complex dishes Tony and the staff prepared every night. The only thing she could do was keep watch on the critic and leak any hints to the staff.

"What do you think?" asked Fred, Gerald's dining companion. "It's damned good. I thought it was all hype, but this place is living up to it."

Gerald looked around. "Good flavor, nice technique. You're right. It's a pleasant surprise." He smirked. "Too bad that when I think about it, it's proof of hackneyed technique and a lack of seasoning. It's an overall disappointment."

Fred laughed. He kept his voice low, but Zaena's spell kept the conversation clear. "You're going to go through with it? I wasn't sure, but you know, sometimes when the opportunity strikes, you got to take it. Will people buy you trashing this place?"

"It's easy," Gerald replied. "The thing you have to understand about restaurants is that they involve a lot of people and moving parts, and everyone has a bad night now and again. It doesn't matter how many other reviewers say this place is great. I can say it was awful, and they can't say I'm wrong. It might just be those plates on this night went out wrong. They can ask me to come back, but everyone knows I don't do that kind of thing. You have to be perfect all the time to be able to claim a reviewer is wrong."

"You're okay with this? I mean, I know why I would be, but I thought you were more about your rep."

"I have my reasons," insisted Gerald. "Yes, I'm getting some benefits out of this, but this is also for the entire food culture of the Bay Area. It might seem unfair to this place, but sometimes you need to sacrifice the little guys for the greater good."

"You've read the other reviews, right?" Fred replied. "They say this place is a big symbol. The good restaurant on top of an old triad base and all that. I'm not saying don't do it, but I want you to feel comfortable with it and not blame me later for getting you involved."

Gerald rolled his eyes. "Who cares about the past? My responsibility is to Bay Area food, not bullshit criminal history. It's not like I'll be destroying the world by taking down one restaurant." He narrowed his eyes. "The waitress is coming back. Let's keep it quiet for a while."

Zaena frowned. She didn't mind high standards, but she would not allow the hard work of Tony and others to be dismissed without just cause.

"You helped me out on that thing with my wife." Fred grinned. "It's not like I'd ever screw you over, which is why I hooked you up with those guys. They were pointed my way by another friend." His smile dimmed. "They said it'd be a good opportunity."

"It will be." Gerald shook his head. "Don't worry. I'm not afraid of them if that's what you're asking."

"You know their type," Fred said, "All businessmen in the end. I've dealt with their kind more than a few times, and they weren't so bad."

She had not worried when she heard the Star Killer

wasn't a hitman, but that didn't make this any less a hit. It sounded far too much like he was mixed up with real criminals.

"Eat for now and enjoy, Mr. Right," Zaena whispered. "Given what you've said, there's nothing I can do that would make it worse."

The minutes passed, with Gerald and Fred eating in near silence. They both kept smiling like they enjoyed the food, but each bite fed a growing wave of anger in Zaena.

Something bothered her about the whole incident. A food critic needed a reputation to have any influence. Contrarian critics were common in American media, but unsupported opinions were easily ignored.

Tony had insisted the Star Killer had legitimate influence and power. That meant the majority of his reviews were accurate. Otherwise, it would have been easy for restaurants to fight back and doom his career.

Why, then, would he risk that reputation by targeting the Sleeping Dragon? There was something deeper, and the conversation pointed to dangerous outside influences.

Zaena finished her cup of tea with a scowl. She no longer believed this was a simple food review.

Direct intervention had been too risky before, but now she didn't see that she had any choice. She had to follow her new guest home and have a little conversation about why he lacked journalistic ethics and who encouraged him to indulge his baser instincts.

She pulled out her phone and texted Karl.

Keep an eye on the place. Something's odd about our food critic. I need to check him out.

Karl's response was instant.

Okay. Don't go overboard.

Zaena smiled and texted back.

I assure you I intend fully to stay on board the metaphorical ship.

Something else bothered Zaena about Right. As the meal continued, he kept eating, but his expression grew more annoyed. She didn't understand what it meant.

"Something wrong, Gerald?" asked Fred.

"Nothing, just a lot on my mind." Right chuckled. "Don't worry about it."

CHAPTER NINE

Zaena's wig flew off her head as she soared through the air. Anyone watching would have seen an auburn wig appear out of nowhere and tumble to the ground.

She didn't have time to worry about it. Keeping up with Gerald Right's car took all her attention and power.

This was the problem with Americans. They were always zooming around in cars.

She flew behind and above Right, camouflaged and wigless. Tony had been right about Right's lair. The food critic had left San Francisco and was heading toward Oakland.

Patrols, exploration, and joy flights had given Zaena a deep understanding of the Bay Area from the air. That provided useful insight into how to catch up with cars exceeding her top speed, which happened far too often.

Fortunately, being able to ignore traffic and lights meant she rarely was outpaced for long by a vehicle. She might not be able to keep up with a car on the highway leaving town, but once she anticipated a car would be taking the 80, it was a simple matter to head straight toward the other side.

Her focus on following Right had only temporarily freed her of a pressing concern. She had no idea how to handle things when she caught up with him.

His admission that he intended to deliver a bad review no matter what was dishonorable, but it didn't merit a confrontation by the Crimson Wind or violence. There were darker hints in the conversation that worried her.

Gerald Right had alluded to criminal backers. Despite Karl's and Zaena's efforts at convincing criminals not to mess with the restaurant, somebody might have decided to get revenge using a different method.

Allies of Amanda Morton might be behind the incident. The turmoil at her company following her disappearance could be traced to Zaena. Her servant in Iceland and his mercenary hirelings might not have been the only ones who knew the truth.

In any event, taking down Right might only be the beginning of a lengthy campaign against a new and dangerous enemy. She needed to interrogate him and learn the truth.

Gerald's car slowed at an intersection, then he turned and headed into a dilapidated industrial neighborhood. For all his zooming along the highway, his car was now moving at a crawl as if he were looking for something. That made it easy for her to follow him without special shortcuts.

Zaena doubted he lived in an old office building or a factory. She lowered her altitude and scanned the area for anything out of the ordinary.

She sensed no magic other than her own. It was a small relief.

One could never be too careful. Paranoia was hard to define in a world where an elf was hiding her identity and relying on mysterious government officials to help her do that.

Gerald pulled into the parking lot of an abandoned warehouse. Zaena flew toward him and frowned.

A dark van also sat in the parking lot. Two men in jackets stood beside it. One was smoking. Gerald pulled up beside him and got out of his car.

Zaena floated in the air. The few working light poles were on the edges of the parking lot. They provided enough light to keep everyone visible but not enough to make it easy to see. Landing might increase the chance that someone recognized the subtle distortions marking her camouflage.

The smoker and his friend looked around but didn't look up. She had found that criminals rarely looked up. No one ever expected an attack from on high.

Gerald cleared his throat and adjusted his tie. "Good evening, gentlemen. I'm here as agreed. I'm even a few minutes early, despite traffic being a nightmare."

The smoker dropped his cigarette and ground it into the pavement with his heel. He reached into his jacket and pulled out a thick envelope.

"Hey, Mr. Right," the man greeted the critic with a grin. "Did you know God did you a solid by letting you be born with that name? Who wouldn't want to be a critic with the name Right? Of course, that's why you have that fancy blog name."

Gerald averted his eyes. "I don't like this. I tried to set up a situation with my friend to provide cover, but my involvement with this situation risks making me look like an unprofessional bastard. Being a contrarian is not the same thing as being a troll, despite what my critics think."

The smoker waved the envelope. "Professionalism is in the eye of the beholder, right? We've heard all about you, Mr. Right. They call you the Star Killer. They say you're a bastard who takes people down for the littlest of things."

"There's no shame in having high standards," thundered Gerald. "All my negative reviews are based on a fundamental truth. At least, they have been before now."

The smoker's eyebrows lifted. He laughed and motioned at Gerald. "Get a load of this guy. He's ready to plug me because I'm dissing his stupid food reviews."

"I've never lied in my reviews," Gerald insisted, "but I'm about to, and I bragged about it to a friend. I thought it was clever at the time, but as I was driving over here, I couldn't help but ask myself why I did that."

"You did it because you're about to make a shitload of money," the smoker answered. "Ain't no shame in making a little cash. In the end, the man with the most points wins. Dollars are the closest thing we have to a scoring system in life. You won't have to write a review for months after you get this payday."

"This is pathetic." Gerald scoffed. "I'm not a wealthy man by any means, but I've earned my reputation through brutal honesty. Why do you even care about some new Chinese fusion restaurant? What does it benefit you for them to be hurt? If it weren't for those unexpected medical bills, I wouldn't even be entertaining this nonsense." He waved his hand. "This is stupid. I can make payments. I'll arrange something. It's better than selling off my dignity."

The smoker shook the envelope again. "Our reasons ain't your problem, Mr. Right. You were offered a deal, and you agreed. Oral contract, asshole. Too late to back out now. Take the money, and make this easy for everyone."

"Oral contract?" Gerald rolled his eyes. "What? Do you intend to sue me? No, I've spent years of my life dedicated to destroying awful food, and I won't waste my efforts and dignity as a paid assassin. I don't need your money."

"You don't need our money?" The smoker turned to his friend. "You hear that? He don't need our money. He's a big man. He's too ethical to write a fake review. Isn't that funny?"

His friend chuckled. "It's funny he thinks he has a choice."

"Oh, come on," Gerald replied. "Be reasonable. I've not taken anything from you, and you can hire some other reviewer to do your dirty work. I, of course, see no reason to risk my reputation by mentioning my interactions with you. There's no net loss for you other than time. We can all walk away from this and never talk to each other again."

"Nah." The smoker clucked his tongue. "It's got to be you. You're the only one who can do what we want and have it stick. We need that damned reputation for brutal honesty and a local connection." He tossed the envelope at Gerald's feet. "My buddy here's got a point. You think you have a choice. You might have had a choice when we first talked to you, but you agreed to do this, which means things have been set in motion. Everyone has a price." He pointed at the envelope. "If that's not enough, let me sweeten the deal."

"My dignity and reputation aren't for sale," Gerald insisted. "More money won't change my mind."

The smoker grinned. "How 'bout your face, asshole?" He slammed his fist into the van so hard it left a dent. "You either take this money and write the review we were promised, or we rearrange your face. We might make your legs point in ways God never intended. How 'bout that for medical bills?" He shook out his hand. "Now my hand hurts. Might make it feel better if I punch you in the face."

Gerald swallowed. "This is insane. You might be hoodlums, but you can't possibly want to hurt someone of my stature like that for something so petty."

"Oh, keep talking, asshole. It'll only make me enjoy this that much more." The smoker slammed his fist into his palm. "I love humiliating guys like you who think they're better than everybody."

"Very well." Gerald lifted his chin. "Principles are all a man has in the end. If I must be beaten rather than betray them, so be it."

The smoker threw back his head and laughed. "It's my birthday and Christmas all rolled up into one."

Zaena landed behind the van. She had not expected anything like this. The arrogant man on display in the restaurant was easy to hate. That same pretention oozed out of him even as he faced off against these likely mobsters, but a man willing to put his life on the line for his beliefs was a warrior, even if he never picked up a weapon.

There was a loud thud from the other side of the van. Gerald groaned.

"That hurt, asshole?" the smoker asked. "You're about to suffer a robbery gone wrong. That's what you're gonna tell the cops because if you tell them anything else, you're gonna end up in the bay. You understand me?"

"You can't do this," Gerald replied.

"Wrong answer. This ain't about restaurants no more, asshole."

Zaena grabbed her ruby and whispered the activation incantation. Her armor spread over her body, taking the invisibility with it.

She jumped on top of the van. Gerald knelt on the ground, clutching his stomach. The smoker stood over him with his fist cocked. His friend stood closer to the van.

All three men looked up at the sound of Zaena's armored boots thudding on the roof. Their eyes widened.

"No way," the smoker shouted. "No damned way. The Crimson Wind? You've got to be kidding me. So much for it being my birthday and Christmas."

"You have one chance," Zaena declared. "You will surrender, or all those awful things you suggested to Mr. Right might happen to you."

The smoker pulled out a pistol. "Back off, bitch. This got nothing to do with you. Go find a cat in a tree to save."

"Bitch?" Zaena replied. "That word used to bother me, but I've become so used to it I barely even notice. Come now, you can't possibly think you two foolish thugs have any chance against me."

"Screw it."

He fired twice. The bullets sparked and bounced off Zaena. They stung but barely left a scratch.

"I see you've made your decision," she offered.

Zaena jumped off the roof. She didn't need her sword, clever spells, or martial arts. An armored woman drop-kicking a man from seven feet in the air was an effective weapon. Her kick nailed the smoker in the chest. He smacked into the ground, and his gun flew out of his hand.

The other thug opened fire. Zaena shoulder-checked him into the side of the van, creating another huge dent. She finished him off with a solid palm strike to his nose. He slid to the ground, unconscious, his nose gushing blood.

"Pathetic," she declared. "Next time, don't assault an unarmed man, and you might not end up in pain on the ground in the middle of a parking lot."

Gerald stood, still holding his stomach. "It's really you, isn't it? They shot you, and you didn't die."

"Some call me the Crimson Wind," Zaena replied. "I serve justice. I deliver it to the wicked."

"How long were you there?" Gerald asked. "I've heard you can turn invisible."

"I've been listening long enough to have questions," Zaena admitted. She marched over to the smoker, who was crawling toward his gun. After knocking him out with a kick to the side of the head, she turned back to Gerald. "A man of true principles is a rare thing indeed. You will call the authorities, and I'll wait here until they arrive to assure your safety, Mr. Right. In exchange, you will answer my questions. I don't care what you tell the police."

"Thank you." Gerald pulled out his phone. "I'll do whatever you want."

Zaena marched over to him. "Who were they?"

"I don't know who they work for other than I presume some sort of criminal group. Someone approached a friend of mine to ask about me, but he'd never met those guys before. They wanted to pay me a lot of money for a nasty review." Gerald shook his head. "I don't understand why anyone would care that much and go that far, and I couldn't do it. The food was genuinely good. What am I if not an honest evaluator of gastronomic efforts?"

"Good for you for sticking to your principles," Zaena declared. "I'll look into it. Before you call the police, I have one question. As you have proven, you are a man who takes your food seriously enough to put his life on the line."

"Yes?" Gerald injected extra haughtiness into his voice.

"What is your preferred fast-food place?" Zaena asked.

"Fast-food?" Gerald snorted. He looked down. "I suppose if pressed, I'd say In-N-Out."

"Interesting." Zaena looked at his phone. "Make a call. I want to leave soon."

"To go save more people?"

Zaena laughed. "No, I'm hungry. I barely touched my dinner earlier. I need to get a burger."

CHAPTER TEN

Karl glowered from beside his dining room table. “I asked Gary if they’d gotten anything out of the guys, but they’re keeping their mouth shut.”

Zaena frowned. “The police don’t want to share?”

“No, it’s not the cops. It’s the thugs. They’re from out of town. Someone hired them but didn’t want the trouble getting back to them. Gary didn’t seem to feel like they were going to get much out of these guys. They’ve got a lot of arrests but no convictions, so they won’t end up serving much time.” Karl grunted in annoyance. “Nothing like a real pro to keep his mouth shut.”

“I should have interrogated them myself,” Zaena offered. “While this pales in comparison to many of our threats, it does disturb me.” She stood. “This represents an unusual strategy to attack the restaurant. Although we’ve had success, it isn’t so vast that I’d expect someone to employ special means to weaken us. We don’t dominate the local culinary scene in either the city or the neighborhood.

I don't understand why someone would go to such lengths unless it's connected to our other activities."

Karl looked thoughtful. "You think something else is in play? You don't think this is just another lead-up to petty extortion?"

"I worry about it, yes." Zaena sighed. "I don't think it's enough of a threat to ask Saelli to aid you in your investigation. It's been too long. She needs to commune. I need to meet with Lae'yul tomorrow. I don't get good reception underneath Alcatraz."

"Don't worry," Karl replied. "This wasn't some clever Mountain Elf trick. I can hold down the fort and figure this out. Whoever was doing this isn't about to raid the place. Otherwise, they wouldn't need two low-rent thugs to intimidate some food critic."

He pulled out his phone. "I'll ask around, and I'll get to the bottom of this. Then we can figure out if you and I are going to go chat with someone or if it's going to be the Crimson Wind. You do what you need to do and let me handle the human crap."

Zaena worried the next morning when her phone lit up with a call from Tony. What was next? Would she find out the Culinary Nuclear Bomb was coming to visit the restaurant? It wouldn't surprise her if some dangerous foreign government targeted her restaurant.

Integrating herself into the human community would benefit elven-human relations in the long run, but it was proving troublesome, given her other appointments for the day. She hoped Karl would find out who was behind the incident quickly.

"Hello?" she answered.

"Have you seen it, boss?" Tony asked. "I didn't think it was going to come out so soon when I heard about how some guys tried to rob Right the other night."

"Seen what?" Zaena asked.

"The review," Tony explained. "It's on the web already. This thing is great. The Star Killer's gushing all over the place about my cooking. He says, 'Some might wonder about the ability of a neophyte chef of questionable provenance. He has had little formal mentorship or training, by his own admission. My meal last night reaffirmed that history doesn't always provide a clear guide to the future. What we have with Chef Tong can only be described as hitherto untapped culinary potential, nay, culinary genius. With what he's already doing at this point in his career, I find my mouth watering in anticipation of what this young man will achieve in the future. I'm willing to risk my reputation by predicting Tony Tong will be a major force in Neo-Chinese-American fusion in the coming years.'"

She'd half-wondered if fear would get to Gerald and he would still write a bad review. He had no reason to associate the Crimson Wind with the restaurant, so she doubted if this was about payback.

"That is unambiguously positive," Zaena observed.

"Yeah, that it is, boss. That it is. Hell, yeah!"

"See?" Zaena offered. "You were too worried."

She wasn't sure if keeping the truth about what had happened from Tony made sense. He was both her chef and an informant, but as the months moved along, she was far more concerned about nurturing the former.

Good news was never unwelcome. She hoped Lae'yul would give her more. Some problems an elf couldn't solve by drop-kicking a man.

Zaena's armored head emerged from the pool leading to Lae'yul's hideout under Alcatraz. Although she didn't anticipate being attacked, she couldn't ignore that Morton had previously traced elven activity to the island and sent mercenaries there. That meant somebody else might come here looking for trouble.

She was halfway out of the water when she stopped and stared. Lae'yul stood near the edge of the pool with a stern look.

That was normal. What wasn't normal was the presence of another Sea Elf, a male. While he was as naked as his kinswoman, he didn't wear any artifact jewelry.

Zaena released the air bubble around her and waded out of the water, then retracted her helmet. "Greetings, Lae'yul." She looked at the other elf. "I see I'm going to need to get more clothes ready. I would have hoped you had anticipated that need when dealing with the surface world."

Lae'yul laughed. "Greetings, Princess Zaena. Don't blame us for your unnecessary surface customs." She inclined her head toward the other Sea Elf. "This is Min'tuk."

"I see you were more persuasive than you thought you

would be." Zaena smiled. "I'll admit I had some worries, but this solves everything." She turned to Min'tuk. "I am Princess Zaena vel Tarilan, First Princess and fourth in line for the throne of the Royal Elven Kingdom. I thank you for your valuable assistance in attuning the nexus and advancing our glorious mission to save all elves from the Creeping Azure."

"I'm here because I've been ordered by the council, air-breather," Min'tuk replied with a snort. "I don't approve of allying with a Forest Elf royal."

Lae'yul glared at him. "Show respect. What she does will free all our people. This goes well beyond the Forest Elves."

"I can handle disrespect as long as he provides his aid," Zaena explained with a shrug.

Vokasin's snark had long since inured her to open dismissal of her royal status. She was under no impression that every elf would be happy to work with a Tarilan princess.

"I do what I'm ordered," Min'tuk offered with a sudden glare. "No more than that. Once my task is finished, I'm leaving this wretched place."

"The nexus will be attuned by then, and we won't need as much help," Zaena replied.

In truth, she would have welcomed more allies for the Night Elf raid, but that could wait until she contacted the Mountain Elf enclave. She saw no reason to explain herself to the hostile Sea Elf.

"There are conditions, Princess," Lae'yul noted. "They have been given by the council. I offered my opinion, but I'm a servant of my people, and I must comply with them."

"I understand conditions," Zaena offered. "I imagine they're not yet ready to part with the artifact, but I have no immediate need of it."

"An accurate guess," Lae'yul replied. "They've reconfirmed that they will only send it along with me after you've conquered the Night Elf enclave."

Zaena grimaced. "I see. You'll aid me in that endeavor?"

"Yes, but it remains to be seen if the few others who can swim without risk will come," Lae'yul noted.

"They've not yet ordered me to aid you with that," Min'tuk clarified. "I'm not volunteering."

"So I anticipated," Zaena replied, trying to think of possibilities. The Azure Knives were willing to risk their lives for murder. Asking for the aid of the non-immune in the final raid might be worth it.

The problem was, there was no guarantee that cleansing the Creeping Azure would save elves who were already afflicted. The ritual took a long time to prepare but not long to cast, and there would undoubtedly be a delay between capturing the final artifacts and bringing them together. There was too much of a risk of unnecessary casualties. In the end, she might have to rely on the immune elves.

Min'tuk might be one of the few others available from the Sea Elves. Zaena was the only living Royal Elf with immunity. She had to face the reality that their Night Elf enclave army might struggle to reach two digits. The appeal of bringing along a battalion or two of human soldiers backed up by gunships and tanks grew.

"There are other conditions," Lae'yul continued. "Min'tuk is to aid in the attuning and will return to the enclave when it is finished, but the council has made it clear that I must also be attuned to the nexus. I am to refuse to aid you otherwise."

Zaena responded, "I never intended for it to be only me, though there's little it will do when you're far away. I'm not refusing to accept the condition. I simply seek to understand the position of your people."

"It will serve as proof of your trust of the Sea Elves," Lae'yul explained, "and will allow us to trust you."

"We'll spread out the primary attunement to me, you, Saelli, and Vokasin," Zaena suggested. She inclined her head toward Min'tuk. "There's no reason to complicate things if he's not even going to visit often, and as you and he have made clear, he'll be leaving soon."

Min'tuk narrowed his eyes. He remained quiet.

"Agreed," Lae'yul offered. "He rides the waves the council has produced. He's not here to make his own."

"I have to say I'm very pleased," Zaena admitted. "I wasn't sure when you told me the council might refuse until we recruited the Mountain Elves. I'd love for that to happen soon, but my last two attempts went poorly. I can only hope that doesn't speak of the rest of the tribe."

"The council understands the significance of that particular nexus and your ritual," Lae'yul replied, curling her hand into a fist, "and they understand that not all immune elves will seek freedom for their people. You've acted with strength and honor, Princess. I've made that clear to them, so they have permitted our aid, even if some don't like it."

"Let's commence the ritual so I can leave," Min'tuk

muttered. "The less time I have to spend near so many air-breathers, the better."

Zaena offered him an apologetic smile. "It's more complicated than that, especially since one of our allies is communing and another soon will be. I never expected someone to come back with Lae'yul, so we haven't begun formal preparations for the ritual."

"What a waste of time." Min'tuk snorted.

Lae'yul shot a look of warning to him. "We can wait until the others have returned. Days?"

Zaena agreed, "Yes. I think it makes the most sense to wait for their return before we begin preparing the necessary sigils and glyphs. It takes you far more magic to survive outside your preferred environment than even Saelli. I'd rather you be in peak condition for the actual ritual."

"We are Sea Elves," announced Lae'yul. "We are as patient as the sea as it wears away mountains. We can wait. We will explore the bay and the ocean nearby but come back to this place before the dawn each day to seek you."

"Thank you, Lae'yul," replied Zaena. "For everything. Soon, we'll have control of the nexus, and we'll be one step closer to freeing all elves."

CHAPTER ELEVEN

Karl slid into the too-small booth in the corner of the bar. It was more brightly lit than the typical dive where he met informants, and he now regretted the ketchup stain on his pants. That would teach him to skip laundry day.

Little T grinned at him from across the table. The informant wore a new dark-blue suit and a matching tie. That was something that always bothered Karl, the slicked-back creeps wearing suits that cost thousands of dollars.

In theory, the informant didn't do well enough to afford those kinds of clothes, or if he was doing that well, it didn't make sense he'd still show up. Even with the extra money Zaena had given Karl to pay informants, he wasn't dropping thousands on every encounter.

Maybe Little T lived in a rented room for cheap and spent every last cent on suits. Karl didn't know, and he wasn't sure he wanted to. Whatever else he could say about the man, Little T had never screwed him over.

He was what he claimed to be: a man who gave information for money. He made it clear when he was sure and when he was guessing based on rumors.

"Good evening, my friend," Little T offered in a smooth voice. He gestured at the amber-colored liquid in his glass. "Drinks are on me. I'm feeling generous. It's been a good few weeks. You're giving me money. Other people are giving me money, and it's not about the same things. That's always for the best."

"So you don't have to worry about someone pressuring you to screw the other guy over?" Karl asked.

"Got it in one." Little T held up his drink. "People know I work with you, but I've made it very clear that I'm a businessman, and I don't see how it's smart business to piss off an ex-cop who works for rich people. Besides, when you look at the people who cross you, they end up pissing themselves or dead."

"I don't go looking for trouble. I end it when it comes looking for me."

"Fair enough, my friend. Fair enough. How 'bout that drink?"

"I don't drink during the day." Karl grunted. "Well, I don't feel like drinking today." He reached into his pocket and pulled out a couple of Benjamin Franklins to pass over. "Is your generosity about you knowing I was going to start this conversation this way?"

"You pay me more since you hooked up with those White Ruby people, but you don't come to see me as often. It's sad because I love making money for doing nothing more than passing on information. It's a great racket." Little T lifted his glass and shook it, rattling the ice inside. "You not hanging out with me? It's enough to make a man lonely."

"I pay you enough you can hire someone for that," Karl retorted, "and I've got more money if you can answer my question in a timely manner. You want to make up for me not showing up that often, that's the way to do it."

Little T sipped his drink. "Ask the oracle, my friend, and get your answer, as long as you offer the proper sacrifice. I accept Benjamin Franklin as your sacrifice."

"You hear about the freelancers the Crimson Wind beat the other night?" Karl probed. "If you haven't, it's fine. You can keep one just for showing up."

"No worries. I've heard about that," Little T replied. "You never know where she's going to end up smacking heads. It's kind of creepy." He chuckled. "I've got a bet there's a Crimson Wind cave under Yggdrasil Headquarters, but it's not like anyone has the balls to check there."

"Morton's place?" Karl asked, surprised. "You think the Crimson Wind's based out of there?"

He didn't mind the misconception, but he was surprised Little T harbored it.

"Yeah," Little T replied. "Think about it. This mysterious vigilante shows up in a suit that can fly." He scoffed. "Ask yourself, 'How is she doing that?' What do you think the answer is? Magic?" He laughed. "No such thing as magic, so it's technology, and Amanda Morton conveniently dies in an accident at the height of the Crimson Wind's career." He grinned. "Don't you get it? The answer's obvious. Morton got tired of playing CEO and wanted to go full-time superhero. She's already a billionaire. It's not like she needed more money."

Karl kept a straight face. He'd always worried that there

were too many arrows pointing at Zaena and the White Ruby Building. Having a competing rumor courtesy of the government's heavy-handed reaction to Amanda Morton's betrayal helped.

"Huh." Karl shrugged. "That's interesting, but I care less about the Crimson Wind and where she's sleeping at night than the guys she beat up the other night."

"Why?" Little T leaned forward, his mouth parting in obvious interest. "What's so special about some guys who tried to mug a pompous food critic? You a fan of Gerald Right?"

"I didn't know who he was until the other day," Karl admitted, "but I've heard from other sources they might have been paying him to mess with the restaurant. The Sleeping Dragon is owned by White Ruby, which means it's my responsibility to protect it as chief of security. I've already had to knock heads with certain family men who didn't know to stay away, but it looks like some people didn't get the message."

Little T finished his drink and let out a satisfied sigh. He leaned back, resting an arm over the back of his chair. "Interesting. Very interesting. The pieces are coming together for me."

"It's annoying for me," Karl countered. "I need to find out who's behind this. If you're worried about blowback, I'll make sure they understand not to screw with anyone over this."

"Blowback?" Little T snorted. "I don't care about that. All I care about is do I get a bonus for being quick. Though, when a man considers all the things keeping him busy, setting some of those aside could cost him other opportunities."

"I've got a thousand dollars on me right now that I'll give for a name if you can get it to me by tonight," Karl explained. "I'm in a hurry and impatient. You benefit."

"A thousand for a name?" Little T grinned. "Trevor Conroy. That's your boy."

Karl tried to hide his surprise, but his annoyed grunt betrayed him. The bastard had known from the beginning. He didn't like being played, and it didn't help that he was still behind in the situation.

"The name doesn't ring a bell." Karl pulled out his wallet and started fishing out more Franklins and Grants to stack in front of Little T. "Doesn't sound like he's triad, Russian, or Italian, based on the name. Not that names are everything."

"No, you're right," Little T replied. "He's not any of those guys." His smug grin only grew. "He's not muscled trash with delusions of grandeur. He's a proper white-collar criminal, or so they say. The kind who hurts way more people but generally gets away with it. Not Madoff-level, but still a piece of garbage."

"Huh." Karl frowned. "I wasn't expecting that."

"He's got a lot of interests," Little T offered, "but locally, he's mostly been focused on real estate. I don't know all the ins and outs of his business, but the word on the street is you don't want to cross him. Unsavory. That's what people keep saying about him. They've used that particular word. Who says that anymore? It sounds like something the Queen of England would say."

"Unsavory?" Karl growled. "Another damned billionaire

I have to deal with. I hate those guys. They always have stupid mercs with all the biggest toys."

"Another billionaire?" Little T gave Karl a curious stare. "You having a lot of trouble with billionaires?"

"Something like that."

"The guy's not a billionaire. He's rich and can buy and sell you and me, but nothing like that." Little T pulled his phone out of his pocket. "As a service to you, my friend, I can even give you the address of his mansion. He's a local boy. Convenient, right?"

"Yeah. Real damned convenient." Karl finished stacking bills. "You've earned your speed bonus."

CHAPTER TWELVE

Karl pulled up in front of the intricate gate. He'd thought about discussing things with Zaena before approaching Conroy, but he didn't need the power of an elven princess to go make a few things clear. A quick net search after talking to Little T confirmed Conroy was a businessman and real estate developer rumored to be involved in questionable activities, but he'd never been arrested or indicted. That didn't sound like the kind of man who would make Karl disappear just for talking to him.

A man needed to be able to handle problems. His chief of security position couldn't just be for show. He didn't need magic to handle a human scumbag, no matter how rich he was.

Karl rolled down his window to press the intercom button. A voice came out before he could.

"Park in the circle drive, Mr. Smith," announced a man over the intercom. "Mr. Conroy will see you now. Though in the future, he requests you call ahead and make an appointment."

"That works," Karl replied. "I'll remember that, but I don't think we'll be talking again after this."

The gate opened, and Karl drove toward a circle drive surrounding a colorful rose garden. He didn't spot any armed guards patrolling the area, but the sprawling mansion contained enough windows and hedges that there could be twenty hidden snipers aiming at him and he'd never know.

Karl parked the car and stepped out. No one was there to greet him, so he headed toward the front double doors at the top of the steep porch. They opened as he crested the stairs.

A tall man in an even more expensive suit than Little T's nodded at Karl. "I'm James. I attend to Mr. Conroy's needs. Please follow me. Mr. Conroy is waiting for you in his den. Please be respectful when you see him."

"I'll try, but that's on him."

James wrinkled his nose in disgust. "Very well, Mr. Smith."

Karl stuck his hands in his pockets and followed. Two more suited men strolled out of a hallway and fell in behind Karl and James. Most men would have been intimidated by their size, but Karl was bigger than either of them.

His trip ended in a den almost as large as Karl's apartment at the White Ruby Building. What struck him more was the utter lack of decoration, dark walls, and dark-brown wood floor. A comfortable-looking chair in the center of the room was the only piece of furniture. A dapper bearded and mustached white-haired man in a white suit sat in the chair. His face was lined, but his well-built frame filled out his suit. Conroy had aged well.

James closed the door behind Karl. The two other men headed to corners and folded their arms behind their backs.

"Hello, Mr. Conroy," Karl greeted. "Nice to meet you in person, though I didn't know who you were until a couple of hours ago."

"Hello to you, Mr. Smith," Trevor replied. "I've known about you for a while." He smiled. "May I call you Karl? Feel free to call me Trevor. I've found in my business dealings that first names can go a long way toward making people feel comfortable."

"Sure. You can call me that. It's my name."

His gaze flicked to the side. There was a dark stain on the wall. The paint made it hard to tell, but he thought it was blood.

"Why is the famous Karl Smith here today?" Trevor asked with a broad smile. "Especially if you're honest about not knowing who I am. I could be offended, but you're not the kind of man who normally runs in the same circles as I do."

"Can we cut the crap?" Karl replied. He pulled his hands out of his pockets. "You know who I am, which means you know my rep and what kind of things I've been involved in, and you let me right in. We can sit here and waste each other's time with a big dance and show, each pretending we don't know what the other is talking about, but I'd rather just get to the point. Why the hell were you trying to bribe a man to take down the Sleeping Dragon? What did that restaurant do to you?"

Trevor chuckled. "You're rather passionate about food,

aren't you? You're a big guy, but you strike me as more the protein-powder type."

"I like a good meal, but this isn't about that. This falls under corporate security." Karl locked eyes with Trevor. "I know it was you, but I don't get the play or the logic. If you were connected to the triads or any other pieces of trash, I would have heard your name before now, and this would be easy to understand." He scoffed. "The cops and the Crimson Wind have run out a lot of scum, and that's creating a vacuum. It could be you want to move into some new business opportunities and don't get how dangerous they are."

"I'm no gangster." Trevor wrinkled his nose in disgust. "Those pathetic men aren't anything like me. That's why I'm rich, alive, and not in prison. Criminals are lazy and stupid. That's why they're criminals and not businessmen."

Smug certitude sat on Trevor's face. Whatever else he might be doing, Karl didn't think he was lying.

"Why are you trying to mess with the Sleeping Dragon?" Karl asked.

"I don't deny I've been messing with it," Trevor agreed. "I do feel somewhat uncomfortable with having to hire heavies. Thugs? Goons?" He laughed. "Hired goons. That sounds funny when you say it aloud."

"Not as funny to me. Those guys were going to beat Right bad."

"I assure you that I didn't intend or want any permanent harm to come to anyone, and I would have made sure Mr. Right was well-compensated if something went wrong. Indirectly and discreetly, mind you, but no matter what had happened, he would have finished ahead. He doesn't even realize the medical bills that were weighing on him are soon going to disappear because of an apparent billing reconciliation. See? I'm not a bad man. You could even say I'm a philanthropist."

"Wow. Yeah. Santa Claus in San Francisco."

Karl stared at the man. Trevor smiled back like they were discussing the amusing things his grandkids did in school. The whole situation didn't make any sense.

"Why?" Karl demanded. "You keep telling me what you're not, but I need to know what and who you are. Answer the question."

"Consider it hardball." Trevor shrugged. "You can't be in the real estate game and not play it now and then. I'm more a hobbyist, but I do like to put my full attention to unusual opportunities with good profit potential."

"What's any of this have to do with real estate?"

Trevor stood and wiped his hands together, his smile growing to diabolic proportions. "When I read about how the Demon Overlords had been destroyed, I realized the huge opportunity presenting itself. They had a wonderful centrally located building in one of the most densely packed neighborhoods in the city. The locals were all too traumatized by the gangsters to see the real chance, or so I thought. I thought that explained why there wasn't much interest in the building." His smile disappeared. "Then this foreign company shows up and buys it. That's what I get for hesitating. I thought about approaching your employers and making an offer, but then they started that damned restaurant. They made it clear they had no intention of abandoning the property."

"It's a good restaurant," Karl replied. "With good food. They're making good use of the property."

Trevor snorted. "This is why you're poor."

"I do okay. I might be rich someday, but you'll always be an asshole."

"Trust me," Trevor insisted. "You're poor. Think about it. A restaurant? They're not even using all of the building, let alone the property. They're not maximizing its potential. It's wasted space, which means wasted profit."

"How would they maximize its potential?"

"They should have bulldozed that place and put up luxury condos immediately."

Karl scoffed. "Condos? Freaking condos?"

"Do you have any understanding of the Bay Area residential real estate market? The board is myopic, but their shortsightedness creates opportunities for men of vision."

"That's what you are? A man of vision?"

"Yes. There are too many groups running around crying and wringing their hands about gentrification, but in the end, it means there's not enough housing for the people who want it, and a lot of those people have a lot of money."

"That's all this about?" Karl snickered. "You want to build a bunch of condos to sell to rich tech bros? Give me a freaking break. It almost makes me wish you were more like Mark Wong."

"I'm going to do what you say and make a lot of money doing it while not breaking any laws," Trevor insisted.

Karl interjected, "Hiring thugs to bribe, threaten, and beat people is illegal."

"Okay, not breaking a lot of laws." Trevor spread his

arms out. "I've got influence on the board, and I've made a lot of charitable donations in Chinatown, too. I've been looking for opportunities like that one, but I never anticipated the Demon Overlords would get taken out by a superpowered vigilante. Now, your employers are wasting that lot with that pathetic restaurant and not even using most of the building. I could have those condos up in a year. I could have a line from here to LA of people ready to pay cash up front for them. Pure profit." He dropped back into his chair. "This is what I get for being too subtle, but I thought if I came sniffing around, the White Ruby people would squeeze me."

"Why is that?" Karl asked.

"I've dealt with the Swiss before," Trevor replied. "You have to be careful with them. Cagey people."

Karl frowned. "Oh, you know about Zaena?"

"I've done my homework. It's not hard to find someone willing to talk about the gorgeous woman who speaks Cantonese and is beloved in the neighborhood. I know that Chinese college-girl poster child isn't the real power behind White Ruby." Trevor scoffed. "She's donated to charity quietly and hired a lot of locals, including that stupid boy chef, also a local."

He flung his hand up. "I know her type. I don't even need to talk to her to imagine she's a stuck-up bitch obsessed with keeping her word with a ridiculous old-world view of honor. If I showed up and made an offer with a profit incentive, she would reject it and claim I don't understand what's important. She'd probably subject me to a preening and a pompous speech."

"Yeah, that's mostly accurate. I wouldn't call her a bitch,

but you know, Trevor, the rest is pretty spot-on." He glanced at the still-immobile guards. "Don't you think it's pretty stupid to admit all this?"

Trevor replied, "I'm admitting it to you, not to the police. You go to the police, you have no proof, and I'd bury you in lawsuits before you leave the station. By the time anyone even tried to look at me, you'd be selling plasma to afford a hot dog, and you can bet it wouldn't be all-beef." He hopped back up, the smile returning. "You're not a stuck-up Swiss bitch. You're a local boy, born and bred. Ex-cop, a man who worked hard. You said it yourself; I'm not gangster gutter trash." He fluffed his lapels. "I'm a businessman. A good businessman wants people to make money." He grinned. "You're right, Karl. You can become rich."

"You're going to make me rich?" Karl asked.

"I can make a lot of money from that property, a lot more than your boss and her bosses," replied Trevor. "I understand the local market, and I'm willing to pay a reasonable premium for the property. If you could facilitate convincing your people to sell the property, I'm sure that I could pay a reasonable finder's fee. Doesn't that sound fair to everybody involved?"

Karl sighed. This was the problem with clueless people stepping too close to the criminal line without going over. A true and honest thug like a gangster understood on some level that the world didn't revolve around them. They didn't expect everything to go their way. Wannabes like Conroy had enough money and success to expect things to go their way even when they were wandering into underworld deals.

"See, here's the thing. I was hired for security," Karl explained, "and that's why I'm here. I'm not paid to worry about business deals. I don't like that the Crimson Wind had to get involved in this. It makes me look like I can't do my job. I'm not a chump who needs a vigilante to do his job for him."

Trevor sighed. "That's unfortunate, but she should be spending time dealing with actual criminals, not interfering with my business plans." He pointed at Karl. "I like you. You're a straightforward guy, and you've got balls. You drove up here and got right to the point. I could utilize you a lot better than that Swiss bitch playing at being a restaurateur. Think about it; a bunch of foreigners showing up out of the blue to buy a property? That's not American. We should benefit when criminals get taken out, not foreigners, let alone Europeans. I know you work there to piss on the grave of the Demon Overlords, and I'm happy if you want to be the head of security for the condo building. It could be a selling point. The famous Karl Smith watching over everyone in our lovely, secure condo community."

"I'm not that famous," Karl suggested.

Trevor grinned. "You're famous enough to squeak out another one or two percent on the price. I was thinking about hiring you away from those people anyway. If the Crimson Wind hadn't screwed up my plans, that restaurant would have been wounded, and I could have snatched it up. Trust me. The Swiss know when to sell."

"Nope." Karl sighed. "You don't get it. I thought you might, but you just don't."

"What don't I get? Explain it to me, Karl."

"I don't need the Crimson Wind to clean up my messes." Karl cracked his knuckles. "Trying to take down that restaurant falls into my area of responsibility. That makes handling you my responsibility."

Trevor frowned. "Don't be an idiot, Karl. I can pay you more than the Swiss, and I'll be offering more value to the community. Think of the property tax revenue alone."

"You're going to agree to back the hell off right now, or you're going to have to see what real hardball is. Is that clear enough for you?"

"You don't know what you're doing."

"Am I supposed to be impressed by you?" Karl gestured at Trevor. "You're rich. Big deal. I've stared down billionaires and federal agents. I'm not impressed by your stupid beating room or your stupid outfit."

"This is no longer amusing." Trevor snapped his fingers. "James, teach him some manners, but make sure he can leave on his own. I'm nothing if not civilized."

James and his two lackeys stepped away from the wall. They didn't go for guns. Karl pitied them. That might have been their only chance.

The two lackeys rushed Karl. He crushed the face of the first with a right hook. The man crumpled to the ground.

His partner threw his arms around Karl in a feeble attempt at a grapple. Karl had a good half-foot and thirty pounds of muscle on him.

"Oh, come on, pal. You're not even trying."

Two elbow blows to the head made the man's grip slacken. Karl grabbed him by the collar and headbutted him before tossing him to the ground. Blood dripped on the wood floor.

"This is where you beat people, right?" Karl asked. "All

nice and easy to clean up? Maid shows up the next day and takes care of it all. I hope you give her a big bonus."

James raised his fists. "Mr. Conroy isn't a gangster. He's never killed anyone. He's not a savage like you."

"Gee, I feel all warm and fuzzy inside. Nobody's ever called me a savage before."

James came in faster than the other men. He nailed Karl in the face with two quick jabs and a body blow before ducking Karl's follow-up punch.

"I was a Golden Gloves champ before I went into private security," James explained with a sneer. "I was going to go pro, but Mr. Conroy made me a better offer. He always makes a better offer. You should have understood that, but now it's too late."

Karl threw a hook, but James bobbed out of the way and nailed him again in the face. Grunting, Karl staggered back.

Trevor clapped. "You see, Karl? I don't employ the kind of pathetic trash you're used to dealing with. I only hire the best. That could have been you, but you had to be stubborn. I feel bad about it, but you can't say I didn't give you a chance. Don't come begging later."

Karl charged forward. He took another blow on the chin. Growling, he threw his arms around James and wrapped in him a bear hug, squeezing hard. He hammered the man's head with his own before releasing the swaying security guard and punching him again.

James groaned and fell to his knees. Karl kicked him in the stomach. The security guard fell forward, groaning.

"The competition must have been weak that year if you won a Golden Gloves championship." Karl wiped the blood off his face. His head throbbed. "This is why I don't wear expensive suits."

Trevor stared at his fallen guard with his mouth open. "I can't believe this. You're a thug."

"Yeah, sure, pal." Karl stomped toward Trevor and loomed over him. "I'm not a gangster, but I've killed a lot of gangsters. I'm through letting idiots with delusions of grandeur think they can push me or the people I care about around." He grabbed Trevor by his jacket and yanked him up. "Now, you listen to me, you piece of crap who thinks he's the world's most interesting man. I don't care how much money you have, and I give even less of a crap about the state of the San Francisco real estate market." He threw Trevor on the floor. "You're going to back the hell off."

"I'll write you a check for a million dollars right now!" shouted Trevor.

"I don't want your money." Karl gritted his teeth. "I don't need your money, but here's how we're going to play this. I'm not going to give myself a bigger headache by going to the cops with this because the last thing I or my boss needs is wasting a lot of time talking to the cops or testifying." He bent over and jabbed his finger into Trevor's chest. "I don't care what crap you're pulling elsewhere, but you're going to leave the White Ruby Company, that building, and that restaurant alone, or you're going to see what I'm like when I'm *really* mad. Is that clear, or do I need to break a few bones to make it clearer?"

Trevor swallowed. "That seems reasonable. Very clear."

"I don't want any money. I don't want any favors. I don't want anything to do with you ever again." Karl leaned forward until his face hovered inches from Trevor's. "All you need to do is keep asking yourself if you want to piss off a guy who wasn't afraid of the Demon Overlords or the Russian Mafia."

Trevor let out a nervous titter. "This was supposed to be a low-risk investment, but I can see upon reflection that it isn't. I think it's best if I go to my backup plan. There's a great property in Alameda with promise. It's not as profitable, but life isn't only about profit."

Karl backed away. "Yeah, you do that. You go become King of Alameda." He headed toward the door. "I'll show myself out, and I trust we'll never have to speak again."

"I still want to hire you," called out Trevor. "I know I said I wouldn't, but I'm even more impressed with you now. Not many men frighten me."

"Too bad." Karl threw open the door. "I like my job and my boss. She's not a bitch, but you are."

He stomped out and slammed the door behind him.

Karl's annoyance didn't begin to ebb until he'd pulled away from the mansion. He was trying to help Zaena stop a deadly magical disease and deal with rogue magic in the world, and idiots like Conroy were only concerned with squeezing out a little extra cash when they already had millions.

It was time to call Zaena and arrange a debriefing.

He snickered as he pulled onto the street. "What an asshole."

CHAPTER THIRTEEN

Sitting at Karl's dining table, Zaena finished her pastrami on rye sandwich as Karl finished his story. "Sorry. I fly over Goldman's Deli every time I come here, and I decided to take the chance today. I couldn't help but stop when I realized there was no line."

Karl chuckled. "Hey, no problem. Sometimes a woman just needs her sandwich."

Zaena took a drink of water to chase the food. "The deliciousness of my sandwich aside, I'm disappointed by your revelations."

"Huh? I thought I did a good job of shutting this down."

"You did, but I had hoped this sort of problem would have gone away after our last major incident. Must we forever worry about duplicitous and greedy humans seeking to take this land?"

"I don't think so. We got the mob-affiliated types off our back, and yes, this guy was a piece of shit, but there isn't a line of wealthy real estate developers ready to pull that kind of crap waiting around. I also suspect D'Arcy's pushing some buttons in the background to keep people away, which is why we've only had local idiots to deal with."

"Is it that easy for the human government to control their people?" Zaena asked. "This country is vast in its size, population, and diversity."

"Sure, but most of those vast numbers of people aren't rich real estate developers," Karl countered. "It's not like she's got to keep an eye on everyone."

"I see," Zaena said. "It makes sense when you put it that way."

"You're not pissed that I didn't get you involved, are you?"

"I already handled my part as the Crimson Wind." Zaena folded her paper sandwich wrapper and took it to the garbage can. "I do have worries. I'm going to be distracted soon by the attunement preparations. Saelli will be leaving tomorrow for her communing. I won't be as available for incidental delivery of justice."

"It's fine, Zaena," Karl insisted. "I've got Little T and other guys with their ears to the ground to listen around about anything else happening. You worry about defending us from great doomsday beasts, and I'll worry about the assholes trying Scooby Doo plots. If the problem is human, I can handle it."

Zaena tilted her head. "He was pretending to be a monster? You didn't mention that."

"What are you… Oh, Scooby Doo." Karl laughed. "He didn't pretend to be a monster. Don't worry about it. The point is, I've got it. Let the human handle the human crap, and you handle the elf crap. I think between the Crimson

Wind showing up and the beatdowns and threats we've delivered, we're safe for long enough to do what you need. This place isn't going to blow up over the next week."

"Thank you. Vokasin will be returning briefly tomorrow, but then he is setting out again, so it'll be a few days before anyone but me does serious work on the nexus."

"What's Dino Boy up to, anyway?" Karl asked. "Why commune, come back, and then leave again?"

Zaena shrugged. "Sometimes I believe he's difficult to make a point, but as long as he aids me when it's important, I see no reason to chastise him." She headed toward the door. "Thank you again for all your aid this past year. This would have all been impossible without your and Grace's help."

Karl walked over to his recliner. "Glad to be of service."

The next morning, Zaena shot a bright smile around the living room of Saelli's apartment. Vokasin lingered near the door. A frowning Lae'yul sat on the edge of the couch. The Sea Elf tugged at her shirt, her face expressing her feelings about air-breathers' clothes. Min'tuk, who sat on the other side of the couch, glared straight ahead as if his presence on the surface world was an insult to his very existence.

Saelli watched Zaena from the corner of the room, her arms folded behind her back. Melancholy clung to her in posture and expression, but she'd deflected Zaena's questions and concerns, noting she'd be fine once she communed. Zaena held onto her doubts, but she didn't want to embarrass

Saelli. It was harder for the Ice Elf to get around than Vokasin or Zaena. The dependency must have frustrated her.

"Thank you for joining me," Zaena expressed. "You're the varsity of Team Princess, and I value your efforts to free our people."

"Varsity?" echoed Vokasin in a curious tone. "What's a varsity?"

"Would you prefer a different method of identification?" Zaena asked.

Her binging of *Blonde Cheerleader Dark Faerie Huntress* a couple of weeks prior had put her in an American high school frame of mind, but it'd take too long to explain to the others.

Vokasin replied, "I'm unfamiliar with what that term means, but I don't care that much."

"We should move along," insisted Min'tuk in an annoyed tone. "The council didn't send me here to listen to drivel."

"Drivel's relative," Zaena insisted.

She could appreciate that constantly having to use magic to breathe might be challenging, but she'd dealt with Lae'yul enough to know Min'tuk was in no danger. His unpleasant personality was unfortunate, but at least he was helping.

"I intend to begin inscribing the sigils today," Zaena announced. "Per our earlier discussion, we're going to prepare for an attunement that keeps the power of the nexus focused near the nexus."

Min'tuk narrowed his eyes. "Are you trying to trick us, Forest Elf?"

Lae'yul shot him a sharp look. "Watch your tongue."

"The council offered its conditions, and now this air-breather tries to violate them." Min'tuk glared at Zaena. "I won't stand for it."

Vokasin laughed. "You're amusing, Sea Elf. You're a fool but an amusing fool."

"I didn't ask your opinion, anarchist," spat Min'tuk.

"Enough," snapped Zaena. She swept her gaze to Vokasin before staring down Min'tuk. "I appreciate the aid of the Sea Elves, and I understand the discomfort many will encounter having to deal with different tribes for the first time in a long time, but what we do, we do for all elves everywhere. It will *not* be derailed by petty complaints and old rivalries."

She marched up to Min'tuk. "Your tribe values strength. If you want to test mine, I'm more than willing to indulge you. I won't even use the Ruby of Tarilan. If you think I'm so dishonorable, prove it in battle."

Min'tuk averted his eyes. "I will follow the will of the council."

Zaena stepped away and brought back her smile. "Excellent. Now, before I was so rudely interrupted, I didn't get to explain that though the power will remain local, we will directly attune the tribal representatives as per my agreements. The final choices won't affect the sigil preparation, but I wanted to clarify that I understood this to mean direct attunement. I will represent the Forest Elves, Vokasin the Desert Elves, Lae'yul the Sea Elves, and Saelli the Ice Elves. We can attune a Mountain Elf representative after we locate one. Any objections?"

Everyone stared at Min'tuk. He remained quiet, but his sullen look said enough.

"Perfect." Zaena clapped once. "I'll begin sigil preparation, and Vokasin will join me after he's finished his business. Saelli can return in a few days and help. I don't see a reason to strain our Sea Elf representatives until the execution of the ritual. Unless either of you has an objection?"

Lae'yul shook her head. "We don't."

She glared at Min'tuk, daring him to disagree. He kept quiet.

"In that case, I think we can all agree to meet again in one week," Zaena said. "Then we'll take the first concrete step toward stopping the Creeping Azure."

CHAPTER FOURTEEN

Grace shouldn't have been so nervous. She'd been living on and off with an elven princess for almost a year. She'd seen the power of elven magic wielded against her murderous ex-boyfriend and witnessed the elf responsible laughing at ridiculous low-rent television.

Her life had become a bizarre fantasy story. That should have prepared her for anything.

She shouldn't have been nervous, but there was something about sitting next to Saelli in her car that did just that. Grace's heart had been pounding for minutes. Her smartwatch even buzzed a warning about her heart rate.

Grace cleared her throat. The ride had been so quiet she thought a sound curtain might be up. Human and elf passengers had focused on everything but each other. Grace had tried to come up with something to say about Saelli's outfit, but the bland and functional look, including the gray beanie being worn to conceal the Ice Elf's ears without wasting magic, didn't lead to great discussions.

Unlike Zaena, Saelli didn't have any relatable human

hobbies. From what little Grace had seen, she spent most of her time meditating.

Even turning on the car radio seemed like too much, as if the silence was keeping the awkwardness from exploding. It had not been as bad when they were in the city, but now as they zoomed along the highway, it was harder to focus on the road and not the apprentice priestess in the passenger seat.

This was wrong. Grace didn't dislike Saelli, but she also couldn't dismiss a certain creepy aura around the elf. They'd talked plenty of times, but only at length when Zaena was around. This was their first trip alone together, and all the residual discomfort had wiggled out of Grace's subconscious.

Saelli wasn't like Vokasin, who flitted in and out, or Lae'yul, who wanted nothing to do with humans. Grace saw Saelli every day at the White Ruby Building. She could easily become a neighbor or a roommate someday.

More importantly, Saelli was helping Zaena, which meant Grace needed to be on good terms with her. Having a creepy vibe wasn't a sin. It was time to grow up.

Fighting discomfort with jokes was always a good strategy. Saelli was a foreign elf in a strange land. She shouldn't have to break the ice.

Grace chuckled. "I was just thinking I've had a strange career path."

Saelli's red eyes flicked in her direction. She stared at Grace for a moment before speaking. "I don't understand."

Grace hadn't thought much about it with Vokasin, but the elves all had different accents when they spoke English. Vokasin's sounded closer to Zaena's than Saelli's did.

"I was in college, you know, before meeting Zaena and getting sucked into the world of the elves and the Creeping Azure," Grace explained. "I was getting an education, and I wanted to be a social worker. We don't need to go into the details of that, but it's way different than helping out an elven princess. On paper, it looks like I was a college student who became a CEO, but now I'm a CEO who's a chauffeur for a prophetic priestess. That's a pretty crazy series of jobs."

Saelli's gaze shifted until she stared at a huge trailer swaying in the wind. "Do you resent having to help me? Do you wish I could travel to the glacier myself like the princess or Vokasin? It's not impossible. I could use earth magic, but it'd be more difficult to conceal my travel, and the distances involved would make it difficult, especially with my magic already so depleted."

Grace grimaced. "No, it's nothing like that. It's not like I was busy today, and it was supposed to be a joke."

"Human humor is strange," Saelli began. "American humor is even stranger. The Icelanders are more intelligible to me. You people are so chaotic."

"I don't know a lot about Icelandic humor, so I can't argue that, but I'm sorry if I offended you."

"My feelings are irrelevant," Saelli offered. "I need to serve the grand task and the prophecy. Whatever inadequacies and indignities I suffer are meaningless compared to the suffering of my people and all elves from the Creeping Azure."

"It's okay to get frustrated," Grace offered. "I know you've dealt with humans longer than Zaena, but by your admission, your experience is limited. Not to mention, she had all these specialty tutors training her to get her set up for this. She had understood for a while that she was going to have to leave her family, but it kind of happened to you without you realizing it was going to happen."

"The prophecy is important. The elements blessed me with this ability for a reason. I shall not ignore their blessing because of something as transitory as personal feelings."

Grace sighed. She wished Saelli would spend more time watching trash TV and less time obsessing about prophecy and self-flagellation. Zaena might have been mission-focused to the point of self-destruction at times, but the elf could still have fun.

"I'm only saying you've sacrificed a lot," Grace replied evenly, "and we recognize and appreciate that, Zaena more than anyone. I'm just a crazy human who got swept up in all this, but she's been doing her best to gather you all and save you from the Creeping Azure. I know she doubts herself more than she lets on at times. Don't let her fool you. It's okay to feel strange about all this."

"I don't believe she will bring our doom," Saelli offered. She kept looking ahead. "I apologize if the prophecy has made her think that."

"She doesn't act like it has, and she would have told me if she knew you felt that way." Grace grinned. "I think even if doom showed up, Zaena would kick its ass after giving it a big speech about justice and quoting daytime TV at it." She chuckled. "It's cool, though. You get a glimpse into the future, and that's got to be comforting. I know it's a scary prophecy, but it cuts down on uncertainty."

Saelli glanced her way. "You believe in my abilities?"

"Sure. Why wouldn't I?"

"Princess Zaena still seems to harbor doubts," Saelli explained in a weary voice. "Belief was split, even amongst members of my tribe."

Grace concentrated on passing the truck in front of them before replying. "She's starting from a different spot with all this."

"A different spot?"

"Yeah. I'm a modern human, and I'm like a lot of people. I always believed there was more out there, but that wasn't the same thing as believing in powerful and obvious magic, let alone elves. Once I understood that elves and magic were real, it made it easy to accept everything else. Prophecy doesn't seem strange compared to a guy turning into a dinosaur or a different guy making an army of rock soldiers and using a magic mask to mind-control people."

"I see." Saelli's face softened. "It's difficult for me to think like a human. I've tried and always fail."

"I can't think like an elf," Grace offered. "It's a good thing Zaena's got humans helping her."

Saelli looked at her lap. "You seem to be more than a servant."

"It's been two months, and you're just getting that?" Grace shook her head. "I'm not anybody's servant. Zaena's my friend, and I'm helping her because she's convinced me it's cruel and awful that a killer disease is keeping the elves from enjoying the rest of the world. I also think the world will be better off with two intelligent species sharing it and providing different perspectives."

"A friend," Saelli whispered. "Yes, that does seem to be the case. You and Karl are both genuine human friends."

"Zaena's done a lot for me," Grace noted. "Including saving my life when I was kidnapped."

"She briefly mentioned that," Saelli explained. "You were taken by a criminal who worked for the Mountain Elf."

"Sure, but it wasn't about that," Grace clarified. "My ex didn't grab me as a Demon Overlord plot. He was just a psycho who didn't want to hear the word no. Zaena could have taken control of the building and taken Mark Wong on without helping me. I was nothing more than a human who helped her out when she first arrived."

"That's why you help her? A life debt?"

"That's kind of how it started, but it's different now. To be honest, I'm glad you showed up and took over the apartment because it made her come back and live with me. I missed her. She's strange by human standards and has terrible taste in television, but she's also kind, generous, funny, and beyond loyal. I'm her friend because she's a good person. Who doesn't want to be friends with a good person?"

"She's not even your kind," Saelli insisted. "She's not a person in the sense of a human. She's an elf. You are a flower blooming and dying while she stands above the garden, smiling at the generations of flowers. You are transitory. To you, she is all but eternal."

"Always glad to hear about my coming death." Grace snickered. "Since humans don't have as many years on this Earth, I think we take them more seriously. I don't care that Zaena's going to be around long after me and a lot of my descendants are dead. For now, we're friends, and I've become a better person because of that friendship."

Saelli let out a soft sigh. She stared at the side window at a building in the distance. "I envy her."

"Zaena? Why? You might not have her royal aura thing, but you're both ridiculously gorgeous in that elf way." Grace rolled her eyes. "It's somehow more frustrating to know that it doesn't matter what type of elf."

"No, I envy her having true human friends," Saelli explained.

"We want to be your friends, too," Grace insisted.

"I understand and appreciate that. I wish I hadn't waited so long to mix more openly with humans, including Helga."

Grace's breath caught. "From what I understand, it wasn't your fault."

"It was, but it was perhaps also fate," Saelli replied with a shake of her head. "If I'd known her better before she died, I could help keep her memory alive far longer than any human."

Grace frowned for a moment at a car in the mirror. She'd thought they were following her, but they broke away to turn onto a county road. "All I can do is offer to be your friend now. I know it's not the same, but there are always second chances in life, and you've got a lot more life for those second chances."

"Aren't you afraid of what will come?" Saelli asked. "Aren't you afraid to be around Princess Zaena and the rest of us?"

"I choose to believe in Zaena. Don't you?"

"I believe in her too, but there is still darkness and great struggle ahead." Saelli squeezed her eyes shut. "There will be blood and suffering and pain. That's a given. I don't need the prophecy to know that."

Grace scoffed. "Is that all you've got?"

Saelli's eyes shot open, and she turned her head to gape at Grace. "What?"

"You didn't spend a lot of time studying human history during priestess school, did you?" Grace asked. "You elves have the Creeping Azure, but it's going to be eradicated probably within a year. We humans have all sorts of darkness and great struggle, and there are a lot more of us feeding a lot of darkness." A smile broke out despite her grim words. "I wanted to be a social worker to help people, but part of me thought it was pointless and suffering and darkness might take us all out. I had a stupid psycho killer ex-boyfriend and everyone acted like he was untouchable, and then she came."

"Princess Zaena?"

Grace nodded. "Yeah, a crazy, stubborn woman who could barely get through three sentences in English without being confused. It wasn't just her taking out Benny that impressed me. It was her whole attitude and the way she didn't let anything stop her from doing what she thought was right. At first, I thought it was crazy. When I finally understood what she was doing, I thought just because magic was real, it didn't mean she could find all these other elves, but she kept finding them and convincing them to help. She's got people from tribes who hated each other working together for a common goal, and she even has suspicious defense officials in my government onboard. It's got to mean something, and I've seen that Zaena's royal aura is only a start. It's not mind control."

"The hands of prophecy move us forward," Saelli suggested. "We advance steadily toward our fates with only a few brief opportunities to control them."

"That's one way of looking at it." Grace smiled. "Hey, but even you're admitting that we can fight for a better fate, at least a little."

"I suppose that is true."

Grace's smile drifted away. Traffic had grown sparser over the last few minutes. It was down to a single car. The lone survivor, a Camaro, weaved in the lane in front of Grace's Fusion, smoke pouring out the front. The car cut toward the shoulder before bouncing off the road entirely and spinning to a stop in the grass.

She glanced in her mirror. There was no one behind her. She tapped her brakes and headed toward the side of the road.

"I know we're on our way to take you to commune and all," Grace began, "but you're not totally out of magic, are you?"

Saelli shook her head. "No, I'm not totally without power."

Smoke poured out of the front of the stopped car. The driver's side door opened, and a man tumbled out, coughing.

"Good because I think we might need some magic to stop a fire," Grace replied.

CHAPTER FIFTEEN

Grace skidded to a halt close to the smoking car. She looked over her shoulder and didn't see anyone coming up the road. She threw open the door and rushed toward the man.

"Hey, you all right?"

The man didn't respond. Grace sucked in a breath. She was glad she had gotten a CPR certification last year. Relief flooded her when he groaned. That meant he was breathing.

Saelli stepped out of the car with a pensive look on her face. "Are you sure this is safe?"

"Nope," Grace replied. She knelt by the groaning man. "Hey, you awake? We need to get you away from the car. It might blow up or catch on fire. Just a few yards, come on. You're a big guy, and I'm a small woman."

The man groaned again and staggered to his feet. There was a gash across his forehead, and his leather jacket was torn.

Grace grabbed his arm and led him away from the vehicle. "Come on. We're almost safe."

Flames erupted from under the hood and spread to the front. There wasn't an explosion, but the man had barely escaped nasty burns.

"Thanks," the guy offered in a low voice. He pulled his arm away from Grace and unzipped his jacket. "Damn. That was close." He blinked and wiped the blood off his forehead. "Wow. Too close."

Grace waved smoke out of her face. "Sorry about your car."

The fire didn't look like it could spread anywhere. With the man safe, risking using Saelli's magic wasn't worth it.

"It's okay," the man replied, reaching into his jacket. "Since you're about to give me a new one."

"Excuse me?"

He yanked out a gun. "I need your car. The pigs already tagged me, and I barely lost them." He grunted and motioned toward the car. "Assholes put a bullet in my car just because I was trying to run 'em down, so I would have had to get rid of it anyway."

Grace rolled her eyes. "Wow. That's crazy that a cop didn't stand there and let you try to run him over. It's sooooo sad they jacked up your engine."

"I didn't say that, bitch." The man snorted. "That's the fault of my dumbass brother-in-law. That bitch was supposed to be taking care of my baby while I was paying my debt to society." He growled. "He told me he changed the oil. He didn't change the damned oil. I'm sure my baby would have pulled through the cops putting bullets in her if it wasn't for that."

Grace folded her arms. "It couldn't have happened to a nicer guy. I'm reconsidering my not-letting-random-guys-burn-to-death-in-cars policy."

She took a deep breath. Annoyance stifled her fear. She couldn't believe the gall of this jerk. Who robbed the woman who'd saved his life? He was less than pond scum.

"Yeah, I'm nice, bitch." The carjacker shook his gun. "I'm so nice I'm not putting a bullet in you, and..." He glanced at Saelli and licked his lips. "Damn. Are all albino chicks that hot? I never seen one up this close before. My head hurts and my car's trash, but she almost makes it worth it."

"When they're from Iceland, yes. They are all that hot." Grace narrowed her eyes. "You don't want to do this. You don't have to believe in karma to accept how dumb it is."

"I want your car," the carjacker replied. "I want your purse and any jewelry." He motioned with the gun toward Saelli. "Phones, too. I got to buy a new car after all this. I'll need some crap to sell."

Saelli sighed. "You should listen to my friend. One doesn't escape from the darkness by moving deeper into the shadows. This doesn't yet have to end in sadness if you're reasonable."

"Don't feed me that," the carjacker yelled. "What? You going to send me to church next? Give me your stuff before I take it the hard way."

"Should I comply, Grace?" Saelli asked. "I don't wish to create trouble for her."

"You talking about Zaena?" Grace sighed. "I don't think she would tell us to sit here and let some asshole carjack us. There's no way we should hand anything over to this guy."

"Do you bitches understand the situation you're in?" the carjacker shouted. "I've got a headache and I'm already pissed off, and you're acting like I'm not even here. I *will* shoot you."

He lifted his gun and fired once. The loud boom sent birds scattering nearby.

"Touchy," Grace muttered, "and rude."

He narrowed his eyes at Saelli. "Don't think I didn't see the diamond ring, bitch. Hand it over before I put holes in your mouthy friend and decide to rearrange that pretty face."

"I can't give you this," Saelli replied. "This is a sacred artifact of my people. I'd sooner die than hand it over."

"Don't tempt me."

"Kick his ass, but keep it subtle," Grace replied. "I don't want to have to shoot him and answer a lot of cop questions."

The carjacker jumped back, gripping his gun tightly. "You're packing, bitch?"

"My employer runs into a lot of undesirable people," Grace explained with a smile. "Our security chief taught me to shoot. No one needs to get hurt. You can just walk away, find some trees, and hide behind them. It's easy."

She didn't want to admit her gun was in her purse in the car. Being trained to shoot wasn't the same thing as being ready to walk around with a shoulder holster.

He ground his teeth. "You two bitches think this is a big joke? You think I won't do this? You don't know me. I've got all sorts of warrants. Cops all over the state are looking for me. I'll kill cops, and I'll kill bitches."

"I think you don't have to do any of this." Grace summoned her best defiant stare.

Her heart pounded. Fear was now swallowing the annoyance.

Hanging around Zaena and Karl made it easy to pretend to be a badass, but she hadn't been in many fights. Even having an elf backing her up didn't mean she'd escape unscathed, but giving in to a man she'd saved was too much.

"Last ch—" the carjacker began.

Saelli lifted her hand. The robber grunted and tripped over the uneven terrain, then stumbled forward. A large stone hurtled through the air and knocked the gun out of his hand. Another rock ripped from the edge of the road and slammed into his already bleeding head.

He threw up his hands to protect his head. "What the hell is going on? How did you do that without me seeing?"

"A magician never reveals her tricks," Grace offered with a grin, "but now you don't have a gun, and I do." She patted her jacket to try to trick him.

"Should I kill him?" Saelli asked, sounding uncertain. "This man preys upon innocents, but I'd rather not spill blood. I've killed enough in recent weeks."

"Whoa, whoa, whoa." The carjacker backed up. "Who the hell *are* you two?"

Grace ignored the man. "He's going to rot in jail, and he'll have a lot of time to think about what he should do the next time two pretty young women offer him roadside assistance."

"A couple of rocks aren't going to stop me," the

carjacker insisted, panic in his eyes. "I'm going to shoot you with your own gun, bitch."

He launched at Grace. A tendril of dirt shot up from the ground and snagged his leg. It broke but sent him to the ground with an audible thump.

"Why couldn't I have done that the other day?" asked Saelli with a sigh. "Habit breeds poor practical ability despite potential."

"I'll kill you," screamed the robber, who was now face-first in the grass. "I'll take you down."

"Is one of your warrants for being a professional dumb-ass?" Grace asked. She pointed at his head. "Knock him out before he forces us to do something serious."

She glanced at the car. Digging her gun out of her purse was the last resort.

The carjacker pushed his body up. His face contorted in rage. Another rock flew from the side of the road and nailed him in the side of the head. His eyes rolled up, and he collapsed into the grass.

Grace sighed. "Keep an eye on him. I'm going to tie him up and call the Highway Patrol."

Grace nodded approvingly at her handiwork. She'd never been great with knots, but she was surprised by what a woman on a mission could do with a set of jumper cables and an unconscious man. It wouldn't stop him if he woke up and was serious about escaping, but he couldn't get up before Grace could draw on him or Saelli could practice earth magic anesthesia.

"Hey." Grace motioned to his legs. "Just kind of cuff him with some rock until the cops get here."

Saelli looked uncertain. "Please be more mindful of your life, Grace. I would have avenged you, but he could have hurt you. I wouldn't have been able to get up a spell in time to save you if he shot."

"I wasn't giving him my car," Grace insisted. "I wouldn't have done that. I spent too long being afraid of jerks like him. I told you already, I kind of believe in fate and destiny, and I know it's not my destiny to get killed by a random carjacker on the side of the highway."

Sirens wailed in the distance. The Highway Patrol was close.

"There we go." She marched over to the unconscious, bound man. "Who's the bitch now?"

CHAPTER SIXTEEN

Grace leaned against the side of her car with her arms folded. She saw no reason to escalate the situation by carrying a weapon when the police arrived. A Highway Patrol vehicle pulled up in front of her car and an officer in a wide-brimmed hat hopped out, his hand already on his gun.

Grim-faced, he glanced between the women and the bound carjacker with a frown. "You two ladies okay? I've got an ambulance on the way, but it'll be a couple of minutes."

Grace smiled at him. "We got lucky, Officer. Like I told the dispatcher, this idiot stumbled out of his car, threatened us, and then tripped and knocked himself out. We took the opportunity to tie him up."

Saelli smiled her agreement. She looked away when the cop stared at her.

"You shouldn't have stayed," the officer insisted with a disapproving look. "Once he was unconscious, you should have gotten out of here for your safety. I'm glad everything turned out okay for you, but this man is extremely dangerous."

Grace snorted. "This tweaker bastard couldn't even go a foot without tripping over himself. We are fine, but do we have to stay here long? Since you want us out of here, I'd love to take off. We stayed because we didn't want him carjacking some poor old man."

"I'll just take a brief statement." The cop inclined his head toward the car. "You got lucky. You don't know how much. This guy's nasty. Dispatch told me he tried to run over a cop in Oakland earlier today, and he's on probation for aggravated assault. I'll just need a brief statement, and you two can be on your way."

Grace kept her smile pasted on to hide the tension suffusing her muscles. "We won't have to testify or anything, will we? My boss is very sensitive about her company's image."

"Nah, nothing like that. You should be fine." The cop knelt and undid the jumper cables, then handcuffed the unconscious carjacker. "This guy's going away for a long time for a lot of other stuff, starting with violating his parole."

Saelli stared at the carjacker. "It's so sad he attempted to repay kindness with vile deeds."

"Yeah, criminals are like that." The cop shook his head. "Don't worry, ladies. This guy's now got to worry about finishing his original sentence before we even get to the new charges."

Twenty minutes and three more Highway Patrol cars later, the now-awake carjacker sat in the back of a police car, his head bandaged, muttering to himself. Every once in a while, he looked at Grace and Saelli with a mixture of anger and doubt.

Grace was worried that he might have figured something out, but she stopped caring after a few minutes. No one was going to listen to what a parole-violating attempted cop-killer had to say about girls knocking him out with rocks.

Grace and Saelli had finished their brief statements. Saelli had impressed Grace with her ability to follow her lead and lie to the police. The police didn't mind her odd accent or word choices once Grace explained that Saelli was a tourist from Iceland.

After climbing back into her car, Grace rolled down her window and waved at the first officer. "Thanks for all your help. Next time we'll just run and let you guys do your thing."

He tapped the brim of his hat. "You two ladies take care of yourself, and I'm sorry your friend had to have such an unpleasant experience. Make sure she gets this isn't what America is about."

"She knows," Grace replied and rolled up her window. She pulled out and continued down the highway.

The earlier thick silence had returned. Grace didn't wait as long this time. Once the police lights had disappeared in the rearview mirror, she spoke.

"He's right, and I'm sorry," Grace insisted. "You had those mercenaries trying to kill you and now a random criminal. This is what I'm talking about. My species can be real garbage sometimes, but I hope you know that we're not all like that. I can honestly say out of all the crimes I've suffered, this is the first time somebody on the highway tried to take my car after I saved them from burning to death."

She cringed when she realized how it sounded. Saelli had come from one of the safest human countries on Earth. After her experience, she had to be convinced she was trapped in the Wild West.

Saelli did something Grace hadn't seen in a while; she smiled. "Petty criminals and paid killers don't worry me or mar my opinion of this beautiful land. I'll admit I've had my troubles, but attacks on me don't prove anything. The Azure Knives were willing to trade their lives to murder me. My people participated in the culling of humans in the distant past. I'm not one to judge humanity or your country for a tendency toward violence."

A shiver ran down Grace's spine. Sometimes she let herself forget how strange her new world could be. She was happy Saelli wasn't upset, but it was messed up that the elf didn't care because a fanatical group of cultists had tried to murder her not that long ago.

"Onward to Cold Town," Grace announced. "It's not like we have any polar bears in California to mess with you."

Grace pulled to a stop at the end of the dirt road. The bright white of the glacier peeked through the trees. She didn't envy trying to climb up there, but Saelli would use magic to do it quickly.

They'd scouted out scientist instrumentation packages a long time ago. Other than researchers, there weren't a lot of people in the state who visited this small patch of ice. It provided enough for Saelli to commune without attracting the serious numbers of tourists that might have made her trips difficult or required coordination with the DIA.

"Here we are at one of the few slices of permanent frigidness in California," Grace noted. "You haven't had any trouble the last few times, have you?"

"What sort of trouble are you referring to?" Saelli asked.

"People, rangers, that sort of thing. Just wanted to make sure."

"There are no humans where I stay." Saelli stared at the glacier longingly. "I do miss my home, but this is a minor sacrifice for a much greater good."

"That's a great attitude." Grace smiled. "Zaena only needs to line up the Mountain Elves, then it'll be on, right?"

Saelli kept looking at the glacier as she spoke in low tones. "I want to believe the Night Elves' monsters have faded from existence, but their nexus wasn't destroyed. The prophecy makes it clear we will face something terrible, and that is the place it's most expected."

Grace shivered and rubbed her shoulders. "I guess Zaena can't just ask the government to nuke it since she needs the Onyx of Shaping, but there's no way she could fail, not after all this."

Saelli turned her head slowly to stare at Grace. "You believe in the princess."

"Yeah, I suppose I do."

"A lot."

Grace shrugged. "Yes."

"Are you willing to risk your life for her?" Saelli asked. "For her mission? It is something that doesn't help humans at all."

Grace swallowed. "I believe in Zaena, and I believe the world will be a better place in the future when elves and humans can freely mix. Do I believe it's going to be perfect? No, but nothing ever is."

"You didn't answer my question," Saelli insisted, her tone strident. She grabbed Grace's arm. "Would you risk your life for hers?"

"I don't know," Grace replied. "If I thought I could save her, yes. She saved me when she didn't have to."

Saelli let go of Grace and looked at the glacier again. "Thank you for your help and honesty." She opened the door. "I will see you in a few days."

"Is everything all right?" Grace asked. "I don't just mean about your need to commune. You're sure there's nothing else you need to get off your chest or something you want me to take back to Zaena? I know your phone doesn't work out here."

"No," Saelli replied. "I'll be fine once I get to the glacier."

She lifted her hands. A disk of earth lifted her off the ground and carried her away.

Grace frowned. Something was wrong, but she didn't know what. It was hard for a human to question an elven priestess.

CHAPTER SEVENTEEN

Zaena gritted her teeth, then stretched out her hands and focused on a wall in the nexus chamber. Sweat beaded on her forehead as she infused tiny gusts of air with maximum magic.

Karl watched with his arms folded from a chamber entrance. "Is there anything I can do to help?"

"No." Zaena shook her head. A complex sigil on the wall glowed as her magic-infused air touched it before disappearing in a bright flash. "It's tedious and challenging work. Preparing the ritual sigils isn't that complicated provided you're familiar with the techniques, but then having to pass magic into them means retracing them with your power and maximum precision."

"That's tough for you?"

"Even without the Ruby of Tarilan, my magic is strong," Zaena replied, "so power isn't the issue. Nuance and precision aren't needed if one can overwhelm with sheer power. I don't particularly enjoy precision magic."

Karl chuckled. "Even the great Princess Zaena isn't

good at everything. It's almost enough to restore my faith in the world."

Zaena released her spell and leaned over, panting. She wiped her brow and stood up. "No individual, human or elf, is beyond the need for improvement."

"Hey, you're talking to a guy in need of a lot of improvement." Karl's gaze scoured the nexus chamber. "All these tunnels make this look like some weird crap out of a sci-fi horror movie. You know, like the alien queen is going to burst out and eat everyone?"

"Saelli suggested this of her own accord," Zaena began, "but I gave my full approval. It improves the defensibility of this structure. I hope we're never attacked, but I won't be as arrogant as Mark Wong and assume a few sentinels and guards will be enough."

Karl answered, "Not saying she should have set it up differently. I'm just saying it's weird-looking. It kind of gets under your skin, but since you brought up our local priestess, I wanted to talk to you about her when no one else was around. Now is a good as time as any to get something off my chest."

"I find that idiom more puzzling than many," Zaena admitted. She knelt. "I need a moment before my next set of spells. What is worrying you?"

"It's not that she's worrying me." Karl furrowed his brow. "She's okay but strange."

Zaena laughed. "Stranger than me? It's taken a concerted effort to talk to you without bewilderment and vice versa. Is she so different?"

"Yeah." Karl frowned. "She's more distant."

"I don't understand."

Karl spent a moment inspecting a carved sigil. "You not knowing about human and American culture has been a problem. We all get that, but you also had an excuse. It was all theory for you, not real-life, but she's been dealing with humans for decades. She still stands out a lot more, and I don't just mean because of the way she looks."

Zaena raised her eyebrows. "That disturbs you?"

"Nah. I wouldn't say it disturbs me."

"Do you feel it threatens the mission?"

"You'd know better than I do, but I'd say no. We don't need Saelli to do a lot with humans, and she can get around without causing a major scene, so she's doing better than you did your first few months here." Karl grinned.

"Very amusing, Karl. You wanted to have this conversation, so that suggests a more concrete worry."

"Worry's putting it too strongly," Karl replied. "It's interesting the way you two princesses are different. I'm not sure I buy into the prophecy stuff, but it's obvious she believes it. I'd put money on her being nothing but honest. I wasn't sure at first."

"Really?" Zaena stood and dusted off her jeans. "What did you think?"

"It's not crazy for someone being hunted to seek help," Karl noted. "It wasn't impossible she wanted you to protect her from the Azure Knives. I didn't want to accuse her of anything without evidence."

"That's the honorable path. You now believe she's following her prophecy with full honesty?"

"Yeah, that's the gist. What about you? It's been a couple of months, and I still can't tell if you think she's crazy or not."

"She's not mad," Zaena stated, "I don't think that of her. I don't know what to believe. I want to be cautious about assuming a glorious destiny will come regardless of work."

Karl chuckled. "Yeah, it's like we humans sometimes say, 'God helps those who help themselves.'"

"That is my concern." Zaena motioned around the cavern and at the complex carvings covering many of the walls. "Despite what so many assume, I wish for my success, but I don't believe it is preordained by the station of my birth. The simple reality is we can't proceed to the most important part of this mission without the cooperation of a Mountain Elf and ultimately their leadership."

"You'll find one," Karl suggested. "Why wouldn't you when you've found the others?"

"I was hoping one of the other tribes might have insight into the location of the Mountain Elf enclave," Zaena admitted, "but that plan has failed. When this nexus is attuned, it puts more pressure on me to move the mission along."

"Why?" Karl asked. "From what you told me, you've got centuries."

"I don't have centuries of guaranteed cooperation among the tribes and the US government," Zaena noted. "The political situation could change at any moment. Min'tuk is proof that not all elves are eager to participate in this task. Fortune has smiled on me, and I've sought to create opportunities, but I can't ignore the possibility that if I wait too long, I might lose the cooperation of any one of my newfound allies." She held up one finger. "Vokasin follows me out of whim." She held up another finger. "Saelli follows me because of a prophecy she might interpret differently with time." She held up a third finger. "Lae'yul and the others value my strength. They might have reason to doubt me if I can't bring the Mountain Elves in."

Karl chuckled. "Come on, Zaena. You've managed to lure a bunch of other elves here. I know you've had bad luck with the Mountain Elves, but from what you told me, the Ice Elves were a lot worse back in the day, and you have them on your side, or at least the most important one. You're overthinking all this."

"A possibility," Zaena admitted. "I suspect tracking down the Mountain Elves might come to something far more unpleasant and tedious than I desired."

"Are you talking about flying all around the world and checking out any major concentrations of magic?" Karl asked.

"Yes. I suspect if a Mountain Elf was going to show up in San Francisco because of my activities as the Crimson Wind, that would have already happened." Zaena walked over to a wall and ran her fingers over a sigil. "There's nothing I can do now but prepare for the nexus ritual. At least we'll be safer once that happens."

Karl looked toward a tunnel. "Hey, before you start up again, can you lead me out? I forgot my flashlight, and my phone's almost out of power."

"Gladly, my friend. Gladly."

Zaena motioned at a tunnel. Her arguments sounded logical, but the others were right. She'd had wild successes. Even if the Mountain Elves despised the royal family, it would be hard to ignore the cooperation of the other tribes.

No new elven arrivals meant no attacks. Amanda Morton was no longer a threat, and the government placed few demands on Zaena. Everything was going well—almost too well.

"It's not true," Zaena insisted.

"Huh?" Karl looked confused.

"Not everything that can go wrong will go wrong," Zaena explained.

"Oh. Murphy's Law, huh?" Karl chuckled. "Do you elves have an equivalent saying?"

"I know one common in the kingdom." Zaena rattled off Elvish before offering the best English translation she could manage. "Cast away your confidence. The wind can blow the leaf both toward and away from the fire."

Karl blinked. "Okay, I don't know if that's more cynical than the human version, but it's less catchy."

CHAPTER EIGHTEEN

Saelli sat in the center of the hollowed-out circular chamber deep within the ice. The blue, white, and green of the Diamond of Protection's forcefield lit the area. A simple static field adjusted to let many things through, including air, could last days if unchallenged.

Her sleeping bag wasn't much of a bed, but between the bag and a chair she'd carved from the wall, the chamber provided a comfortable place to commune and regain her magical power.

The utter quiet provided real peace. There were no large crowds or honking horns to overwhelm her.

She lay on the sleeping bag and let out a long sigh. Some of it she couldn't blame on being around others. Even when she'd lived in the enclave, she'd kept her distance from other Ice Elves, and not only because of her status as an apprentice priestess.

Saelli lifted her hand and spread out her fingers. She stared at the glowing roof through them.

Being a prophet didn't grant her greater insight into the

nature of fate. She couldn't be sure if fate was an inescapable destiny or a path to different destinations.

Could she force fate to her will? Is that what came with knowing a prophecy?

Saelli sat up. The other, more frightening possibility was that knowing a prophecy locked in the future. Serving Princess Zaena by delivering a useful prophecy might help them find a Mountain Elf, but it could also doom them all.

Locking in someone else's fate without asking their permission was questionable. The most honest path would have been for her to ask Zaena what she wanted.

The answer was obvious. The princess was honorable, and she was determined to take the burden of the great mission on herself. Inducing prophecy via a serious injury would be something Zaena would never allow.

Saelli didn't seek death. She sat nestled in the perfect environment for communing. Grievous injuries would heal in days.

She swallowed and lifted her hand. A blade of ice tore itself from the floor. It shot toward her and stabbed her chest.

Saelli gritted her teeth. Knowing pain was coming didn't make it hurt any less. She closed her eyes and lay back on her sleeping bag. Her chest throbbed.

"I beg of the elements to give me a prophecy of the Mountain Elves," she whispered. After voicing the thought aloud, she kept it in her mind, a prayer-filled meditation to distract her from the pain in her body until she passed out.

On the day the sun wishes most not to leave, go to where two ancient rivals are connected under the crushing depths by lines of three. He will come, but he will not come without pain.

Saelli gasped and shot up. Between ragged breaths, she ran her hand over the hole in her shirt. Dark stains covered the clothes and her skin, but her wound had healed. A dull ache had replaced the throbbing fire from before. The skin around the wound remained discolored.

She couldn't be sure how long she had slept, but given how badly she'd stabbed herself and her current state of health, it must have been at least a couple of days.

Saelli grabbed the phone gifted to her by the princess. It'd been two days, but she also needed to type in the prophecy while it remained fresh in her mind. She whispered each word as she typed it.

After finishing, she stared at the words. She'd prayed for a Mountain Elf prophecy. That had to be what this represented.

Grace would return the next day. Leaving the glacier would allow for a call, but another day of healing and communing made the most sense.

"I've done it, Princess," Saelli murmured. "I've done it."

CHAPTER NINETEEN

Grace hummed to herself and drummed her fingers on her steering wheel. She was doing her best not to look at Saelli.

Dealing with elves had put Grace in many awkward situations. Zaena was a lot better after so long in San Francisco, but she'd been a walking embarrassment factory when they first met. That forced Grace to accept that any encounter with an elf might put her in an uncomfortable situation she had no previous experience with.

Such was the case that afternoon. When Saelli got in the car, there wasn't a problem, but when she'd unzipped her jacket, it was hard to miss the huge hole in her shirt and the bloodstains.

Saelli's nonchalance made it hard to broach the subject. There could be some strange elf custom that Grace might be insulting by asking about it.

The elf didn't look or sound distressed, and the blood had dried. Whatever happened was long since over. It might not be best to pry.

"Have a good trip?" Grace asked. "Or communing session, whatever you want to call it."

Saelli nodded. "The people of San Francisco are kind, but every second I'm there, I'm reminded it's not my home. It's pleasing to be in a place that isn't so hot, but that won't be for some time."

"It's weird to hear someone complain about San Francisco being too hot," Grace replied with a chuckle. She glanced at Saelli and tried not to look at the hole. "There are all sorts of humans, and there are certain traits that make different types of people a little better for one environment or another, but elves take it to another level."

"Because we chose to change ourselves," Saelli noted. "We were not changed from outside like your kind."

"Hey..." Grace checked the rearview mirror, paranoid Zaena might be behind them. "Can I ask you something?"

"Yes. I will answer to the best of my ability."

"The way Zaena tells it, everyone used to be a Royal Elf or a Forest Elf. Then you all broke away and changed yourselves, partially over the Creeping Azure response and partially for other reasons." Grace's voice wavered. "It's not that I think she's lying to me, but she grew up a Tarilan princess. Sometimes I wonder how much of what she believes is propaganda. Vokasin has never acted like she was lying, but your tribe and hers didn't get along. You have more reason to challenge her version of history."

"My ancestors committed horrific acts. The Tarilans were right to fight us. They might have saved us."

"Saved you?"

"Yes. The madness of the Night Elves drove them to such extremes that they destroyed themselves." Saelli furrowed her brow. "The justification for culling was to save elves, yet in the end, an entire tribe ceased to be. The Night Elves feared doom but brought it on themselves. The Creeping Azure didn't wipe out the rest of us, and now Princess Zaena's efforts will end it once and for all. Patience was the appropriate strategy rather than genocidal madness."

Grace shivered. Saelli had delivered the speech in a soft tone, the same tone someone might use to discuss their favorite flower.

"So, you don't think the official royal version of history is a big pile of propaganda?" Grace asked.

"No," Saelli replied. "I'm sure there are details I could quibble over, but I wouldn't be aiding Zaena if I thought she was a misguided monster. The elements wouldn't have brought me to her if that were the case. You touched upon it earlier, but fate can be hard to escape."

"Sure, I guess, but what do you mean in particular?"

"Many groups chafed under the control of the Tarilans," Saelli explained. She stared out the front windshield, a distant look in her red eyes. "The only misrepresentation I might accuse them of is minimizing that and suggesting the Creeping Azure policy was mostly responsible for the split."

"Zaena doesn't spend a huge amount of time talking about elven history," Grace replied, "but I kind of got that."

"The Creeping Azure exacerbated things, of course," Saelli continued. "I know it must be difficult for a human to comprehend." She offered an apologetic look. "I don't say this to insult your intelligence, but the timescale of the disaster challenges human perspective. It didn't sweep over the planet like your Black Death in mere years and decades but crawled at first and pressed at the corners of elven civilization, advancing slowly but surely over the centuries. It gave the elves plenty of time to question and challenge each other, but in the end, it only accelerated the schisms that were already happening."

Grace took an opportunity to pass a car in front of her. There was no one ahead for as far as she could see. "You're saying the Creeping Azure policy differences were a symptom, not the cause."

"Yes." Saelli's hand drifted to the hole in her shirt. "The Night Elves might still live, but it was ideology that drove the unified elven race apart. Who can say what a true elf is or is not now? The Forest Elves claim that we should all be as they are, but the Sea Elves point to the greater amount of water and say they are living more in harmony with this planet."

"What about the Ice Elves?"

"The soul of my people is as cold as our ice," Saelli told her with a solemn look. "The Azure Knives are murderous, but in a sense, they are no different than most in my tribe. We all accept one fundamental truth. We all accept that our actions in the past weren't justified. They wouldn't so readily accept the Creeping Azure if they didn't believe that."

"Plenty of human philosophies and religion have similar ideas," Grace noted. "There's nothing wrong with accepting that you aren't inherently perfect and trying to move forward and live a good life despite that."

"Yes." Saelli narrowed her eyes. "I can't help but wonder if we were destined to split up no matter what. Now I wonder what fate has in store for the future. I do believe Princess Zaena will cure the Creeping Azure but are the separate tribes meant to become one?"

Grace whistled. "That'd be impressive. You're right, I'm a human, and I think in human timescales. The idea of things flowing over centuries and thousands of years is weird and, I hate to say it, alien."

Saelli agreed. "Does a butterfly worry about what might happen in fifty years?"

Grace let silence take over. During the conversation, she'd been able to ignore the hole in Saelli's clothes, but the evidence of injury combined with sadness in her voice made Grace want to press forward. The Ice Elf always sounded a little melancholy, but this felt worse.

Another five miles of highway passed before Grace mustered the courage to continue. "What the hell happened up there?"

Saelli tore herself away from her intense review of local trees. "Excuse me?"

"You have bloodstains on your clothes," Grace said, keeping her eyes on the road, "and a big obvious hole. I've seen Zaena get messed up and then heal like a miracle while camp…uh, communing afterward, so I'm not surprised you'd get hurt and be okay, but I'm trying to figure out how it happened. It's not like there are giant ice worms in the glacier, right?"

Saelli laughed. "There are no ice worms in California."

Grace blinked. She'd pulled the creature out of her imagination. She was too afraid to follow up. Confirmation they weren't near her was enough.

"Okay." Grace let out a nervous chuckle. "No ice

worms, and there isn't a nexus nearby, so we know you didn't get attacked by some soul-bound elf running an evil village of the undead. You've also communed here plenty of times without coming back with signs of obvious injury. So, I'd like to know what happened."

Saelli stared at the window for a good twenty seconds before responding, "Why?"

"Because I'm worried about you," Grace replied in an exasperated voice. "You might think I'm going too far in saying you're my friend, but Zaena's my friend, my best friend, and she cares about you, so I care about you. That's how things work with me."

"I was injured," Saelli replied, "but as you have said, I was in my communing spot. The injuries healed. There's no need for concern."

Grace scoffed. "I don't know a lot about your relationship with your mother, but let me tell you a little about my relationship with mine. That woman is the empress of not saying what she feels."

"I don't understand why we're talking about your mother."

"What I'm getting at is that I'm very good at noticing when people are trying to hide something," Grace explained. "Something happened in there. You might as well tell me now because I'm going to go tell Zaena, and she'll be harder to brush off."

Saelli sighed. "There's a new prophecy."

"Whoa." Grace jerked the wheel in surprise. The car swerved. She straightened it out. "Sorry about that. You were saying?"

"I dreamt a new prophecy," Saelli confirmed. "I wrote it on my phone."

"Probably not a great idea," Grace explained. "Everybody and their uncle can hack phones. Let's pull over, write it down on paper, and erase it from the phone as best we can. Do you plan to tell Zaena?"

"I do."

"Then I'll let you tell her in person." Grace grimaced. "This isn't one of those 'Anyone who hears this will die in the next seven days' things, is it?"

"No." Saelli shook her head. "Danger is involved, but I trust the princess."

"That makes two of us."

CHAPTER TWENTY

Zaena read the small slip of paper five times in silence. She'd been shocked when Grace had called her and told her to come to Saelli's apartment to hear about a special dream. After committing the prophecy to memory, she handed it to Karl.

Karl looked at the paper. "I don't know if I buy into this mumbo jumbo as much as the rest of you, but pretending I do, I'm not seeing how this is all that helpful."

"It is directions to a Mountain Elf," Saelli insisted. "I prayed to the elements to give me guidance, and I received this prophecy."

"Why do you think it's directions to a Mountain Elf?" Karl shook the paper. "It doesn't say crap about elves or mountains."

"Royal Elves and Mountain Elves as two ancient rivals?" suggested Grace.

Karl snorted. "Come on. That could apply to a lot of people and things. I'm not saying she's wrong and this is just a dream, but it's nothing we can use."

Saelli bowed her head. "Karl's right. It's useless, after all."

Zaena patted her on the shoulder. "I maintain some skepticism about prophecy, but accepting it, it's a matter of interpretation. The prophecy that led you to me wasn't clear until several other factors came together."

Grace snapped her fingers. She rushed toward a closet. "Have you moved a lot of stuff in here, Saelli?"

Saelli replied, "No. Other than the chilling sigils, I've done little to change this place."

"Good. That means there's stuff left over from when Zaena lived here." Grace threw open a hallway closet door and rummaged for a moment before producing a magnetic whiteboard and a black marker. "Time for Team Princess to brainstorm."

"That sounds unpleasant," Saelli noted with a frown.

"It's an idiom describing an active collaboration process," Zaena replied, feeling proud of herself for her command of the language.

Grace took the whiteboard into the kitchen and hung it on the refrigerator. She wrote out the prophecy neatly before drawing a line beneath it and tapping it. "Now we just throw out stuff to figure out the truth."

Karl scrubbed a hand over his face. "You think we're going to be able to figure out a prophecy by acting like we're a bunch of dumbasses in a corporate meeting?"

She rolled her eyes. "The only person in this room with any experience in interpreting prophecies is Saelli. Do you have a better idea?"

"Crushing depths," Karl replied, rubbing his chin. "I feel like an idiot for admitting it, but that implies underwater to me. Not just under the bay, but somewhere deeper, like the ocean."

"We should be cautious of interpreting anything too literally," suggested Saelli, "but your input is valued."

Grace scribbled Underwater and ocean? on the board, along with an arrow to crushing depths. "Maybe underground?" She added her suggestion to the board. "You're right. It does sound like something to do with water."

"Submarines," Zaena suggested. "I watched a movie the other day that mentioned crush depth."

"We're not going to find a Moun—" Karl stopped speaking when Grace glared at him.

"Would you have ever guessed we'd find a Mountain Elf pretending to be a gangster?" Grace asked. She scribbled down the submarine note.

Karl snickered. "You got me there."

Zaena rubbed her hands together. "If this turns out to be nothing, it'll harm no one to pursue it. The prophecy is useful. It contains a specific day, a location, and a suggestion of an encounter. This is, you might say, actionable intelligence."

"What's the day the sun wishes not to leave the most?" Karl asked with a shrug. "A holiday? An elven holiday?"

"The tribes have different celebrations," Zaena noted. "Royal Elves don't have any holiday involving veneration of the sun."

Saelli shook her head. "My people value the elements, not the sun."

"Maybe a human holiday?" Grace suggested. "Plenty of humans worshipped the sun, but things get obscure if we think about it that way."

Karl pulled out his phone and tapped something in. He grinned. "Prophecy's easier when you have the internet." Everyone looked his way expectantly. "I asked, 'What's the longest day of the year?'"

Grace's eyes widened. "The summer solstice." She scribbled it on the board. "That's less than a month away."

"Prophecy isn't always imminent," Saelli noted.

Zaena pointed at the board. "On the solstice, somewhere under the sea, something important will happen. Who are the two ancient rivals? Two factions among the Sea Elves? They could have internal enemies similar to the Azure Knives."

Grace wrote the suggestion with a frown. "Don't you think Lae'yul would have mentioned that? She's not a friendly little mermaid, but she does want this mission to succeed."

"That's true. She's been straightforward about the political considerations." Zaena stared at the board. "The who is less important than the where or when. I'm comfortable with the idea this represents the summer solstice and something under the sea, but I don't understand what the lines of three might reference."

Karl grunted. "That could be tricky. Three lines? A triangle? The Bermuda Triangle? Is that an elf thing?"

Zaena laughed. "There's nothing unusual about the Bermuda Triangle when you consider the normal frequency of ship disasters. You can make a triangle over any major path of human traffic and get about the same number of lost ships and planes. Presuming it's cursed is nothing more than human pattern-matching at work."

Karl stared at her. "Let me get this straight. You, a

magical elven princess from a hidden kingdom underneath Antarctica, are telling me it's silly to think there's anything special or magical about the Bermuda Triangle?"

"I watched a documentary on it. Very convincing. Neal deGrasse Tyson was in it."

Grace turned and laughed into her hand. The act confused Zaena, but she wanted to keep her focus on the prophecy.

"Are there any sea borders that touch like that?" Zaena asked. "Three seas that touch?"

"Sea borders are weird," Karl noted. "It's not like countries. There are different lines people recognize, and they let you wander over others." He tapped away at this phone. "Yeah, that's not promising."

"What about deep lakes?" Grace suggested.

"Huh." Karl furrowed his brow. "The closest thing I can come up with quick searching is that Michigan touches three of the Great Lakes, but I don't think we can search all of Michigan and three Great Lakes in one day."

"He will come," Saelli intoned. She waited until everyone was looking at her to continue, "He will come, but he will not come without pain."

Zaena agreed. "I'm hardly surprised that violence might be involved, but I'm sure this prophecy isn't intended to lead us astray."

"I thought you didn't buy into this stuff?" Karl noted.

"There's no harm in pursuing potentially useful information," Zaena replied, "and I trust Saelli enough to at least look into it."

Saelli blushed and looked away. "I'm trying my best to help you, Princess."

"You were probably right before, Zaena," Karl offered. "Let's assume whoever is there might come in hot. You bring along Dino Boy and Saelli or Lae'yul as backup, and that shouldn't be a problem. Assuming we've got the day right, it's useless without the location. It'd be nice if we had a time."

"Dawn," Grace declared confidently. She gestured at a clock. "That's the starting point for the day."

Karl shrugged. "Could be true. I can't believe my life's at the point where I'm saying 'could be true' while discussing dream prophecies from Ice Elf priestesses."

Zaena clapped once. "We're halfway there. We can do this. Let us continue our grand brainstorming session!"

An hour later, Zaena stared at the board. Grace had taken a seat, as had Karl. Saelli stood at the edge of the dining table, her eyes downcast. They'd bounced around ideas to the point that they needed to erase most of their notes, but they'd ended up back where they'd started. Someone or something hostile was coming on the summer solstice, most likely underwater, but they had no insight into who that was or where.

"There's not much we can do at this point," Grace offered in a defeated tone. "We still have weeks before the solstice. We can keep thinking about it and trying to come up with something."

Karl looked to Saelli. "You don't have any more hints?"

She smiled. "It doesn't work that way."

"It's fine," Zaena told them with a firm nod. "We know

more about the future than we did yesterday. That is a victory. I'm sure the answer will present itself to us with time, but Karl, without mentioning the source of information, you might broach the subject of international travel with the DIA and Miss D'Arcy. It'd be lovely if we were fortunate enough for our encounter to be close to our home, but my instincts tell me we'll be traveling farther afield this time."

Karl stood and dusted off his pants. "Okay, I'll do my best."

Zaena smiled at Saelli. "Good job. Thank you for your help."

"You're welcome, Princess."

Grace headed toward the door. "Hey, Zaena, can I talk to you about something for a bit since we're done with the Team Princess prophecy brainstorming conference?"

"Of course." Zaena followed her friend into the hallway.

Grace looked over her shoulder and walked up the hall until they reached a turn. "She changed her clothes before you arrived, but when I picked up Saelli, she'd recovered from a nasty wound."

"I doubt if there are any active ice worms in California," Zaena murmured.

Grace groaned. "Am I the only one who doesn't know about ice worms? Anyway, she's hiding something. I don't like it. I'm not saying she's planning to screw you, but she reminds me of the early you."

"The early me?" Zaena cocked her head. "What does that mean?"

"You thought you had to handle everything yourself in the beginning," Grace explained. She gestured down the hall. "I think Saelli thinks she's protecting you. It's just my instinct. Call me the Elf Whisperer if you want."

Zaena considered the possibilities. Saelli would have no reason to conceal a monster attack. That limited the options.

"The surviving Azure Knives might have tracked her to California," Zaena suggested. "She's had some worries about her battle abilities outside of Iceland." Something didn't sit right. "If they attacked her on the glacier, she would have been well-prepared to fight them off."

"Remember that carjacker we ran into?" Grace asked. "What if she ran into someone like him? Some psycho killer human, and she had to take him out?"

Zaena shook her head. "I doubt she'd conceal it. If anything, she seems to feel human deaths more keenly than I do because of her experiences in Iceland and the oath she made to that Helga woman. Don't worry." She smiled. "I'll give her time to calm down and then speak to her."

CHAPTER TWENTY-ONE

Zaena sipped her hot coffee, smiling to herself at a sudden realization. She'd wrapped a layer of hot air around herself to counter the magical chilliness of Saelli's apartment. For all their concern about preserving magic, while they were outside their enclaves, they used it for the most basic of creature comforts, as they now used spells to cancel the effects of other spells.

That would change soon. With Saelli's return, the nexus preparation could proceed quicker. Although Vokasin was nowhere to be found, he had a habit of showing up exactly when he was needed. After she collected Lae'yul and Min'tuk from Alcatraz the following morning, they'd be ready for attunement. She frowned, realizing that Vokasin had managed to escape having to prepare sigils.

Saelli sat at her dining room table across from Zaena. "What did you wish to speak to me about, Princess? Did you have some other ideas about the prophecy?"

Zaena shook her head. "I think we should absorb the

prophecy and think about it. Vokasin and Lae'yul might have some ideas. No, I came to talk about something else."

"What?"

Zaena leaned forward, adopting her best haughty princess stare. Her father stressed that being royalty went far beyond their bloodline aura. It was far less effective with elves anyway.

Saelli averted her eyes. "I didn't mean to offend you, Princess."

"You haven't offended me," Zaena said. "You have worried me."

"I had to bring you the prophecy," Saelli insisted. "It was the only way I could think of to help you. I'm less familiar with the human world than Vokasin. I can't travel as easily as Lae'yul. I lack the ability to speak to human contacts like Grace and Karl. My prophecy is my best tool."

"I'm not upset with you for bringing the prophecy," Zaena noted. "I'm overjoyed if anything. I know we haven't solved it, but we know more than we did when you first received it. I'm confident we'll figure out where we need to go, and we will travel there and find a Mountain Elf, or at least a lead on a Mountain Elf. I don't worship the elements like you, but I'm finding it difficult to deny your special power. In this case, your prayer must have been answered."

Saelli bowed her head. "I only wish to be of service. The shadow of my fate has hung over me my entire life, but now rays of light push through."

Zaena picked up her hot chocolate and took a sip. "I was so excited to hear about the prophecy it made me almost forget something else."

"Something important?"

Zaena nodded. "The convenient timing."

"My prayers were answered."

"Yet I'm sure you've prayed to the elements many times in your life." Zaena narrowed her eyes. "I feel like there's something you're not telling me."

Saelli looked away. "Is this because of what Grace saw?"

"Perhaps, but now that you've mentioned it, I find I'm more curious." Zaena stood and leaned over Saelli. "If you wish to aid me, you need to be honest with me. Something is disturbing here. A prophecy is surprising but not disturbing, but there's no reason you should have suffered an injury on the glacier. It's beyond absurd that an Ice Elf would have an accident there. Animals in the area would respect your presence, and you'd sense any wounded creatures."

"I brought you the prophecy."

Zaena sighed and knelt in front of Saelli, trying to dampen her intimidation. "We're about to participate in an extremely dangerous ritual. I've let you live here near the nexus and trusted you around my human allies. I'm going to attune you to the nexus and give you power. If that doesn't prove my trust, what does? I'm not your princess, but I am your leader, and I deserve your honesty. What happened up there?"

Saelli stared at her hands. "We needed a lead, Princess, and I gave you that lead."

Zaena's breath caught. "What does the injury have to do with the prophecy?"

"I recently realized something. Now that I'm not running away from my gift, it lets me reflect more on when I've received prophecies." Saelli's mouth twitched, and she hesitated. "I realized that a serious injury had the potential of summoning a prophecy—not a guarantee but a chance. We needed one."

Zaena gasped. "You did it to yourself?"

"I wasn't in danger, Princess," Saelli insisted. "Not really. I was in my communing room. I was protected by the diamond. I awakened a couple of days—"

"Days?" shouted Zaena. "You hurt yourself badly enough that you slept for days?"

Saelli looked down. "I survived."

"You're a fool," Zaena insisted. She frowned at Saelli. "You were alone, and worse, you were protected by the diamond. Even if someone became aware of what you'd done, they might not have been able to save you."

Saelli swallowed. "I was worried about enemies like the Knives, but it worked."

"You admitted you weren't sure it would," Zaena snapped. "You risked your life without any backup. We both know communing is powerful, but it's not perfect. You could have quite literally made a fatal mistake."

Saelli stood. She couldn't make eye contact with Zaena, but she shoved more passion into her voice. "You've risked your life on countless occasions for causes you thought were just, both protecting humans and fighting evil elves."

"That's not the same," Zaena insisted.

"I've heard you talk about your battles. In Iceland, Vokasin and I fought at your side, but you challenged that Mountain Elf and his army by yourself."

"That's not true," Zaena replied. "I had the aid of humans."

"They didn't engage the Demon Overlords inside this building," Saelli replied. "I've heard you discuss it with Karl and Grace. You fought the humans, the creations of Mark Wong, an elf infused with the direct power of a nexus. You were nearly killed."

Zaena sighed. "That is overstating things, and I had little choice. Mark Wong intended a massacre. His power was growing unchecked. It was fortunate I arrived when I did, or he might have become unstoppable."

"You're saying fate put you where you needed to be at the right time."

"I don't know. What I'm saying is that I attempted to deal with Wong and the Overlords without violence." Zaena looked sad. "He left me no choice, and I worked closely with others who were aware of the risks to themselves and me. I didn't make a unilateral decision without informing anyone. Now I wonder…"

"Wonder what?"

"What would have happened if you'd asked me and I'd ordered you not to?"

Saelli managed to lift her head and offer something close to a defiant look. "As you've said to me, you're not my princess."

Zaena scoffed. "And you've told me we're entwined by fate. Please, Saelli, your decision was made without even informing me. It's obvious you didn't want me to forbid you from doing it, and it's obvious that you wouldn't have obeyed."

"We could have every elf in the world and all the power of every nexus," Saelli replied in a near-whisper, "but we still can't turn back time. The storm has begun. The raindrops can't return to their clouds because they're frightened."

"I'm ordering you never to do that again," Zaena said in a commanding tone. "If you can't take this order, you can stay in the glacier. I won't have an elf throw her life away on a guess and a possibility."

Saelli sank into her chair. "I needed to do it. The elements gave me the prophecy for a reason."

Zaena sighed and squeezed Saelli's shoulder. "We won the gamble this time, but that is something you do when you have no other options. We still had time and a choice, but the risk of failure isn't worth it. It makes no strategic sense. The balance of risk and reward was off."

"I wanted to be useful. I wanted to serve the great mission."

"You have." Zaena inclined her head toward the floor. "Your work with the nexus chamber has been critical." She backed away. "Perhaps I'm a hypocrite. If I truly had the courage of my convictions, I would refuse to use the information your gamble netted, but since you've already done it, I will honor your commitment by doing my best to take advantage of it. That's the other reason this was a foolish gamble. A prophecy remains a riddle until solved, and a riddle isn't worth your life, even if it's a riddle about the future."

Saelli gave a shallow nod. "I understand, Princess."

"Again, I'm being a hypocrite, but let me give you the same advice I was recently given. We're elves. We don't need to be so impatient. For now, get a good rest. Tomorrow we're attuning the nexus."

CHAPTER TWENTY-TWO

Pulses of crimson light blasted from the sparking nexus heart. A sharp, resounding crack accompanied each. Zaena squinted but didn't look away. She concentrated on imbuing the air in front of her with magical energy.

The attuning theory was simple, especially because she wasn't casting a spell. She was doing nothing more than forcefully leaking magical power without channeling it into her elemental spells. It was an exercise in raw power.

When she'd been a child learning to control her abilities, this sort of display was held up as the ultimate example of failed and wasteful magic. She was emitting massive amounts of power to produce no direct magic. Her powerful magical potential had led to lazy tactics in the past, but ironically, that was exactly what the ritual called for—all power and no technique.

Zaena took slow, deep breaths. Remembering to breathe was proving to be the hardest part of the ritual.

Despite the complex preparation work, the final steps in the process were straightforward. There were no complicated spells or incantations. All the participating elves projected their raw magic power directly into the nexus, and it responded in kind. Those standing, sitting, or kneeling over the appropriate channeling sigils would increase their connection until they were linked on a fundamental level.

The loud cracking noises began to overlap with the echoes of their predecessors. The pulses had been increasing in frequency since the beginning of the ritual. When the elves had begun, the pulses had erupted every couple of minutes, but now they came several times a second.

Zaena wasn't sure how much time had passed since the start of the ritual. No one spoke. Everyone concentrated on shoving magic into the nexus while also doing their best to ignore the pain. She couldn't remember the last time she'd been forced to focus with such rigid determination.

With enough participants, the attunement could have been a routine, almost boring procedure. With fewer than five people, it was dangerous and potentially lethal. Zaena had gathered just enough assistants to eliminate the chance of magical backlash killing anyone, but not enough to avoid discomfort, pain, and intense effort.

Another pulse. Another crack. Agonizing heat replaced the distracting warmth Zaena normally felt when exposed to strong magic. Kneeling in front of the heart with her arms stretched toward the nexus, she gritted her teeth.

The ritual wouldn't kill her. She trusted that, but giving up would mean having to start the whole process again.

With exhaustion weighing her down, it might take a day or two to be ready again.

She didn't want to ignore the truth of this ritual. Five elves surrounded the heart, all going through the same suffering. They represented all but one of the living tribes.

Zaena forced a smile through the pain. They lacked the aid of the Mountain Elves, but this alliance couldn't be dismissed. Decades and centuries of work had been reduced to a year. Fate was smiling on them.

Karl and Grace had been right; she'd forged something that hadn't existed in thousands of years. What was starting with a handful of elves would spread to the other tribes after they cured the Creeping Azure. The elves might never live as one again, but they didn't need to be enemies.

A tutor in her early childhood had told her it would take a miracle for the elven tribes to turn their efforts to one shared purpose. She was creating that miracle.

Vokasin growled, drawing Zaena's attention. Sweat bathed Saelli's face. Min'tuk and Lae'yul both wore the same stony-faced expression of concentration as if they'd practiced it together before coming to the nexus.

Buoyed by the efforts of the others, Zaena continued pushing magic and regulating her breathing. Her eyelids and arms had grown heavy. Her heart thundered in her chest. She almost welcomed the numbness spreading through her body. It made it easier to ignore the fiery pain.

The pulsing sped up so much that Zaena could feel the light more than perceive it. Pain spread through every cell in her body. She hissed but didn't move. The pain proved their ritual was working. They were almost there.

Sparks stopped erupting from the nexus. Red light spread over Zaena before covering Saelli, Vokasin, Lae'yul, and Min'tuk in turn.

Zaena kept her breathing even. Everything was proceeding as they'd planned and discussed. They could do it. They *had* to do it.

Saelli slumped but kept her arms up. She vomited. They'd not planned on that.

"Don't stop," she whispered. "Please don't stop."

Zaena chanced another look at the Sea Elves. Min'tuk had the added distraction of having to split his magic between their surface breathing spell and the ritual, where Lae'yul had her breathing artifact. Both had their eyes closed, but their chests still rose and fell. Vokasin looked less distressed than the others until Zaena noticed his eyes had turned reptilian and his breathing was ragged.

"We're almost there," Zaena announced in a strained voice. "Steel yourself for what's coming, but we shall have victory."

"Just don't fail now, Fourth Born," Vokasin growled. "This isn't as amusing as I'd hoped."

"Many things are more necessary than amusing."

"Less talking," Min'tuk demanded. "Finish the ritual."

The loud cracks made it hard to hear anyone. The nexus heart swelled, consuming the stone cage around it. Tremors shook the chamber.

Zaena forced herself to her feet. She could barely feel her legs or feet. "I am Princess Zaena vel Tarilan, First Princess and fourth in line for the throne of the Royal Elven Kingdom," she declared loudly, forcing her eyes open and staring directly into the nexus.

"What are you doing, air-breather?" Min'tuk spat, barely audible under the thunder of the nexus. "This is no time for your pretentiousness."

Zaena didn't bother to look at him. "I'm here to represent the Royal Elves, alongside Vokasin, bearer of the Sun Gem of the Desert Elves, Saelli who bears the Diamond of Protection of the Ice Elves, and Min'tuk and Lae'yul of the Sea Elves, who will bear the Pearl of Summoning in the future. We come here today representing all tribes."

Min'tuk tried to say something else, but only a grunt of pain came out. He doubled over but kept his arms up.

Speaking took Zaena's mind off the pain. "This attunement isn't about power or glory. This isn't about revenge against Mark Wong. This attunement represents the first step in freeing elves from the tyranny of the Creeping Azure, the evil cursed disease that has forced our people to hide from the rest of the world for thousands of years."

"Is this really the time?" Vokasin asked with his jaws clenched.

"Hear me now, anything and anyone who might be listening," Zaena shouted. "We will be free!"

It was a turning point in history. They all had discussed theories and the future, but the others didn't appreciate that truth. Such moments needed to be marked. It wasn't just the time for such declarations; she'd argue it was required.

Every elf in that room walked without fear of the Creeping Azure. It'd become a nuisance to them, not a deadly threat, but the scarcity of immune elves meant the occasional free elf had only minimal influence on the cultures of the tribes.

Everything would be different soon. The others present needed to understand they'd taken the first step in changing the entire world.

Min'tuk slumped onto his side, his eyes clenched shut. The pain of the nexus flared in the others. Their faces contorted.

Zaena looked at the Sea Elf, her vision swimming. The power now flowed through only four of them, but they'd completed the bulk of the ritual.

"Do we stop?" Vokasin shouted.

"No," Zaena insisted. "We're close now. We can do it."

Lae'yul pointed one arm at Min'tuk. "He lives, but I must maintain his breathing spell."

"We won't stop," Zaena insisted, blinking sweat out of her eyes. "Do what you must to save his life. I'll finish it myself if necessary. I can survive it at this point."

Saelli sat up. She was even paler than usual, her fine veins standing out. Stretching out her arms and raising her palms, she offered, "I will help you, Princess, no matter what."

Pain overwhelmed Zaena. She dropped to her knees.

The nexus grew again. Zaena fought her instinct to close her eyes as bright light consumed her and washed out everyone and everything else in the room. The ritual demanded that she stare into the heart of the nexus near the end.

Zaena's eyes burned. Her chest burned.

The heart of the nexus snapped back to its normal size. Saelli's stone cage provided a snug fit.

Zaena's pain vanished as if it'd never been there. Her heart continued pounding but slowed when a comforting warmth soaked her body. It washed away her fatigue and concern, leaving her feeling refreshed and relaxed.

Min'tuk's eyes fluttered open. He frowned and looked away. Lae'yul grimaced.

"We did it," Zaena announced, standing and swaying. "I can feel it." She took slow, even breaths. "It almost feels like I've been communing."

Saelli hugged her shoulders, the color returning to her cheeks. "I don't feel drained anymore."

"Remember, our power is tied to this place, so it won't help when we're away from the area," Zaena noted.

Vokasin's eyes returned to normal. He lifted his hand and summoned a flame. "It's not what I expected. It doesn't feel like I thought it would."

"What did you expect?" Zaena asked.

"To feel powerful and stronger, but this feels comfortable. It's relaxing. Soothing."

Lae'yul tugged Min'tuk to his feet. "This one is ready to return to the water, as am I. We've done what you need, Princess. We would take our leave of this place of rock and little water."

"Thank you both for your assistance." Zaena's gaze flicked to the nexus. "Thank you all for your help. Your names will go down in elven history."

CHAPTER TWENTY-THREE

Karl stared at the glowing elven sigils lining the smooth tunnel. The elaborate maze might not have been necessary anymore, but to his annoyance, no one had mentioned getting rid of it.

Although he hadn't studied Elven, spending a year around Zaena and dealing with Mark Wong's creations had impressed certain repeating patterns into his mind. He had no idea what most of the sigils did, nor had he asked, but he recognized enough to learn the patterns for the correct tunnels.

Karl cared less about the sigils than the warmth on his skin. He'd expected to feel something different given the massive surge of magic he'd felt in the main building during the ceremony, but now that it was all over, the nexus hadn't changed for him. It was exactly like it'd been before and after Mark Wong's death, stronger than any magic Zaena or others might pull but not overwhelming.

Karl turned a corner. A rock statue covered with

glowing brown sigils stood in the center of the tunnel, one of Saelli's new stone guardians. It lacked the artistic flair of Mark Wong's terracotta soldiers, but with two legs, two arms, and three sharp fingers, it had what it needed to fight.

The statue stepped aside. There was something unnerving about magical soldiers working for their side. At least Saelli had created them to recognize Karl and Grace, along with the other core members of Team Princess.

When he arrived in the main nexus chamber, he spotted Zaena standing near a rock wall, slight magic emanating from her. She ran her finger along the wall, carving into it with a thin, invisible blade of air.

"You sure you should be doing this so soon?" Karl asked. "It's not even been twenty-four hours. From what you described, I figured you'd want to be sleeping it off."

"I think you misunderstood," Zaena replied with a smile. "The ritual was unpleasant, but now I'm thoroughly recharged. I don't think I've ever been this powerful in my life."

She kept carving the wall. Intricate glowing arcane symbols decorated the top portion.

"Really?" Karl stuck his hands in his pockets and sat on a boulder. "What about back in the kingdom? Weren't you plugged into the nexus? Isn't that how it works? The Royals are the ones connected up?"

That made the most sense to him. It was how he imagined most human countries would run things if they had magic.

"Even my father wasn't directly attuned to the nexus in the kingdom. My family's distant ancestors helped attune the nexus when my people first moved to Antarctica to create the enclave, but it's the responsibility of an elite order in our kingdom and has been passed down through the centuries to their descendants. When one member dies, a new one is attuned. They are the elves most directly responsible for maintaining the livability of the kingdom and are respected as such."

"Sounds like a bunch of magical power engineers," Karl suggested. "Or magical bureaucrats?"

"That's not an incorrect way of thinking of them." Zaena finished her latest sigil. "The more I think about what we can do with his nexus, the more disappointed I am with Mark Wong."

Karl chuckled. "I'm not disappointed with him. He died. He did us a favor, or do you mean you're disappointed with him for being a big asshole?"

"I mean, his greed for personal power blinded him to the overall potential." Zaena stepped away from the wall and surveyed the sigils. "He was more interested in using it to fuel himself than to do things like setting up proper defenses."

"What about all his terracotta soldiers? Those things were enough of a threat that we had to go begging for help."

"Only because he was using them as terror tools." Zaena walked across the chamber to a barren patch of wall. "The nexus' power let him field a lot of them, but he could have kept me out of his room with a shield spell fueled by the nexus if he'd focused it locally rather than relying on a tether to empower himself wherever he went. He could have made it all but impossible for a single elf to invade with such ease, even one bearing the Ruby of Tarilan."

"Huh." Karl looked at the closest tunnel. "You're going to put up a shield?"

"Of sorts. We'll be implementing a spell that will block everyone but members of Team Princess. It's not impregnable, but it's another thing that will slow potential enemies. We'll also be setting up alarm wards to detect magic not coming from us. First, it'll be in the nexus area, and then it'll be over the entire building."

"Can't you already sense magic?"

"Sensing an elf entering the building from across it and knowing exactly where he is would be better than a vague sense of spells being cast nearby," Zaena explained. "Especially since these would make it clear it's not any of the elves attuned to the nexus."

"That makes sense, and for the shield, could you plug in the Diamond of Protection?"

"Potentially." Zaena carved the first line of a new sigil. "I think it's too much to ask from Saelli. That's a sacred artifact of her people. I'd never ask her not to have direct control over it."

"I was just thinking if some crazy guy brought in a bomb, it'd be a nice defense."

Zaena shook her head. "A human bomb won't destroy the nexus." She motioned around. "Although Saelli has the power now, it takes time to create stone guardians. We plan to station at least six here and numerous others in the tunnels."

"Why not the ice guys you told me about?" Karl asked. "From what you said, it's easier for her to make them. Sometimes quantity beats quality."

Zaena wrinkled her nose. "That would require this entire tunnel system to be frigid. In this case, we'll follow the American example of democracy. There are more of us who are uncomfortable and less effective in cold temperatures."

Karl chuckled. "Just wear a sweater."

"Your question does bring to mind other environmental restrictions." Zaena stepped away from her carving. "This place is very inconvenient for our Sea Elf allies."

"Why don't you build them a pool down here?" Karl joked.

Zaena nodded once. "That's exactly what I was thinking."

"Seriously?"

Karl imagined an Olympic-sized lap pool filled with naked Sea Elves. His life could always get weirder.

"We're not doing it immediately," Zaena clarified. "Lae'yul won't be back until the first of the month anyway, but one of our upcoming projects will be to build accessible water tunnels for Lae'yul, along with pools in the main nexus chamber for maximum comfort."

"She's got that artifact."

"Which she shouldn't have to constantly rely on," Zaena noted. "It could be lost, damaged, or taken, like in my first encounter with her. Then it's a matter of constantly using magic, which can be draining even with a link to the nexus."

Karl looked at the nexus. It was beautiful. The sparks were hypnotic.

"If you're thinking like that, why not an industrial-sized refrigerator room for Saelli?" he asked. "She keeps her apartment cold, but if you're expanding this place into a mini-enclave, shouldn't everyone have what they need?"

Zaena blinked. "I suppose you're right. I was so fixated on the idea of her doing the entire tunnel system, I didn't think of the other opportunities for improvements."

"So, in other words, eventually, this place is going to have a bunch of water-filled tunnels, ponds, stone statues, and crazy ice soldiers?"

"Yes." Zaena gestured grandly. "This isn't an enclave, but it must become a symbol of cooperation among the tribes. Small gestures such as the one you suggested will be helpful for that, but there are other things we should include if we're planning."

"Such as?"

"A training facility," Zaena suggested. "Something vast enough that we can practice fighting without having to risk damage to a forest or being spied upon by the government. I don't feel the need to constantly demonstrate my abilities to them."

"Huh. That's a good idea. You can use the same ground survey data Grace's already gathered for the initial expansion, but I have a hard time thinking you're going to have trouble going deeper. I don't think the city's running much in the way of water and gas this deep."

"I'd hope not, but you're right. We don't want to create problems for anyone else."

Karl stood and walked over to the stone cage. "While

you're planning things, is there going to be a desert room for Dino Boy? Bring in a bunch of sand? Have Saelli make some?"

"It's beyond our power and ability to produce what he truly needs. It goes beyond a place that is both hot and dry. I should note these small home comforts won't be enough for true communing."

"You have the nexus." Karl pointed at the cage. "Isn't that all the power you need?"

"Communing isn't only about magical power," Zaena insisted. "It's about soothing the very soul of an elf."

Karl asked, "Do you think Mark Wong was communing in the mountains somewhere?"

"I don't know. I believe so. For all the difficulties Saelli faced, this state provides plenty of mountainous terrain if one doesn't care about ice. If he wasn't doing it, that explains his unpleasant personality traits."

Karl waved toward the tunnel. "By the way, it's nice to know that the next time mercs show up, we'll have an army of weird-ass magical creatures."

"You think they're that strange?" Zaena looked vaguely offended.

"I don't know." Karl backed away from the nexus' heart. "It's just kind of odd to go from beating down magical creations to using them. I saw Saelli working on them, so I knew it was coming, but now that some are walking around, it's a lot to take in. I will have to train myself not to smash activation sigils."

"My specialties are focused on personal combat and related techniques. It's possible that a different immune Royal Elf might have come on this mission and created servants to aid her in her mission. In that case, she might have faced off against a Mark Wong as a master of earth magic, and you'd find the use of statues more normal than flying and air blasts."

Karl pondered that. He'd never believed in anything supernatural before, and now it was commonplace in his life. It was ironic given his elven blood, but he hadn't known about that until last June.

When he'd met Zaena, it hadn't taken him long to accept her magic. He attributed that to his pragmatism. There wasn't much point in pretending not to see what was right in front of you.

"You're good?" Karl asked. "I've been trying to think about the prophecy, but I still haven't figured out anything other than what we did before. The DIA is tentatively willing to help us, but I didn't tell them the details. I just asked them if they could help us out if we became aware of trouble."

"Thank you for that. We should control access to our information." Zaena's smile brightened. "We have weeks before the deadline. We also have true control of the nexus. We have a multitribal coalition of allies. I'm confident we'll be able to figure out the location the prophecy mentioned, then we can make a more concrete request."

"You think a Mountain Elf is waiting there for you?" Karl asked.

"If not, then a clue that will lead us to one," Zaena replied. "But I admit my experiences are beginning to coarsen my expectations."

Karl chuckled. "You think he's going to be a dick, don't

you? You think this is the Great Prophecy of the Coming Dick."

Zaena's face scrunched in disgust. "Min'tuk provided a useful reminder that many elves are not murderous but can still be, as you put it, dicks. I anticipate, based on the prophecy, that this Mountain Elf will display an extreme version of the attitude Lae'yul displayed on our first meeting."

"You think you're going to have to beat his ass to get him on board?"

"Yes. Perhaps more than once." Zaena hissed in annoyance. "If only they could all be like Saelli."

"Recruiting her included fighting a bunch of elves and mercs," Karl noted.

"True, but at least she wasn't difficult. I—"

The piercing, echoing sound of Karl's ringtone cut Zaena off. She and Karl stared at one another, surprised.

"I get reception here now?" Karl laughed. "You did that with the nexus?"

Zaena looked at the chamber's roof. "I wouldn't even begin to know how to ensure that magically. It's not something we intended to do. It must be a side effect of the ritual, but I like the convenience."

Karl pulled out his phone. "Hey, that means I won't miss anything important when I'm hanging out here." He frowned. "Why the hell is my brother calling? My dad's out there visiting. Probably driving him crazy."

"What is it, Bryan?" Karl answered gruffly. "You could have just sent me a text."

"You need to catch a flight to NYC right away," Bryan replied, his voice tight. "It's about Dad."

"Hey, Dad and I don't talk," Karl insisted. "He's supposed to be visiting you. I'm not coming over there to break up any fights. He likes you better than he likes me."

"No. That's not it." Bryan took a deep breath. "Dad's in the hospital. He just had a heart attack."

CHAPTER TWENTY-FOUR

Zaena's ears perked and she watched quietly, curious about what was going on. She could have used magic to hear the conversation, but that would have been rude. She trusted Karl to tell her anything of importance that was relevant to her. She valued Karl's friendship and aid, but she accepted that he was a volunteer, not a Royal Elf serving the royal family.

"Uh-huh," Karl said into his phone. "A heart attack? Is he alive? Oh."

She hadn't met his brother or his father. They'd discussed his family troubles in the past, but it wasn't her place to press him on such painful memories. She was always there if he needed to talk.

"Yeah," Karl continued. His face tightened. "Uh-huh. I've got a lot going on here. What? No, I am being reasonable. Look, just give me a few minutes to digest all this, and I'll call you back. It's not every day you get ambushed with news like 'Your dad had a heart attack and is in intensive care.' Just let me think. I'll call back soon."

Zaena offered him a comforting look. "I'm deeply sorry."

Karl lowered his phone with a frown. "My brother wants me to fly to New York. It's not like he's expecting me to stay until my dad's fully recovered, but Bryan thinks it'd be best if I came. I'm not so sure that's a great idea. We've got a lot going on here."

His reluctance surprised her. Even with the trouble he'd had with his father, she'd assumed he'd want to be at the man's bedside at such a concerning time.

"You should go," Zaena insisted, keeping her tone soothing, "and you're wrong. Overall, we don't have a lot going on."

"What about the nexus?" Karl motioned around the chamber. "You don't think all this is something going on?"

"What comes next doesn't require human assistance," Zaena noted. "I don't believe fate conspired to give your father a heart attack at a time of maximum convenience, but I have complete control of the nexus now and two stone guardians already. Vokasin might have departed to indulge his latest whims, but Saelli and I can defend this place with our power while we continue improving and strengthening it."

Karl furrowed his brow. "Which means you'll be in the basement all day? Humans could ambush you."

"Alarm wards," Zaena countered. "Different ones than those designed to detect magic."

Karl pointed at the ceiling. "What if they attack the restaurant?"

"That would be foolish," Zaena replied. "It'd result in an immediate police response. Such a terror tactic would draw a lot of attention and ensure whoever did it would be investigated. Your phone will inform you of any conventional intrusions." She smiled. "It's not that I don't value or need your aid on a normal basis, but I think there is a window where you could leave without significantly weakening this place or my mission."

"I don't know." Karl rubbed the back of his neck. "Now that I think about the nexus, this isn't the best time to leave because you attuned it."

Zaena understood he was looking for excuses, but his logic was twisted.

"I don't see how that could be true," she offered. "I don't see how that's different than what you suggested earlier."

"The nexus might not feel different now, but there was that big spike during the ceremony," Karl replied. "Elves probably could feel it from far away. You might have thrown up a flare for elves not paying attention to things like human news reports. Grace can help with some stuff, but she can't sense magic. I can."

Zaena nodded. "That's true, but it's not as if every attunement announces the existence of the nexus to the entire world. I came to San Francisco because the kingdom's scholars determined its location was critical for the curing ritual. We didn't know or expect an elf to already be in control. For anyone to have felt it, they would have had to be close to this place. I'm dubious about the risk, and an elven attack would be best defended by elves and stone guardians, would it not?"

"Would it?" Karl stopped himself. "What am I saying? What the hell do I know about magic nexuses? Spend a year around you, and now I'm acting like I'm freaking Merlin."

"I don't believe he was real."

Karl snickered. "Neither were elves until I met you."

"Getting back to the subject at hand, we'll be fine," Zaena reiterated. "You should go see your father. Family is important. Unless…" She stared at her friend, a background concern building. She might be misreading the situation. "Do you not trust Saelli?"

"That's not it. She's kind of weird, but that weirdness works for you. I mean, the woman stabbed herself because she thought it'd help you out. That's serious dedication to your mission."

"I know, and I'm hoping I can stop trouble in the future without her risking her life." Zaena sighed. "Are you truly so resistant to seeing your father?"

"I'm not like you, Zaena," Karl explained. "I don't get along with my dad. I get along with my brother okay, but not my dad, and Mom's been dead for a while. We didn't have a good reason to get together as a family, so we've just been drifting farther apart."

"Don't you have regrets about the past?" Zaena asked. "I understand you weren't what he expected and he mistreated you because of it, but it's not too late for him to change."

"It's not a big deal."

"You don't want to see him. That suggests it's important to you."

"It's not like we hate each other, but we both do best when we're not talking to each other." Karl tucked his phone back into his pocket. "The guy lives in Oakland, and

I barely see him. Bryan sees him more than I do, and he lives in New York. Dad hasn't traveled in a couple of years. I didn't realize he was in such bad shape. I guess that explains why."

Zaena offered Karl a soft smile. "I know you have your problems with him, but I've never heard you wish for his death. That has to mean something. It has to be something you can build on."

Karl snorted. "Yeah, I can pass the low bar of not wanting my dad dead, but there's a lot of people I don't want dead that I wouldn't take time to see."

"Think of this as a good chance to conceal the ax," Zaena suggested. "I know he should be the one initiating the process, but you shouldn't pass up the opportunity."

"Conceal the ax?" Karl stared at her. "Sometimes you're so close, and sometimes... Oh. Not conceal the ax. That's not the saying. The saying is 'bury the hatchet.'"

"Oh." Zaena gave a firm nod. "That's right. I was thinking of a different saying in Swahili, or was it in Hindi? Watching television isn't as great as communicating, and since I... Never mind. My point is, you should go to your father."

"I get what you're saying, and it's not wrong," Karl continued, "but we need to remember there's a lot of people watching this place, including the government. The DIA might try something while I'm gone, especially with me already having approached them."

"How is that different from what you said earlier about people attacking the restaurant?"

"They have more knowledge of your abilities."

"Let them try. Unless you think they're prepared to

annihilate this place with overwhelming force, there are no valid reasons for worry. Go to your father."

"What about..." Karl grunted. "Fine." He nodded at a tunnel. "I better go pack and buy some tickets. Try not to rough up any food critics while I'm gone."

"I make no promises."

CHAPTER TWENTY-FIVE

Karl yawned as he trudged down the sterile hospital corridor. He hated hospitals. He'd spent far too much time in one after getting shot. Every step in a hospital was a reminder of the fragility of life. No man liked to be reminded he was going to die someday.

He still wasn't sure if flying across the country had been a big mistake, but health scares were the one time families should come together, regardless of what had separated them in the past. At least, that was what everyone had told him, including an elven princess.

A passing nurse offered him a polite nod and a smile. Weariness lined her face. This wasn't just a hospital ward. This was an ICU, where people arrived on the edge of death. He continued on his way. His father's room was close.

After turning the corner, Karl slowed as he spotted his brother Bryan chatting with a nurse. Sometimes Karl wondered how they could be related. While there was a resemblance in their faces, Bryan hadn't gotten any of

Karl's bulk or height. The man was skinny and unimposing. Karl had had to protect his brother from bullies plenty of times when they were growing up.

At least Bryan had never turned his back on Karl. They might not agree on a lot else, but that meant something.

"Thank you for letting me know," Bryan commented to the nurse.

She smiled and walked toward the nursing station down the hall.

Karl walked up to his brother. "Hey. I came. It's against my better judgment, but I still came."

Bryan pulled Karl into a tight hug. Karl grunted and patted his brother before pulling away. He wasn't a hugger.

"I'm glad you came," Bryan replied. The heavy bags under his eyes and his rumpled suit made him look worse than Karl and the poor overworked nurse from earlier. "I'm not trying to be an ass, but I wasn't sure you would. I wouldn't have blamed you if you chose not to come. It doesn't matter. What's important is that you're here now."

Karl nodded toward the door. "Can I see him? Is that a bad idea?"

"You can if you want." An odd expression passed over Bryan's face. "He's sleeping, but I think you should go and see him just to make it real."

"I flew halfway across the country. I know it's real."

"Please. I'll be out here when you're ready to talk."

"Okay."

Karl stepped past his brother and opened the door. His jaw clenched when he spotted his father encased in the web of tubes running everywhere, including up his nose. Machines beeped. Every beep reinforced how much technology was being used to support a man who'd served as a symbol of strength during Karl's early years.

Bryan had inherited their mother's size, but Karl was a clone of his father. His future self was lying there in a bed, asleep. The powerful, sometimes terrifying man looked pale and vulnerable.

It wasn't the Bill Smith Karl knew. If someone had appeared and told him he was a stranger, he might have believed them.

Karl forced himself to watch his father's chest rise and fall. A real man never looked away from death.

He stood there for a good five minutes before heading out and closing the door quietly. "How's he doing? I mean, he looks like shit to me, but he's still alive."

"That he is." Bryan inclined his head toward the nursing station. "He's past the worst of it. He's going to be in the hospital for at least a couple of weeks. They say it could have been a lot worse, and he'll have to take better care of himself in the future."

Karl grunted. "Yeah, doctors tend to say that after you have a heart attack. What else are they going to say? Drink more, smoke, and eat crappy food?"

"You know Dad. He's already bitching about all the diet changes he's going to have to make."

"Somehow…" Karl tried to clear his thoughts. He'd expected to have trouble with the visit, but not this kind of trouble. "Seeing him like that was strange. I know it doesn't make sense, but I always thought I'd die before him. I figured he was too stubborn to die, and I was a cop who focused on anti-gang work. I thought all that before I got shot by a triad enforcer."

"Another terrible time for this family, but we've had a lot of them." Bryan frowned. "As twisted as your plan to die before Dad is, you should know he's not going to die, Karl. It was a nasty heart attack, and he's going to have to take it easy for a while and make some big changes, but he's going to make it through. They say he could easily live another fifteen or twenty years if he takes care of himself."

"Maybe I shouldn't have come," Karl suggested, glancing at the closed door. "The last thing a guy who had a heart attack needs is to wake up to the black sheep hovering over him. There's a reason you see him more than I do."

"It's not like that, and you know it." Bryan folded his arms. "What he needs is his family around. You know how bad things got when Mom died. Dad likes to act like he's the toughest son of a bitch on the planet, but he's a softy. He needs his sons with him. We're the only ones who can give him the support he needs."

Karl snorted. "He's a softy to you." He pinched the bridge of his nose. "No, you're right. This isn't the time for me to be a bitch, but calling it mixed feelings is an understatement. I'm honestly unsure if I would have come a few months ago if the same thing had happened."

"Why is that?" Bryan lowered his arms. His expression softened.

"Because then I'd given up on life," Karl admitted. "I was just going through the motions."

"Things changed because of what happened with Benny Lee?"

"It's more complicated than that. That was part of it, but I made new friends who helped me get a new perspective. I thought I was trying to move on from my past, but all I was doing was ignoring anything good in life, past or present."

"Not healthy."

"Exactly," Karl replied, "but I was ready for a change, and then Gary convinced me around Christmas not to let life pass me by anymore and to reach out to people. I've been reconnecting with old friends to join my new ones. I knew I'd reconnect with Dad at some point, but I didn't figure it'd be like this. I was kind of working my way up to it."

"Better late than never." Bryan motioned to a chair beside the door. "You can take a seat if you want. I'm sure you're exhausted after flying from San Francisco."

"I'm good. I might be a big guy, but I get plenty of exercise."

There was no reason to worry his brother with tales of gangster fights and killer statues.

"I'm sitting." Bryan plopped into the seat. He let his head loll back until it rested against the stark white wall. "I am glad you came. The last conversation you had with Dad could probably be heard from three states away. I kept replaying it in my mind after I called you and wondering if you'd just say screw it and send some flowers."

"You know what they say. Absence makes the heart grow fonder." Karl shrugged. "All our old man had to do to get me to come running was almost die."

Bryan chuckled. "That's one way to look at it." He sat up. "If you're moving on like your old boss told you, why not go all the way with that? You finally moved on from everything that happened with that witness when you got your new fancy security job. Might as well wipe the slate clean with everything, including family. I get why you didn't before, but this provides an opportunity for both you and Dad."

"It's not so simple," Karl replied. "I'm here. Sure. I'm ready to take the first step, and now I'm wondering what was the point?" He gestured at the door. "He's not dying, and it's not like he's gone out of his way to pick up the phone and call me. I'm relieved he's okay, but I'm not sure if my pushing it is how this should go down."

"Sometimes you got to offer a hand if you want someone to take it," Bryan suggested. "His pride's never going to let him admit he was wrong, not completely, and yes, he's not going to die this time, but he's getting older. What about next time? Do you want him to die without having cleared the air? Do you want to hate him until he's dead in the ground?"

Karl growled. "I don't know. None of this got solved when I was shot. Why would it get solved just because he's the one on the edge this time? What's different?"

"Being reminded of one's mortality helps old men realize the mistakes they've made," Bryan replied. "I get that it's more his problem than yours, but short of the three ghosts of Father's Day Past, Present, and Future visiting him, I don't think he's going to be able to make the change himself."

Karl snickered. A brief, ridiculous plan involving Zaena and magic to fake ghostly visitations formed in his mind.

He'd keep the idea in his back pocket for the future. There had to be a time where an elf pretending to be a ghost might be useful.

"Let's be real, Karl," Bryan continued. "In a lot of ways, I think Dad's always been frustrated with you because you didn't turn out to be what he wanted or expected, but you are still twice the man he is. Keep being the better man so you don't die with any regrets about things you can't take back."

"I know it wasn't all his fault." Karl scoffed. "I got my stubbornness from him. The only reason he got along so well with Mom was the woman was a saint who could put up with anyone's crap. She'd need to be with a husband like him and a son like me." He sniffed the air. An unpleasant stench filled his nostrils. "Damn. I don't travel well. I think I'm going to head back to my hotel. I'll visit tomorrow when I've had a chance to get a decent rest and shower. Dad needs his sleep anyway, and I need more time to think."

Bryan smiled. "Whatever you decide, I'm glad you came. I'm sure he will be too."

Karl patted his brother on the shoulder before turning around. He'd faced down gangsters and corrupt businessmen. He'd helped Zaena fight magical statues and challenged mercenaries. Why did that all seem so simple compared to dealing with his father?

CHAPTER TWENTY-SIX

Grace flipped through the channels, desperately seeking a show worth watching. She'd realized something when Zaena moved out. The elf's presence in her home had led to Grace watching a lot of television.

Before, she was doing her stereotypical generational part to murder TV by rarely watching it, instead spending her time on her computer or phone. The princess, being in need of a cultural education had made television a constant part of Grace's life. That, in turn, had led to Grace spending more time watching TV.

With Zaena's return, her entertainment interests had expanded, and the elf was now paying for a ridiculously overpriced high-end cable package. It wasn't like Grace had any right to complain. She wasn't on the hook for any of it, including the rent for the house.

Somehow, though, whenever Zaena wasn't there, Grace's interest in TV dwindled. She tried to tear herself away from the living room, but the act of searching for something gave her something to do.

Zaena was at the White Ruby Building, helping Saelli set up magical defenses. As much as Grace wanted to help, there were some areas where a human couldn't offer much.

Despite all the discussions and discoveries about magic, including that some humans had elven blood, human magic wasn't a thing as far as Zaena had explained. Grace didn't mind. She wasn't interested in slinging spells, but she didn't like the idea of not being able to help her best friend.

She kept flipping through channels, refocused on finding anything to distract her. An earlier hour of scrolling through social media on her phone had left her unsatisfied.

It didn't help that she was worried about Karl, too. Grace could understand having trouble with parents, but as far as she was concerned, everyone should be on good terms with their parents. It was hard to imagine not talking to her father for months or years at a time.

"Come on, fate. Saelli speaks so highly of you. Can't you do this a girl a solid and give me a nostalgic movie that makes me feel like I'm fifteen again with no responsibilities?"

So many channels, so little on. Grace stopped on BBC America. Somehow, adding an English accent to a show, no matter how inane, always made it seem more interesting. Even trashy British reality TV came off more cultured, despite featuring the same depressing scenarios and personality types.

Grace's eyes widened at the news. "You've got to be kidding me! Could it be? No. Yes!"

She snatched her phone off her coffee table and sent a

text to Zaena. She couldn't risk passing information over the phone where the DIA or somebody else might intercept it.

Fate had done her the requested solid.

On my way to the WRB. I think I've solved the riddle.

Grace couldn't stop herself from pacing in Saelli's chilly apartment. Zaena and Saelli watched her from the couch as she explained how she'd been watching television and stumbled upon what she believed was the answer to at least one of their major remaining questions about the prophecy.

"Wait." Grace stopped. "Should I text Karl?" Her words sped up. "No, no. He's got enough on his mind, and we don't need to deal with the DIA right away. We need to figure out what we're going to do before we handle it, but I do think we might need them after all, or maybe not. We could go find a guy who does fake documents. Karl must know someone."

Zaena cleared her throat. "I appreciate your adherence to security practices, but I think you're forgetting something important."

Grace spun toward her. "What?"

"You've yet to explain what you discovered," Zaena explained. "I'm not claiming any of your suggestions are inappropriate, but without knowing what you've uncovered, it'll be hard for me to comment with reasonable authority."

Saelli offered a shallow nod. "Prophecy can be all-consuming. You're not the first I've seen react this way, Grace. Take time to reflect and share what you feel will be useful to the princess. I'm sure it will be."

Grace cringed. "You're right. Sorry. It just feels so weird to figure out something like this. I feel like I just realized the secret of the One Ring, and I'm running back to the shire to make sure that stupid hobbit has it safe."

Zaena scoffed and flung her wrist in dismissal. "Gandalf's a terrible wizard. He should have been able to sense the magic from the beginning. Having to figure out the ultimate weapon of his ultimate enemy from research in a library? Imagine my ancestor having to do that with the Night Elves. They would have taken over the planet and destroyed all humans."

"Who is Gandalf?" Saelli asked. "Is he a human who has magic powers? Might we seek his aid in these matters?"

"No, he's a fictional wizard from a human movie and book series."

Grace grimaced. "Sorry. I'm getting us off track. Living with you has led to too many movie marathons, Zaena." She took a deep breath and slowly let it out. "So, here it is. I've figured out the prophecy." She chuckled. "There's a sentence I never thought I'd say in my life, but anyway, I was watching the news on BBC America, and an interesting little report popped up. They were talking about potential repairs being needed in the Chunnel."

Saelli looked confused. "That word sounds like something I should understand, yet I don't."

"It's an underwater rail passage between England and France," Zaena noted. "Also known as the Eurotunnel, among other names. It's an impressive feat of human technological prowess. What does this have to do with the prophecy?"

Grace licked her lips in excitement. "Because the initial headline or whatever they call that thing on the bottom caught my attention. 'Do all three Channel tunnels need maintenance?' That confused me because I'd only heard of the Chunnel. I looked it up after. It turns out the Chunnel is three tunnels, two rail service tunnels, one running from France to England, one the opposite, and a service tunnel between them where trucks and carts and stuff can go through."

Zaena gasped. "I've read about the Chunnel, but I didn't realize. It seems so obvious now that you say it."

"That does fit, based on what you've said," Saelli confirmed. "Underwater and lines of three. We have our location."

"We know the time, the summer solstice," Grace observed, "and we know the place, or at least the general place. The tunnels are pretty long, but they aren't that wide. If it's magic and you guys just move along them, you should be able to sense something, right?"

Zaena agreed with a nod, "There aren't any other clues that will let us narrow things farther."

"What about the ancient rivals?" Saelli asked. "Does knowing the location help figure that out?"

"Yes, actually," Grace replied. "Sure, you've got all that cooperation and frenemy stuff nowadays, and the UK's a bigger deal than England, but you're talking about something connecting England and France. Those countries have been fighting on and off for a thousand years. That might be nothing by elf standards, but human standards, that's a pretty old rivalry. Positively ancient."

"I see. Yes. That does match what I've learned from my tutors." Zaena gave a firm nod. "Excellent. I think you're right about this. We know where and when we need to go. That makes an impossible task merely inconvenient."

Saelli brought up her phone and a map of the English Channel. "I believe the prophecy suggests a Mountain Elf is waiting for us there, but if Princess Zaena must subdue him, it might prove dangerous to fight in a tunnel."

"I'm not sure," Zaena countered. "If he's contained, it might be easier. At least three of us can wield water magic. If he attempts something of that nature, we'll be able to counter him."

Grace furrowed her brow. "Saelli's right. Those tunnels are used by trains carrying people. If you have a big elf fight, a lot of people could get hurt. As much as I hate to say it after all my concerns about secrecy, you might need to reach out to Selene D'Arcy on this. I'm sure she can do some government voodoo and convince somebody over there to stop traffic for a day while you hunt for trouble."

Zaena stood with a concerned look on her face. "We can't focus relentlessly on a single prophecy and ignore the potential threats implied by others."

"Huh? We know there might be trouble from the prophecy."

"Saelli's other prophecy spoke of a great beast," Zaena reminded her. "Perhaps there's not a Mountain Elf waiting for us but a dragon or something similar."

Grace swallowed. "I'm not sure you want to pass that

along to the government. Once Karl gets back, he can work something out."

Zaena frowned. "No."

"What?"

"I understand that I should not attempt to do all things by myself," Zaena explained, "but I am a representative of an elven kingdom and the de facto representative of the other enclaves to the US government. I cannot continue relying on Karl. I can contact the DIA without him, so it's time I...what is the saying? It's time I took off the training wheels."

Grace snickered. "Says someone who flies everywhere and has never ridden a bike in her life."

"Be that as it may, I can arrange a meeting via Agents Lyle and Waves with Miss D'Arcy. I'm not ready to suggest a dragon attack, but it wouldn't harm things to have human military assets nearby in case something unexpected happens."

"You're going to arrange a meeting?" Grace replied. "You mean a teleconference?"

"It's still a meeting." Zaena looked at Saelli. "Your prophecy has `given us useful information. Whether there's a dragon in need of slaying or a new ally, we will move forward thanks to your gift."

CHAPTER TWENTY-SEVEN

Karl was sitting in a chair next to the ICU bed when his father's eyes blinked open. He'd expected something dramatic, as if the simple act would solve all the problems between them without Karl needing to do anything else. Instead, he felt nothing but simple relief.

Bill Smith turned his way, a brief flash of surprise shifting into something unreadable. The lack of a second heart attack was a good start. They could salvage something.

"You came," Bill commented, his voice hoarse and quiet, "but you have a funny look on your face. What's wrong? Disappointed I survived?"

"You know that's not true," Karl replied. He kept his voice calm and controlled. "I wouldn't have bothered to fly across the country if that was true."

"Do I know that's true?" Bill's face twitched. "I thought you told me once the wrong parent had died. You've said it more than once, so it's not just me misremembering something."

Karl's stomach twisted. A man's own words were the greatest weapon another could wield against him.

He looked away. "I'm sorry for saying that. I'm not going to try to excuse it, but we've both said a lot of dumb crap in the past when things got heated, and I'm sure we're both sorry for a lot of it. I'm not saying I'll get over Mom dying so young, but I didn't want you dead. I just wanted you not to be such a dick and accept me for who I am."

"You're right." Bill closed his eyes and gave a shallow nod. "I'm not a saint. I'm such a dick the Devil probably calls me a prick." He managed a weak grin. "I've said all sorts of shit to you for stupid reasons I had no business saying. We both know the kinds of things I said when we last talked about your mom." He took a deep, slow breath. "Now we share something in common, something I doubt Bryan will ever share with us because I bet we'll both be dead before he ever experiences it."

"What's that?" Karl leaned forward to better make out his father's quiet words.

"We know what it's like to come close to dying," Bill replied. "His fancy internet-connected exercise bike and healthy eating are going to keep him alive for a lot longer than assholes like us who don't know how to take care of themselves or who throw themselves in front of bullets. What's he going to die from at work? A papercut? A poisoned latte?"

Karl chuckled. "His desk might collapse on him when he's leaning down to get something, or the latte's too hot, and he jumps back and falls out of his window."

Bill's hoarse laugh sounded painful. "He'll never get near anything dangerous. I never could understand how I had two sons who were so different. You'd been taking down bullies twice your size since grade school, and Bryan always had to run away while you cleaned up for him."

"Yet you were always harder on me," Karl noted in a cool tone. He wanted to patch things up with his father, but closing the gap between them meant genuine apologies about everything, not brushing it away and pretending it never happened.

"We doing this?" Bill asked. There was no anger in his voice, only resignation. "Right here? Right now? I just had a heart attack."

"If we're going to move on, then yeah, we're doing this. It's because you just had a heart attack that we need to do it."

"Okay." Bill nodded. "Fair enough."

"Really?"

"Almost dying makes a man think," Bill explained. "I didn't see no fancy tunnels of light, no saints ready to ask me where I wanted to go. I don't know if that's because it wasn't my time yet, or if I'm meant for the heated basement when it's all over. My life didn't flash before my eyes, but when I've been awake, I've had a lot of time to think about everything I've done. I know about my mistakes. I can't do anything but think about them."

"Was the way you treated me a mistake?" Karl asked.

"Some of it, yeah. Not going to say all of it, but at least some of it."

"How generous of you."

"I'm trying." Bill forced his eyes open and stared at the ceiling. "I knew from early on you weren't going to be what I expected, but when I saw you were going to take after me and Bryan would take after your mother, I don't know. I wanted you to be strong."

Karl scoffed. "You've said a lot of crap over the years."

"You stood up to me," Bill replied. "Especially when I was saying all sorts of crap to you. All I can say is I'm sorry. I thought what you were made you weak, but I was wrong about that. I'm not going to apologize for wanting you to be strong, but I am going to apologize for giving you more crap than you needed."

"Okay." Karl's jaw clenched.

"You're my son, and I love you. Pushing you away just because you weren't what I expected wasn't fair, but you grew up to be a cop who took on gangsters, and now you're doing fancy security work. I'm sorry, and I want you to know I couldn't be prouder of you. I've got nothing but regrets now. Your mother, God bless her soul, tried her best to make me see, but I didn't because I was a stubborn son of a bitch. I'm not dead, which means it's not too late for us. I'm sorry, Karl. That's all I can say. This time with no reservations. I'm sorry, and I'll do better."

Karl averted his eyes. He didn't know what to say. He could count on one hand the number of times he'd heard his father apologize, and those had all been to Bryan or their mother.

"I'm sorry, too, Dad," Karl offered. "I should have tried to keep in touch."

"You were too busy making the world a better place and taking down street garbage," Bill replied. "While I was busy being an asshole."

"I'd hug you," Karl noted, "but it would probably kill you right now."

Bill let out a chuckle before groaning. "There are worse ways to go."

Karl fell back-first onto this hotel bed. It creaked in protest over his massive frame. He'd not done much that day but watch and talk to his father and brother, but he felt as exhausted as he did after a heavy session in the gym.

He didn't think this meant he'd be meeting with his father for weekly brunch or watching games together. The whole thing felt strange.

A man got used to a heavy weight pressing on him. After a while, he learned to compensate and ignore it. Now that it was gone, he felt freer than he had in years.

Karl pulled out his phone to check for messages. He'd turned it off on his way to the hospital and forgotten to turn it back on. He frowned at a message from Zaena.

Everything is going smoothly here. There's no need for concern.

"What the hell?"

She never sent messages like that. Zaena enjoyed texting far too much for someone centuries past her teenage years, but she preferred passing along actual information in them.

Was it a code? Was the White Ruby Building under siege, and she was trying to warn him? She understood the government could intercept their phone messages.

It might be a different problem. A surprise attack by

murderous elves who had mind-controlled the local SWAT team might have pinned her down, and she needed him to bring in the DIA.

Karl called her. He sat up on the edge of his bed.

"Hello," Zaena answered in a guarded voice. "How is everything with your father?"

"He's doing okay," Karl replied. "He'll be staying here a couple of weeks at least, but they don't think he's going to drop dead. We did the whole concealing the ax thing, as you might say. This whole thing turned out pretty well."

He could hear her smile over the line.

"That's wonderful. I'm glad you went. I know you were reluctant to leave, but now that you've passed along your news, I feel more comfortable passing along my own."

"What? Your dad had a heart attack, too?"

"Oh, I'm doubtful my father would suffer that way." Zaena sounded amused. "No, because of Grace's television-watching, certain important riddles have been solved, including the meaning of my houseguest's poem concerning where the poem takes place."

Karl jumped to his feet. "Are you serious?"

"Yes," Zaena confirmed. "The nature of the primary subject of the poem remains unclear, but the rest of it makes sense. Don't you worry. I'm going to talk to your professional friends and attempt to negotiate some aid. I don't see why you can't spend a few days with your father while I do so."

Karl wished Zaena knew some way to protect their conversation over the phone. "Do you think it's a good idea to talk to them without me? They can be tricky. Remember, they're used to manipulating people."

"I think talking to them is not only a good idea but a necessary one," Zaena suggested. "Besides, we have time before our deadline if the discussion goes poorly."

"I guess. You sure you don't want me to come back on the next flight?"

"Family is paramount," Zaena insisted. "I'll see you soon, but not too soon. For now, know that everything is going well. Have a good afternoon."

"Yeah, you too."

Karl lowered his phone. There was no reason his presence would have helped with solving a prophecy interpretation problem, so it didn't surprise him that they'd figured something out. However, he wasn't sure about Zaena negotiating directly with the government.

"I hope she doesn't start World War Elf before I get back."

CHAPTER TWENTY-EIGHT

Zaena offered a polite nod to Selene, who was on a laptop on the center console of the car. Agent Lyle drove their vehicle away from the park where they'd met. Agent Waves wasn't present, which was a rarity.

She continued to be annoyed by Selene's utter refusal to meet in person. Soon, she'd need to make it a condition of further dealings. Trust needed to go both ways if they were going to establish a lasting relationship.

"Good afternoon, Princess," Selene greeted her. "I'm very pleased you decided to reach out to me directly. I have nothing against Mr. Smith, but a human intermediary can't help but add their own bias to discussions."

Zaena didn't know what to make of Selene D'Arcy, but the woman's speech was always cold and devoid of most emotions. She wanted to attribute it to professionalism, but the agents spoke with more human feeling. It made her wonder if all high-level government defense officials were as dispassionate. That made her worry about the future.

"Karl is handling some personal business," Zaena

replied, "but he has my full confidence and support. I don't believe I would have been as successful in my endeavors among humanity without his aid."

"Those are words of high praise," Selene replied, "and I'm well aware his father had a heart attack."

"You're following his family around?" Zaena asked.

"We're the government," Selene offered. "It's our responsibility to protect the American people from all threats foreign and domestic. I think it's a good idea to keep an eye on the close family members of your primary human contacts for their safety. If at any time a foreign power becomes aware of your existence and the link between Mr. Smith, Miss Kwan, and yourself, a natural leverage point would be their family members. Given your past interactions, I'm sure you understand that."

Zaena stared at the cold blue eyes of the woman on the laptop. The lack of inflection made it hard to interpret what she'd just heard.

A charitable reading pointed to Selene protecting the families of Zaena's human friends. A cynical interpretation pointed to a veiled threat. Zaena hoped that wasn't the case, but making things clear to Selene and whatever government officials gave her orders could only help in the future.

"Anyone, regardless of who they work for, who threatens my friends or those they love will answer to me," Zaena noted. "I will not hesitate to deliver justice to them. You're well aware of my capabilities and my willingness to use force when I feel justified."

"I see," Selene said, nodding, "That has implications. Is your elven justice more important than geopolitical stability? A rogue nation assassinating one of your friends would be a tragedy, but acting harshly could result in war."

It sounded reasonable, but it also sounded like a convenient excuse. What was the point of having strength if you let villains harm those you cared about?

"I will protect my friends and those they love," Zaena insisted. Her hands balled into fists. "I would love to protect all innocent people, but I'm but one woman with a small number of allies. It would be too much for me to deliver justice to every human who deserves it. That doesn't mean killers will escape because they hide behind a flag of convenience."

"I see. Sometimes foreign powers commit acts of violence that can't be responded to immediately without risking war. That's something anyone in the Defense Department has to come to terms with. Justice and security aren't always the same thing."

Zaena scoffed. "I'd suggest you make sure none of those foreign powers harm my friends then, since I will not restrain myself because of diplomatic concerns. Technically, I have no diplomatic status in any nation. As I understand it, that includes the United States, so any hostile foreign powers that see fit to commit heinous acts against my friends can be dealt with by me without implicating you or your government. I'm sure you wouldn't object to that, would you? If necessary, you can disavow me, and I can disappear. There are certain lines I won't allow to be crossed, regardless of who is involved."

"You're very passionate about your friends," Selene commented.

"Yes, I am."

Selene offered a thin smile. "Let's just hope no complicated situations ever arise and all these discussions remain theoretical."

Zaena still didn't know what to make of the woman. Every indication suggested Selene had assassinated or secretly imprisoned Amanda Morton after the incident in Iceland. That spoke to a ruthlessness that could threaten Team Princess, but at the same time, Zaena might have well killed Morton after the betrayal. She'd admitted as much in the speech she'd just given.

Selene's secrecy made sense, given her involvement in such strange matters as American-elven relations, but she'd also originally been an ally of Amanda Morton's. Zaena appreciated the government's help, but she maintained no illusion that they were her friends. She could be disappeared by an aggressive US government just like Amanda Morton with enough effort.

However, that didn't have to happen. Their interests converged, and Zaena intended to establish full and open diplomatic relations with the United States. That said, she wasn't naïve enough anymore to believe every human she dealt with would be as honorable as her close friends.

"I hate to hurry you, Princess," Selene continued, "but you're not the only appointment I have today. I assume you set up a meeting to discuss something in particular. Has there been a change in the status quo you need to make me aware of?"

"There has." Zaena had spent the past two months trying to figure out the best way to pass along information about the prophecy without revealing too much. "I have other intelligence sources available to me. They point to a possible incident where I might require your assistance to ensure a lack of collateral damage, among other things."

"Are these intelligence sources of a magical nature?" Selene asked, her voice filled with curiosity.

"That would be an accurate summary," Zaena replied. "But you have to understand, I have to protect my sources, just as the American intelligence community has to protect theirs."

"You're saying it's classified?" Agent Lyle asked from up front with a chuckle. "Glad to see elves and humans aren't so different."

Selene glared, but the position of her laptop only allowed it to reach Zaena. "We don't need your commentary, Agent."

"Sorry, ma'am." Agent Lyle smirked. "I'll keep my mouth shut."

Zaena smiled. "He's right, though. Sharing information with your government doesn't mean I'm required to tell you everything about where and how I get my information. I do have actionable intelligence, to use your terminology, concerning a major magical incident occurring on the summer solstice in the Chunnel. I'd rather innocent people not be harmed, and I'm prepared to use magic to intervene to end any potential incidents."

"I see," Selene replied in a disinterested tone. "Where exactly will this occur? The Chunnel is a decent length."

"I don't have that specific information at this time," Zaena admitted. "I only have the day and the general location, along with an indication a hostile elf might come there, or a magical encounter might happen there."

Even if she wanted to admit she was relying on

prophecy, those portions of the prophecy were the one part they hadn't solved. She couldn't tell Selene with any confidence what they'd find.

Selene looked down for a moment with a slight frown. "What is your plan?"

"I intend to lead a force of allied elves there," Zaena explained. "Three, potentially four, to check things out. If there is a hostile elf or other magical threat there, that would be enough power to capture them and minimize the threat to the Chunnel's tunnels."

"Are you saying you believe an elven terrorist is threatening a major transportation corridor?" Selene asked.

"I honestly can't say," Zaena replied. "I'm not trying to hide anything. I don't know that information at this time, but I doubt there is a terrorist threat. I am concerned about the possibility of innocent people getting hurt during an encounter. Thus, I'll need your help. It'll be easier if you facilitate our travel to that location and you assure that the Chunnel is shut down that day to minimize the risk."

Selene's brow lifted. "You want the Chunnel shut for an entire day?"

"At least until we can confirm there's no risk," Zaena suggested. "It might take less than a day."

Selene leaned back in her chair and steepled her fingers. "Forgive me for saying so, Princess, but why should you even be involved? You've given us the location and day. Why shouldn't we handle it ourselves? Your kind is tough, but they're not immortal or immune to every weapon humanity has to offer."

"That's true, but your ability to handle elven magic remains limited. Keep in mind that three of us were able to hold off an entire group of well-equipped mercenaries despite them ambushing us. Not only that, but this coming encounter will also likely involve close-quarters battle in cramped tunnels. A team of your soldiers could easily be seriously injured and killed if they don't know what they're walking into, and you can't easily collapse these tunnels without massive repercussions."

"Can you face off against our mystery elf in a safer manner?" Selene asked.

"My team can," Zaena insisted. "If there is a hostile elf, he might be far less willing to engage three elves than a group of humans. I can offer no confirmations that anyone specific will be there, but I think my plan is the best overall risk versus reward scenario. Forgive me for saying so, Miss D'Arcy, but if this somehow goes awry, it might be useful to have a scapegoat. I don't know who you answer to, but I assume at least some of them are aware of my existence."

"Be careful what you offer," Selene replied with a ghost of a smile. "Missions have a way of going badly even when you have accurate intelligence, and by your admission, you aren't sure what you'll be facing."

"If you follow my plan, we can minimize risk," Zaena offered. "There can be no certainty, and there might not be anything there, but if there is, I can't risk a train full of people getting hurt, even by accident. I assume you feel the same, even if these are mostly citizens of different lands."

"Looking the other way concerning potential mass casualty events in allied nations is frowned upon. Very well. I need to consult my superiors. This will require much more diplomatic finesse than the Iceland incident given the scale of intervention, especially since we're not prepared to admit your true nature to the UK or French governments."

"Won't they assume I'm Amanda Morton in a powered suit?" Zaena asked. "Like so many others?"

"Oh." Selene's face contorted into something approaching a genuine grin. "That is still a strong rumor, isn't it? You're right. Humans tend to explain away the strange in terms they understand. That's one advantage of dealing with elves. When the truth is stranger than fiction, no one will guess. Have a good day, Princess. I'll contact you soon."

The screen went black before Zaena could reply.

She sighed. The whole thing might have been a mistake. Selene's superiors might order a human force to capture anything involved and not care about their elven assets.

On the other hand, every action by Selene in recent months suggested she was interested in making use of Zaena as a tool. There was no reason for her to take an unnecessary risk now.

"Whatever happens, be careful," Agent Lyle offered from the front. "There could be someone way worse than Mark Wong down there."

"Unfortunately, Agent," Zaena replied, "the best options aren't always the safest."

"Don't I know it," he grumbled.

CHAPTER TWENTY-NINE

Karl stood near the door to his dad's room. His brother sat in the chair. The family had been chatting about the merits of different golf courses for the last couple of hours.

He couldn't remember the last time he'd talked so long with his dad without yelling. Doing it in an ICU room was even stranger, though the nurses said they'd be able to transfer him out of ICU by the next day.

"I'm glad you're back on the course," Bill noted. "All men should golf. It's a real sport that takes real skill and finesse. Plus, you can still do it when you're not a young stud anymore."

Bryan smiled. "Here in a few months, we should have a golfing weekend, all three Smith men."

"You that eager to get your ass kicked?" Karl asked.

"Hey, I've been practicing," Bryan insisted. "It helps impress the boss at work."

"Figures, not that I can say much. I golf with my old boss."

"Yeah, I'd like to have a Smith men weekend. Bryan, you can take us to one of your fancy New York courses at one of those clubs that'd normally be too good to let people like Karl or me inside. I'm not going to be impressed, and I'm going to be loud the entire time."

"Dad, don't be that way." Bryan looked pained.

Karl grinned. "He's right. You're the one making the most money. I promise not to be loud."

"You're working for a bunch of rich Europeans," Bryan countered. "Your company name even has 'ruby' in the title. Sure, I'll figure something out." He shook a finger. "Only when Dad's better. I don't want to have to come back here in two months because he overexerted himself and dropped on the course."

"We can use a cart," Karl suggested.

"I'm not dead yet," Bill insisted. "Yeah, I'll admit I let myself go a little because your mother's not around to glare some sense into me, but I'm also not ready to see what kind of golf course they have upstairs." He smirked. "Let alone downstairs."

"Probably nothing but sand traps," Karl suggested, "and the Devil's your caddy and always gives you the worst club for your shot."

"No." Bryan gave him a serious look. "He gives you a tennis racket instead of a golf club."

"Probably." Bill laughed before grimacing. "Doc says I have to be careful about that. It'd be pretty embarrassing to die laughing."

"There are worse ways," Karl replied.

"Sure. Don't we both know it?" Bill gave him a stern look. "Now, I want you to get the hell out of here."

Karl frowned. "Excuse me?"

He wasn't sure what had happened. His dad had been nothing but jokes and smiles the entire time, despite being plugged in to all the machines.

"We've had our big touchy-feely father-sons bonding moment," Bill explained, "and I'm not going to do anything but lie in a bed, then get transferred to a different room to lie in a bed for longer. You finally got a decent job after leaving the force, and I'm not going to be one to screw that up because I didn't know how to take care of myself and ended up having a heart attack."

"They can live without me for a few more days," Karl insisted. "My boss is very supportive. To quote her, 'Family is paramount.'"

"Go back to work." Bill shook his head. "Both of you. You don't need to sit here and stare at my boring face."

"I was already on vacation," Bryan noted with a shrug.

"Then don't spend all day sitting here staring at me. It makes me feel like I'm an invalid."

"You just had a major heart attack, Dad. You *are* an invalid." Bryan rolled his eyes. "It's okay to rest for a while."

Bill pointed at Karl. "He should go back, at least. Smith men don't sit around and mope. They get crap done. I live close to you, Karl. You can visit me soon enough. Bryan can stay until he gets killed by a papercut."

"A papercut? What are you talking about?"

"It's nothing." Bill frowned. "Karl, come on."

"I don't know." Karl rubbed the back of his neck. "This doesn't feel right. You're not even out of the ICU yet."

"I'll be out tomorrow, and it doesn't feel right because we're not supposed to be sharing so many feelings," Bill insisted, averting his eyes. "I love you, son. I love both of you, but if I have to spend the next two weeks spending all my time with you, I think I'd rather have another heart attack and go join your mother."

Bryan laughed. "Fine, Dad, I don't need to spend all my time here, but I'm not going back to work yet."

"I've always got crap to do back in San Francisco," Karl admitted. "My boss has a big thing coming up in a few weeks. It's going to involve international travel, so it'd be helpful if I headed back sooner rather than later."

"You should be back there helping her." Bill closed his eyes. "For now, I think I need to sleep. I'll call you after I'm back and settled in."

Karl looked at Bryan for direction.

"I'll handle everything," Bryan assured him. "I had the vacation time scheduled anyway, so it's easy to extend it a little. I'll also get some in-home help arranged for when he goes back to Oakland, so you don't have to worry."

"Okay." Karl grabbed the door handle. "I'll talk to you both soon."

He stepped outside. He hadn't been sure what to expect when he came. His father might not be his best friend anytime soon, but at least they were talking again. That was progress, and as long as a man was moving forward, he could reach his goal.

Zaena was right. Family *was* important.

Zaena smiled into the rearview mirror of Agent Lyle's car. It'd been only a day since her last trip. Unlike before, Agent Waves also rode with them.

She preferred the cheerful younger agent, though Agent Lyle took the lead in most conversations. Not that she disliked either man. Her previous encounters with them had proven they were reasonable men with at least a modicum of honor.

"You two could just come to the White Ruby Building to discuss things," she suggested. "I'm sure you're aware I've added entrances that are harder to see from the street. I can guarantee absolute privacy there with magic. As amusing as it is meeting you in parks and parking lots, it's inconvenient for me."

Agent Lyle shook his head. "Sorry, Princess. We have our protocols. Until more people know about you, it's the best way to protect both our interests and yours. I'm sure you've got all sorts of magic power, but all it takes is one missile to ruin your day. No offense, but I don't think you've got a spell to cover every possible type of eaves-dropping."

"Yet," Zaena offered. "Once elves and humans are working more closely together, we'll be able to develop all manner of impressive magic."

"Huh. Never thought of it that way. Missiles are still a big threat, though."

Zaena had begun working with Saelli to harden the nexus and the connected portions of the building. She wasn't sure how well it'd stand up against massive attack, and every new suggestion laid bare how Mark Wong's arrogance and assumptions had undermined the best use of the nexus. A less egomaniacal elf could have ensured his success.

She'd thought long and hard about it and come up with a single answer. Mark Wong must never have anticipated an elf of her power would become interested in the nexus. He must have assumed the rarity of immunity would assure that anyone who came sniffing around could be handled by his army of humans and terracotta soldiers.

While it didn't make him any less arrogant, it wasn't an unreasonable position. Zaena's public activities had drawn other elves to her. Mark Wong had been trying to be subtle before her arrival. Without Zaena's mission, he might have succeeded in taking over San Francisco.

Much of his subtlety had been achieved through his artifact mask. When Saelli had dug out the collapsed nexus, they'd found only the tiniest inert fragments of the once-powerful demon mask. The collected shards joined his remains in the sarcophagus.

She didn't mind its destruction. Some magic was too disgusting to tolerate.

Zaena frowned. She'd not noticed it when she got in the car, but there was no laptop.

"Am I to communicate with Miss Darcy via the phone this time?" she asked. "I'd prefer to look her in the eye when I talk to her."

"No meeting with her. We're messenger boys today. She's got a bunch of meetings with people way more important than us."

Zaena smiled. "I see. I hope you come bearing good news."

"Good news." Agent Lyle snorted. "No offense, Princess, but as far as I'm concerned, good news means no news. You're on our side, and I appreciate it, but anything you're worried about could get real nasty."

"Come on, Carson," chided Agent Waves. "It's not her fault. It's like complaining to Superman about property damage because Doomsday showed up and knocked a building down."

"Just saying," Agent Lyle replied. "She mentioned it herself. She's worried about collateral damage with all this."

"You could pass along her message," Zaena suggested. "My feelings are irrelevant. I simply need to know what decisions have been made and what resources are available."

"Okay," Agent Lyle agreed. "You're right." He slowed and made a turn before continuing. "The short version is she's got something worked out. Our top people have convinced the relevant stakeholders there is a potential terrorist incident, and they can get it locked down without anyone watching. Officially, it'll be a small spill from an accident that needs to be cleaned up."

That worked. Zaena understood the difficulty of coming up with plausible excuses. There were far too many dangerous scenarios that might only encourage people to try to come and watch.

"Here's the trick though, Princess," Agent Lyle offered. "One day max. That's the best they can do. If you haven't found whatever you think might be coming at that point, they're going to have to open it back up. I hope for your sake you find something because our boss is going out on a major limb here. She's going to be beyond pissed if this ends up being nothing."

"It's fine," Zaena replied. "I'm confident this incident will be resolved within one day, or I'll at least establish if it's a danger by then."

"If you don't?"

Zaena shrugged. "In that scenario, I'll most likely be dead, and you'll be using massive military force on whoever killed me to stop further damage."

Agent Lyle grimaced. "Do you have to sound so calm when you say it?"

"I don't intend to die, but I do want to be clear about the likely aftermath if I do."

Agent Waves cleared his throat and glanced back into his seat with a concerned look. "There's going to be NATO counter-terrorist forces stationed at every exit on both sides, but they will not be entering. We can provide you a brief insertion window so they won't see you. We know you can do your invisibility thing, but this way, we won't have any misunderstandings. Right now, the idea is that they will not be going in to support you at all. Miss D'Arcy wanted it highlighted that without more concrete intel on what they might face, it's too much of a risk."

"That's also fine. It makes more sense to fight magic with magic. I suggest we travel there before the day so I can patrol the area without entering the tunnels. The other limitations don't worry me."

A hint of doubt crept into her thoughts. She was confident she could handle anything short of a great beast, but the latest prophecy didn't suggest that level of threat. The military presence would ensure a minimum number of civilians were around and rapid response in any other occurrence.

Agent Lyle frowned. "You do understand the situation, right? You'll be in underwater tunnels. This isn't a big warehouse or mountain. You're not going to have a lot of room to maneuver, and you can't just blow up everything you see at full power."

"I've been studying the tunnel configurations since we identified the location," Zaena explained. "Please note that all the limitations you highlight apply to any enemies we might encounter inside. Preferably, this won't be a battle."

"Do you have intel suggesting that's a possibility?"

"It remains unclear," Zaena admitted, "but remember, I won't be going alone."

"The dinosaur guy and the albino chick from Iceland?" Agent Lyle asked.

"Among others, all with strong magical abilities."

Agent Lyle's hands tightened around the wheel. "Your little army keeps growing."

"True, but unlike Mark Wong, they have no interest in harming humans." She smiled. "We have weeks to prepare. There's no reason to think this will go poorly, and I presume your associates are now monitoring the area extensively."

Agent Lyle nodded. "Sure. They're going to try, but we don't have a good way to detect magic. We might get lucky and spot the optical distortions that accompany elven camouflage, but we can offer no guarantees."

"All we can do is prepare for the possibilities," Zaena suggested.

"Prepare for the worst, and you'll never be surprised."

Zaena chuckled. "Ah, a man even more cynical than Karl. That's an impressive feat."

"Spend twenty years in government and see what it does to *you*."

CHAPTER THIRTY

Zaena settled into one of the straight-backed stone chairs Saelli had crafted in the main nexus chamber and made a mental note to suggest the design be changed. They were far too reminiscent of thrones. They were something Mark Wong would have enjoyed.

She might have been a royal, but despite being attuned to the nexus, this wasn't her kingdom. A future where the elven tribes cooperated freely had to start with mutual respect, including the furniture.

For now, the chairs would serve for the meeting. There was no reason to sour things with a complaint. Saelli's rapid accomplishments had been stunning, even with the help of the nexus.

Zaena stared at a stack of papers on the ground beside her. That was a minor inconvenience. Saelli needed to make a table.

It'd been over a week since Zaena had last talked to the DIA agents. She'd had enough time to meet with Lae'yul and request Min'tuk's help in the raid. Unfortunately, the

Sea Elf Council had refused to offer additional help, saying, "the fantastical imaginings of Ice Elves are insufficient to justify the risk of sending two of our tribe."

Lae'yul now sat in a chair in the chamber, along with Vokasin, Saelli, and Karl. Zaena would have preferred as much elven help as possible, but a team of four well-trained elves with diverse elemental masteries wasn't a weak force, and she'd explained that as she outlined the Chunnel mission.

"We don't know what we will face there, but even if it is an elf with powerful artifacts, we should be able to contain them," Zaena offered by way of summary. "They won't be expecting several elves to arrive and confront them."

"Are you sure the intention isn't to destroy the tunnels?" Lae'yul asked. "They aren't trivial for humans to fix. It's not a lethal blow, but it would be grievous."

Zaena shook her head. "We can't be sure of anything at this point, but if we engage based on what we know, we have at least some chance of stopping unnecessary damage and suffering."

Karl folded his arms. "I know I'm not going along since there's not much my human ass can add that you all can't. At least some people with access to major military assets know you're going on this mission. You're going to be underwater in a contained location, and there's already a plausible cover story if anything blows up."

Vokasin offered him a toothy grin. His incisors were so large they must have been the result of a partial transformation. "You think your government will strike this place while we investigate? You're very distrustful, human."

Karl replied, "I prefer pragmatic, and I don't know.

They might do it. Somebody who knows what Zaena and Saelli are could be watching and waiting for the chance. Azure Knives. Morton dead-enders. Leftover Demon Overlords. We can't ignore the possibility."

"It's not worth destroying the Chunnel to kill a handful of elves. We're powerful, but not that powerful, and it'd focus the attention of an entire continent on the incident."

"Yeah, okay, true," Karl admitted, "but what about this place? D'Arcy's going to know it's going to be missing the Crimson Wind and her Spectacular Friends soon, and if an elf shows up, I'm straight-up screwed."

"The human isn't without a point," Lae'yul concluded with a scowl. "The defenses are being strengthened here, but they can't be controlled well by a human with only distant elven blood. Sensing magic isn't enough to stop it."

"I should stay," Saelli offered. "I'm the only one who can properly control the stone guardians and adjust their spells. Simple directions won't be enough. Even if they are overwhelmed, I'm the one who has been digging out the nexus chamber and the environs. I also can use the Diamond of Protection. Combined with the power of the nexus, I'm confident I could defend the nexus for however long you're gone from either humans or elves."

Vokasin looked between Saelli and Zaena. "In terms of pure defense, Fourth Born, there are none who compare. I'm doubtful an elf will attack, but I'm less sure about your people. Saelli could be useful on the trip, but we're trusting your human government friends far too much. It might be best to leave her to ensure all our other efforts aren't wasted."

"Huh." Karl grunted. "I agree. It's a really good plan. I

can help with tactical support if anything happens as long as I know I've got magic at my back. Whoever might show up isn't going to drop a nuke in the middle of Chinatown."

Zaena frowned. "I would have preferred to have four elves when we traveled to the Chunnel, but there's wisdom in not leaving this place undefended." She looked at Lae'yul. "You intend to aid me directly with this investigation? You've not yet made that clear."

Lae'yul nodded. "It's been left up to me by the council, and I choose to aid you."

Zaena was surprised. The Sea Elf might respect her strength, but that wasn't the same thing as trusting all her decisions. She knew Lae'yul far less well than Vokasin or Saelli, with whom she'd spent more time in casual interaction.

"Then it's decided." Zaena picked up the stack of papers, left her chair, and handed one to everyone present. "This is a map of the three tunnels making up the overall Chunnel. One of the things I wanted to discuss is an engagement strategy."

"Hunt and suppress," Lae'yul declared. "Isn't that enough? We find any hostile elves and ask for their surrender. If they refuse, we attack them until they do. If they aren't hostile, we don't attack."

"I suggest something slightly more nuanced," Zaena replied. She held up her paper and pointed at one of the sub tunnels. "Miss D'Arcy has assured me there will be no trains in the tunnels and no humans. We will enter from the English side at dawn, one elf per tunnel, after doing initial sea and air patrols to try to sense magic. We will then advance through the tunnels. There are service tunnel entrances every 410 yards in the main tunnels."

"Will we communicate with air magic?" Vokasin asked. "Will that be possible in those tunnels?"

Zaena answered, "I will be providing us with portable encrypted radios. The agents have assured me we can use them in the tunnel systems without significant disruption, with their help. I'm unfamiliar with the relevant technology, but I have no reason to believe they're lying since there's no benefit to the US government or its allies in allowing unsanctioned magical activity. We will quickly realize if they're lying and can react accordingly."

"Yeah," Karl offered. "Zaena and I had a conversation based on your last couple of training sessions. These won't be headsets; they'll be walkie-talkie-like units attached to your clothes." He looked at Vokasin. "At least until the fun starts. Don't worry if you have to drop them or trash them. The main goal is for no one to get cut off. You're all badasses, but it makes sense to take down anybody with superior numbers."

Lae'yul stared at the map. "If I draw water from the sea, won't that destroy their precious tunnels? I can't bring along enough water to display my true power."

Karl grimaced. "I can field that one. I didn't want to reveal too much to the government, but I asked about water running through in case they're on fire, and they say plenty of pipes will be active, and they'll flood them for our purposes, so draw what you need from those pipes. They'll fix it later."

Zaena tapped her paper. "Once we encounter anything suspicious, we can report our relative locations over the radios. To help our patrol, they'll be opening all the access doors throughout. Every service access door has an identifier, and they are sequential."

Lae'yul narrowed her eyes. "In such a case, potential enemies will also be able to move more easily."

"I'd rather have it this way than be forced to work with the human soldiers," Zaena replied. "We can't operate too freely if we're worrying about humans around us."

Vokasin's gaze roamed the map. "If Lae'yul uses an ice platform, we could all fly through our tunnels. It'll allow us to cover the distances quickly and find the elf who would challenge us."

"There's no guarantee we will encounter an enemy," Zaena insisted. "I think we should be cautious about how much magic we use until we encounter the source of trouble."

Lae'yul inclined her head toward Saelli. "Her prophecy talks of pain. That suggests you won't be able to talk this one down, Princess."

"I don't know about prophecies," Karl interjected, "but I don't think it hurts to go in with the assumption you might have to knock some heads around. I've been wondering if you've been thinking this through too magically."

"How else would we?" Vokasin asked with a sneer. "We are going to this place because of a prophecy. Our strength is in magic."

"Yeah, but Mark Wong was a Mountain Elf who used magic and technology," countered Karl. "You're all assuming you're going to walk into some guy who is going to throw rocks at you. I'm not so worried about the government trying to bury you, but how do we know it's not some elf showing up with a bomb?" He shook his paper. "Without Saelli, how the hell are you going to get out if you get buried?"

Lae'yul scoffed. "I'll tear through their tunnels with the power of the ocean if I must. Princess Zaena can as well. At that point, there's no reason to hold back."

"If I'm to die there, I'll die," Vokasin offered.

Zaena looked at the elves and Karl. "He does raise a good point. If you encounter something that looks like a bomb, we will immediately retreat and inform the human military. They have better resources for dealing with this sort of threat."

Lae'yul's gaze ticked to Saelli. "The priestess could give us the Diamond of Protection. It could seal such a device."

"I cannot give you the artifact," Saelli said, "I value my mission, but this is a sacred artifact of my people. I will use it to aid the princess in her overall task, but I will never willingly hand it over until my death."

"We also might need it as a last line of defense here," Zaena noted, "and she's right. I would never demand any tribe turn over their artifact without a member present. For now, we'll continue training together, and everyone should go and also commune to ensure we're at our best. The day before the solstice, we will be delivered by an American military transport. That should give us time to patrol. The local environments are only suitable for communing for Lae'yul and me, so Vokasin, you should avoid using too much magic until we're inside the tunnels."

"I'm fine letting you do the less amusing tasks."

Zaena placed her hand over the Ruby of Tarilan. "This will be another important day in elven history. Four tribes will cooperate across two continents together. I'm growing confident in this prophecy. I know it will lead us to what we need."

Vokasin eyed Saelli. "Let us hope for all our sakes that we can trust your dreams, priestess."

CHAPTER THIRTY-ONE

A few days before the mission, Karl and Zaena stepped out of a black DIA sedan. The agents had picked them up in a parking lot and driven them to a dockside warehouse. The agents called to arrange a meeting but were strangely reluctant to talk once they'd picked up the Team Princess reps.

Karl was annoyed at having to meet with them yet again, but he didn't worry. Whatever this was, it wasn't an assassination. Unless they killed Zaena right away, there was no way they could win. The agents knew that, as did their boss.

A gull flew overhead, squawking as Karl surveyed the area. It wasn't the place they'd run the anti-terror mission out of a couple of months before. There were no other vehicles nearby. His annoyance shifted to curiosity.

Agents Lyle and Waves led Karl and Zaena through a side door and along a dusty hallway toward another door secured with an electronic keypad lock. Karl wasn't surprised when Agent Lyle opened the door to reveal a clean, well-equipped office with desks and computers.

Karl folded his arms and stood next to a desk. "Okay, so what's the deal with this place? Is this where the *magic* happens?"

Agent Waves laughed. "Kind of."

Agent Lyle closed the door behind them. "We've got a few different ops centers throughout the area, so we can respond to a variety of incidents and conditions." He gestured around the room. "Our boss told us she wanted you to know about this location. Consider it us extending additional trust to you. We'll do our primary briefing here on mission day before we take you to the plane."

"Isn't this place a little undefended?" Karl gestured at the door. "One fancy lock isn't going to stop anyone but junkies."

Agent Lyle smirked. "We've got people here. They just know how to keep out of sight."

Karl surveyed the room. There were eight desks, all with computers. Even if Waves and Lyle were their main contacts, it wasn't like he'd never seen other government agents in their dealings.

Zaena sat at a desk and crossed her legs. "I presume there's a purpose for this visit other than to establish greater trust?"

"That's right, Princess." Agent Lyle's smirk and haughty tone vanished. "We wanted to pass along some additional information in case it changed your plans or strategy. We were made aware of a Chunnel incident this morning. Right now, the news is being kept quiet to stave off additional media attention, and it'll probably work to our advantage once it breaks."

"An incident?" Karl frowned. "I don't like the sound of that."

"There was some sort of construction accident a few hours ago in the France-to-England rail tunnel," Agent Lyle explained. "The exact nature is unclear. Some workers were injured but not killed, and there was no serious damage. Fortunately, this makes one aspect of this a lot easier. They're closing the entire Chunnel until repairs and inspections are completed. We've gone from a day to at least a week."

"That's awfully convenient." Karl glanced at Agent Waves, looking for discomfort.

The younger agent wasn't that good at hiding his emotions. Agent Waves smiled back like they were at a party.

"Sometimes luck goes your way," Agent Lyle replied with a shrug. "I'm not going to complain that everyone's not going to have to work so hard to keep this quiet."

Zaena looked down with a scowl. "Karl's right. It is too convenient. Are we already too late?"

"Whoa. What are you talking about? Do you know something you'd like to share with the rest of the class? Like I said, no deaths, no serious damage."

"You also said the nature of the accident was unclear," Zaena commented. "If a hostile magical attack occurred, the humans involved might not be able to properly interpret it. This might not be a construction accident."

Agent Lyle nodded his head. "I see what you're getting at, but from what I've seen, you can do a lot more damage.

None of the workers have serious injuries. There's some rail damage, but the tunnel's not collapsed. If this was elven magical terrorism, it's pretty low-key stuff. It doesn't make sense."

Karl stopped giving Agent Waves the eye to drill into Agent Lyle with his gaze. "You two know more than unclear details. This isn't a murder investigation where you need to hide details so you can trick the suspects. She needs to know what she's walking into so she can deal with it. That's to her advantage and yours. Right now, doesn't the American government want their favorite elven princess to survive?"

"Initial reports indicate a minor explosion," Agent Waves offered, ignoring the warning glare of his partner. "There was a small fire, but they got it under control. The concern is that there are problems with the electrical lines. They're worried there was a hidden natural gas pocket that somehow escaped previous geological surveys. That's one of the reasons they're being so careful." He stared at his partner expectantly.

Agent Lyle frowned. "Here's the problem. Even finding out that information was like pulling teeth, and no one is acting like or reporting this was terrorism, so we don't understand why our friends across the pond are being that way. It feels off."

"You believe a conspiracy is in play?" Zaena asked.

Karl was glad about how far she'd shifted from trusting everyone's motivation. There was being optimistic, and there was being dangerously naïve.

"Selene's way more uptight than usual," Agent Lyle admitted, "so you're right. I don't think we can dismiss the possibility this incident was magical, but we're far from having evidence confirming that either."

Karl snickered. "Oh, I get it. You're worried because you haven't admitted to these governments that elves exist, and you're not sure they'd do the same."

"That is the concern, but they are still responding positively to our counterterrorism proposal. The mission is still on. We're not sure if they believe this was an attack and would rather just let Americans fall on their face or if they're aware of something else and are holding it back. In either event, we'll still get a full day of clearance, but we could potentially get more if you need it."

Zaena stared at the wall, her brow wrinkling. "We trust our tipster. If the attack has already occurred and been resolved, so be it, but if it was an arrival preparing themselves, my varsity team will sense the relevant magic, and we'll be able to handle the threat."

"Your varsity team?" asked Agent Lyle with a confused look.

"Don't worry about the name," Karl insisted. "It's an internal team thing, and I don't think she's keeping it."

Zaena gave him a disappointed look.

"If you say so." Agent Lyle shrugged.

Karl would have loved to see how two government agents reacted to hearing a mission was going to start based on a prophecy. In his mind, it was no more ridiculous than sending a group of elves led by a princess to investigate another elf threatening the Chunnel.

"Are you going to continue with your initial plan?" Agent Lyle asked. "We can guarantee the tunnels will be bottled up by soldiers on both sides. You'll have a day to play, along with comms provided by an American intel team with appropriate clearance. You don't have to reveal anything to England or France yet. As far as they're concerned, a specialist US unit is being sent in because of potential chemical warfare concerns, and we just happen to have the necessary experts on hand."

Karl chuckled. "We don't have to reveal anything, or you don't want our alleged ally countries to learn about your pet elves?"

He was tired of the government acting like they were doing them a favor. There was nothing seedy about *quid pro quo* as long as both sides understood where the other was coming from.

"We're not in a position to order Princess Zaena not to reveal that," Agent Lyle offered with an annoyed look, "but we would hope she understands that it's not the best time to introduce new complexities to this situation. As far as our official position, this is a need-to-know matter, and they don't need to know."

"I think it's better for the moment that only the US government knows about my elven nature, but I do want to make you aware that position might change within a short time."

"All we want is a heads-up," Agent Lyle suggested.

"I'm sure we can manage that," offered Zaena. She stood. "Then we continue as planned. I see no reason to adjust things now. If anything, it's only proof that the tip we brought you has merit."

"It could be a big coincidence," Karl noted. "That sometimes happens."

Zaena smiled. "Lately, I find coincidences impossible to accept."

It was hard to argue with that on a mission starting because of a prophecy.

"Get your team ready for transport, Princess," Agent Lyle said, "we'll get you on a plane to England. Let's hope nothing happens between now and your mission."

"Don't say crap like that," Karl admonished. "If there's no such thing as coincidences, it's inviting bad luck."

CHAPTER THIRTY-TWO

A harsh, shrill noise blasted Karl awake. He sat up and snatched his phone from the nightstand, understanding what was going on. The noise was his custom sound for the building security system. He'd even tested it, setting it off before to ensure it would wake him up.

"You've got to be freaking kidding me," he growled, snatching up the phone and bringing up the security app. Their system wasn't set up to contact the police. The last thing Karl wanted was cops swarming the White Ruby Building and hampering Saelli's and Zaena's ability to defend it without worrying about tipping off people to the existence of magic.

It might not have helped anyway. He furrowed his brow and stared at the phone. Besides the intrusion alert, there was a phone line failure alert and an internet access failure alert. That was a lot of things breaking at the same time.

That wasn't promising. The main alarm died with the warning, replaced by multiple system failure messages. He didn't need to believe in Zaena to doubt that was a coincidence. Nobody had that much bad luck or timing.

He frowned when he noticed his nightstand clock was off. Combined with the alerts, that suggested someone or something killed the main power. The main security system components had battery backups, but that didn't seem to mean much. He could go hit the generator for this side of the building, too, but that would take time he doubted he had.

A moment later, he lost all the bars on his cellphone. Things were officially ridiculous.

"Oh, come on," he yelled.

Karl tapped in a few commands into his phone to shift security control to a local backup booster that should in theory have a battery backup and operate on different frequencies than the cellphones. Reading crazy websites and having a big budget let him try a lot of things. He couldn't do much about everything else without contacting the outside world, but any info on what was going on would help.

He managed to connect to the cameras and started cycling through feeds after checking the door sensor. Ski-masked men in dark clothes stood crouched next to an open side door. They had pistols and small flashlights.

"I don't know if I would have preferred an elf."

An odd black device with a long silver antenna sat next to the intruders. He had no idea what it was, but it didn't look magical.

"Did these assholes wait until Zaena left to break in here?" Karl muttered, "or are they just trying to give me a restless night?"

He grabbed a gun from his nightstand drawer before heading to the closet to snatch his shoulder holster and strap it on, along with a jacket because he already had extra mags and night-vision goggles in it. That left him half-naked in nothing but boxers, a shoulder holster, and a jacket.

He was reaching Bruce Willis-action-movie levels of underdressed. He hoped the universe would bless him accordingly.

The intruders hadn't entered the restaurant side of the building. That cut down on the chance they were there to steal kitchen equipment. He doubted simple kitchen thieves would take such elaborate measures versus a quick smash and snatch.

After grabbing another set of night-vision goggles from his closet, Karl rushed down the hall and knocked on Saelli's door. She answered with a speed that surprised him until he spotted the open laptop on her coffee table and an article about the Chunnel. She'd tied off her silk robe, though it still showed a lot of smooth leg. That would have distracted him if he didn't play for the other team.

"We have intruders," Karl whispered. "All humans. They have guns, but only pistols from what I've seen. They've gone out of their way to make sure we can't call for help."

Saelli had a grim look. "If they are humans using human weapons, I don't think they are the threat mentioned in the prophecy. Why are they here?"

"I don't know, and we don't have a lot of time," Karl explained. "I can track them with the cameras. There's no way they can easily penetrate the nexus tunnels without explosives." He furrowed his brow. "I'd like to keep the lights off to surprise them, but they've cut the power, so that takes care of that." He offered her the goggles. "Can your stone guardians see in the dark?"

"Yes and no. They sense life force rather than see. Thus light isn't important, but all the active guardians are in the nexus complex," Saelli replied. "There are none on the upper levels. I can summon them here."

So far, so good, but now was the big test. Saelli was polite enough to him when Zaena was around, but tolerating a human and taking orders from him in a dangerous situation were different things. He doubted he'd be able to defend the place without her help, but she needed to understand he was the one with all the tactical knowledge.

Karl shook his head. "That might be overkill anyway," he admitted. "First, we need to figure out what their deal is. If they're petty thieves, we'll knock them out and call the cops, but they've got enough skill that they managed to knock out a lot of things before getting inside, which means they might be more dangerous. If it's serious, we'll do what we need to, understood?"

Saelli stared at him and slid the goggles onto her head. "You mean, you want to kill them?"

"I don't *want* to kill them," Karl stated, "but I'm not going to go out of my way to risk my life for armed intruders who are here to murder us or try to break into the nexus."

"I'd rather not kill if we can avoid it," Saelli admitted. "I've grown weary of it."

"That's up to them," Karl offered. "I don't know about you, but I've never killed anyone who didn't have it coming."

"Has your government betrayed us?" Saelli asked. "They would know exactly when the princess would be too far away to aid us."

Karl grabbed his phone from his pocket to check the feeds. The entire group of intruders had invaded a hallway, but they were advancing slowly as if looking for something or someone. They were far closer to the apartments and offices than the restaurant, and they hadn't entered the building close to the restaurant.

"I'm not sure." Karl shook his head. "D'Arcy's teams would have been Special Forces with top-of-the-line weapons and goggles, but these guys also disabled our power and messed up our phone. They've got some weird gadget set up outside. I think it's a cell phone jammer. That's a lot of serious effort and gear for neighborhood robbers."

"Another enemy?" Saelli mused. "What a depressing thought."

"They might be the government, but not hitting the restaurant first is majorly suspicious, along with the timing." He checked his phone. "Zaena shouldn't have landed yet, but she's far enough away that even if we got hold of her, there's no way she could get back."

"You don't want to contact her?" Saelli asked.

"We'll handle these guys and then worry about it. We need her to concentrate on what she has coming up, and there's nothing she can do unless she can invent teleporting magic in the next two minutes."

"Your plan is reasonable." Saelli raised her hand. Water, dirt, and rock flowed from vases positioned around the living room. "I'll do what I can. I offer my power to you. We shall defend this place from all enemies."

Karl gestured to the water and a vase. "Is that why those are there? I just thought you were really into human art."

"Not all types of magic have the same advantages and disadvantages," Saelli explained, now circled by separate rings of water, dirt, and rock. "Water and earth offer more flexibility than fire and air, but their very nature makes them harder to produce without an existing source or excessive levels of magic. Even with my connection to the nexus, my power isn't unlimited."

"If you need to yank something from pipes, do it. Zaena will understand, and the local contractors will be happy to get more business." He motioned down the hall, then tossed his phone into his left hand, so he could monitor the camera feeds while holding his gun with his right. "I checked exterior cameras earlier, and these guys only came in the one entrance. That is another thing that points away from them being the government. They would have secured all the exits so we couldn't escape. The DIA would also know we've got a ton of cameras in this place."

"I used earth magic in Iceland," Saelli replied. "The government must also know I'm capable of it, even if the princess hasn't explicitly told them. They'd know we can escape by burrowing."

"Nah. I'm not sure we can assume anything about how much people understand about elven magic. They're looking for something, but I don't know what."

"We could retreat to the basement and secure ourselves there."

"Nope. I don't want them looking around. You got your diamond?"

Saelli held up her hand and displayed the diamond, which was set in a bone ring. "I never take it off."

"Use it if you need to," Karl ordered. "I don't care if a bunch of random thieves sees something weird in the dark. They won't tip anybody off, and even if they did, no one would believe them." He frowned. "Damn it."

"What?"

"I just thought of one reason why they might not have hit the apartments," Karl explained. "They might be trying to go to the security room first. Not a good sign, but it gives us more time to get ready. If they trusted their gadgets too much, they might not have realized that the alarms woke me up, even if they didn't go anywhere else."

Saelli nodded. There was no fear or concern on her face. "You want us to get ready here?"

"I'm going to watch them until I figure it out." Karl inclined his head toward her sink. "Rather than using a few gallons here and there, why not get a steady stream going?"

CHAPTER THIRTY-THREE

Karl frowned at his phone. He'd been watching the intruders, and they had proceeded to the security room, as he'd theorized. They'd entered and then killed the entire system after one brought up a familiar camera feed showing him standing just outside Saelli's apartment.

He shoved his phone in his pocket. "I think I've confirmed what they're looking for," he whispered. "Don't leave the apartment until I tell you. We still have a chance to surprise them."

"What have they looked for?" Saelli asked. Large blobs of water floated around her, constantly fed from a stream running to the faucet.

"Me," Karl replied. "Maybe both of us. They got info from contractors or someone since they showed a better understanding of the layout of this place than I would have guessed." He ground his teeth in frustration. People were always the weak link in security. "They were checking a camera for this specific hallway, which means they're coming this way. If it wasn't about looking for the apartment and confirming someone was here, they would have turned before the security room. They were heading to the nexus, and they've passed up storerooms that might have equipment."

"Shall we ambush them?" Saelli suggested. "I can cut through the walls if necessary with my magic."

Karl considered for a moment before shaking his head. "We've got a good position here, and I'm pretty sure they don't know an elf's here, or they would have brought something more impressive than a bunch of Glocks." He inclined his head toward her door. "How much water do you need to make fog?"

"I have the beginnings of enough." Saelli gestured at the floating ring of water. "I can continue to draw from my sink."

"Good plan," Karl replied. "Better that than fixing the pipes again, but do it if you have to. Make me some ice walls to hide behind, then create a fog. I want them unsettled when they get here."

Saelli thrust her arm toward the hallway, and all her rings and blobs flowed that way. They split into two streams, one forming a line of ice, rock, and dirt and the other water stream flowing farther along the hallway before vaporizing into a hazy mist.

Karl looked satisfied. He wasn't sure how things would play out with Saelli. A woman who'd risk her life for a prophecy was a wildcard, but she was proving to be a reliable ally at the moment.

She thickened the line into the base of a shield and grew it inch by inch, with a look of annoyance on her face. Water beaded on the walls, and the fog deepened.

Karl shivered a little. He was used to experiencing water becoming steam by being heated, but Saelli was feeding into the air and keeping it far cooler. Magic didn't play by the rules he'd been taught in school. He still wasn't sure how well that sat with him.

Of course, he might not have been as cold if he'd thrown on some pants. Bruce Willis got to keep his pants on in *Die Hard.* Getting equipped and to Saelli as soon as possible had seemed like a good idea, but he hadn't assumed the intruders would have such a complicated plan.

"Miss living on a glacier?" Karl asked, flexing his fingers. "You could have probably had a wall and the fog up in seconds, and you could throw angry snowmen at these idiots."

"Having ice around is preferable, but this is working." Saelli moved her hands back and forth and continued building the wall. "This is magically strengthened. It's not as strong as rock, but it should take hits better than normal ice. Don't risk your life unnecessarily."

"Who are these assholes?" muttered Karl. He looked at his phone, but the feed was still dead. "I counted six. Assuming they came directly from the security room but don't sprint here, we probably have a couple more minutes to get ready. The way they were moving, I think they're worried about getting jumped, which we can use to our advantage."

"Stay low, please," Saelli suggested. "It takes time to build this and create the fog without ripping water from the pipes, and I'd prefer not to do that unless necessary."

"No more low-flow faucets for us." Karl checked his

gun. “I should start sleeping in kneepads. When the guys get here, stay in your apartment and keep feeding ice and fog here until I call for help. I’ve got an idea that should avoid us having to deal with a pile of bodies, but it’ll require them not to know you’re here for it to have a chance of working. I don’t think they saw you, and I don’t know if they know you live here. It helps that they didn’t have time to hack the system. It looks like they just killed it, so they’re blind too.”

“Understood.” Saelli had grown the wall to a decent size, enough to protect the kneeling Karl. “Handling a situation with less bloodshed is always preferable, even if killing is easier.”

Karl looked her way. “It bothers you that much? You took out those Azure Knives in Iceland, and you didn’t sound all that broken up about it.”

Saelli gave him a bland look. “They tortured an innocent woman, and they sought my life. I had no choice but to take theirs.”

“These guys might not be into torturing innocent women, but they might be all about trying to kill us.”

Saelli shook her head. “The Knives replaced reason with fanaticism. I assume greedy humans cling to reason.”

Karl scoffed. “Lady, you’ve got a lot more faith in humanity than I do.”

Flashlight beams shone on the wall. Footsteps sounded in the distance, along with low murmurs.

“They’re almost here,” Karl whispered, jabbing his finger at the intersection. “That was quicker than I thought, but it doesn’t sound like they’re running.”

Saelli stopped adding to Karl’s shield, opened the door,

and ducked behind it. The stream of water continued flowing from the sink and fed the burgeoning hallway mist.

Karl grinned. He would have liked a few more minutes to set up the atmosphere for his plan, but it wasn't bad. All he needed was lightning and thunder in the background. He crouched and waited for the first man to turn the corner. The swirling fog highlighted the flashlight beam.

"What the hell?" the intruder asked. "Is that ice and fog? Is their AC messed up? Is that even possible with a broken AC?"

"Keep it down, idiot," another man whispered.

A third intruder crouched and turned the corner with his gun in hand. "Yeah, why is it so foggy in here? Someone having a rave? I don't hear no music."

Karl stopped a chuckle from escaping. He'd been expecting hardened professional killers, but he wasn't impressed so far. These idiots were giving up way too much. It was time to begin his psychological offensive.

"You don't want to do this," Karl called out. "Good job on the security system, but you didn't stop it entirely. The alarm already went off. I've been ready for you since you got in here. Your only chance was to come at me right away, but you waited, and now I'm pissed off and armed."

The men ducked back around the corner. Judging by the furtive whispers, they weren't running. He'd hoped mentioning the security system would be enough to drive them off.

"That you, Karl Smith?" called an intruder. It was the voice of the second man. Karl assumed he was in charge.

"That's the name on my birth certificate," Karl called

back. "Think I should change it to Fernando the Ass-kicker? A lot of flair, right? I don't think I have the hair to pull off being a Fernando. Nicholas the Ass-kicker?"

"This doesn't have to go badly, Smith," the leader shouted. "If you want to make it through this alive, you're going to come out from…" His voice faltered. "From behind that ice with your hands up. You have a gun, or you try anything, we'll put bullets in you. That's a guarantee."

Karl scoffed. "You guys want me to walk willingly toward a bunch of armed robbers with guns? I'm not going to walk into an execution. I'm not a complete moron."

"This isn't an execution. This is just a litt—"

"Come out, Mr. Smith," called another intruder. Karl recognized the voice, but he was having trouble placing it. "I'm tired of games. You're not going to die today, but you're going to have to suffer the kind of savage beating a savage like you deserves. Now, man up and come with us to take your licks."

"Wait." Karl narrowed his eyes. "I know you. You're that asshole that works for Conroy."

A masked man stuck his head around the corner. He pulled off the balaclava. It was James, his face still bruised from their last encounter and bandages over his nose.

"Damn." Karl laughed. "I didn't think I hit you that hard. You still look that messed up? I was trying to hold back so I didn't kill you."

"I had to get surgery to fix my nose because of you," James bellowed. "You're a damned barbarian, and you're going to come out right now with your big paws behind your head if you want to have any chance of surviving this.

No boxing this time, Mr. Smith, only guns, and there are six of us and one of you."

Karl stayed low. "Yeah, how about no, asshole? You want me, you can come and get me. I'm feeling mighty Spartan today."

"Oh, we'll come and get you, but you should come out if you want to get by with only the beating." James offered a sick grin. "Mr. Conroy has made it clear there's to be no deaths despite the unfortunate disrespect you displayed in our last meeting with you. Unlike you, he's civilized. If you had chosen to be civilized, we wouldn't be in this position, and everyone would have been richer and happier."

Conroy's involvement explained that strange mix of expensive jamming equipment and amateurish intrusion. The rich bastard probably hadn't wanted to outsource his beatings anymore. This was what Karl got for showing them mercy.

"No deaths?" he called back. "All the guns could have fooled me."

Karl glanced at Saelli. She stayed behind the door, still feeding the thick mist. There was no fear or reluctance on her face, only resignation.

The flashlights of the intruders couldn't pick Karl out between the fog and the ice, but he had a good view of them with his googles.

He dismissed the idea that this was a Zaena-targeted plot. There was no way Conroy and his half-assed goons knew she was the Crimson Wind. It was a coincidence, after all. Unfortunately, sometimes a man drew a crap hand.

"You damned arrogant bastard," James shouted, waving

his gun. "You ruined everything. You and the Crimson Wind, but it's not like you're always going to get that lucky to have her help you out. All you had to do was take his offer, and you'd be living in comfort with a man who values his employees. Now you're going to take a beating, and your employers are going to have to sell this building out from under you. Fortunately for you, Mr. Conroy isn't interested in hurting anyone but you."

There was another chance for Karl to bluff his way out of it. They hadn't started shooting yet, which meant he still could play his cards.

"I don't know," Karl commented. "You don't think the Crimson Wind will show up? She did help clear this place out. She probably watches it."

"She's not here, now, is she?" James noted. He swung his gun around. "This is why Mr. Conroy shouldn't have hired outsiders to do his work. Those idiots screwed up and drew her attention. I was more careful, and now it's just you and me and my associates. Too bad for you, Mr. Smith."

"Just you and your dumbass friends, huh?" Karl asked. "You've never broken into a building before, have you? That's why I was ready for you. The only reason you're not dead is that I don't want to have to waste my night talking to cops."

"It doesn't matter that you weren't surprised. I know you didn't make a call." James scoffed. "I'm not a thug. We hire thugs to do this sort of thing, normally. They have their uses."

Every second Karl stalled, the fog grew thicker. He was

proud of this plan. He was starting to get what magic could do with a little thought.

"Not a thug, huh?" Karl replied. "You tried to bash my face in. That was mighty gentlemanly of you."

"That was for your disrespect of Mr. Conroy." James gritted his teeth. "Now we're reduced to this. You only have yourself to blame. Be a real man and accept your punishment."

"The cops are on their way," Karl lied. "You should leave before they show up. You probably only have a couple of minutes at most."

James let out a cold chuckle. "Nice try, Mr. Smith. We brought special gear, and we hired some specialists. We both know no one's coming, which is why you keep throwing out those sad little lies to get us to go away."

"Special gear?" Karl snickered. "Yet I'm awake and waiting for you. If it's just about me, it would have made more sense to grab me off the street. More amateur hour crap."

"A break-in is easier to explain. Shut your damned mouth."

"Then there was your original plan with the critic." Karl barked a mocking laugh. "It's all overly complicated. Your boss thinks he's a super mastermind, but he's an amateur who's way out of his depth. If he wants to be a supervillain, he needs to study. Hire some retired mobsters for advice. I'm sure you can find instructional videos on YouTube."

"Shut up," James yelled. "I've grown tired of you and your mouth."

"You should leave and go kiss your girlfriend," Karl suggested. "Because if you try to take me out, you're all going to die. Your only choice is to go home and wait to be arrested, dumbasses. I'm starting to lose my patience."

"I've lost mine." James pulled the trigger. The bullet went wide, missing the shield. He walked forward, screaming and firing. A couple of bullets blasted chunks out of the shield, but most passed overhead. "Come on!" he yelled. "Let's finish this! Mr. Conroy wanted you alive, but accidents happen. You're dead, Smith! Dead!"

The other men rushed around the corner and opened fire. Karl ducked. More chunks flew into the hallway. His shield wouldn't last long.

Karl hadn't been lying about avoiding the police, and he didn't want to gun them down now that he knew they weren't a serious threat. A pile of bodies would be hard to explain.

Fortunately, the men were shooting down the hall with no real accuracy. The thick fog and darkness pushed them to near-blind firing. It was time for the next step in his plan.

"They're all in the hall now," Karl whispered to Saelli. "Send some ice through the hallway a couple of times to knock them over. I'll call you out when it's time and they can't see you, and you can disarm them and pin them against the wall."

She hadn't questioned him or asked for details on his plan. He was surprised.

Saelli flicked her wrists. Thick chunks of ice crystallized out of the fog and flew down the hall. Two smashed into James. He stumbled backward, firing into the ceiling.

"W-what? What the f—"

An ice chunk shattered against another man's head. He pitched forward, tripping over another.

Saelli swirled the fog into a spinning ring of ice. Bobbing flashlight beams highlighted the men. They had stopped their forward advance after her first ice attack, but they hadn't retreated around the corner.

The ice shot spread out, leaving no room to escape. Men groaned and yelped as they got nailed by demon hail. They dropped their flashlights and weapons.

No one fired. Stray light revealed shattered ice and the outlines of downed men.

"Come out now and pin them," Karl ordered. "Their lights aren't pointing this way, but stay low."

Saelli spun around the edge of the door. Karl wasn't sure which was more absurd, his boxers, jacket, and night-vision goggle combination or the pale elf in her silk robe and goggles.

Ice flowed from the ground and flew toward the men, forming cuffs around their arms and legs. Saelli's attacks and follow-up had repurposed most of the fog, clearing out the hallway. James and his team groaned and struggled.

"Now the fun part begins." Karl tucked his pistol back into his holster and rubbed his hands together. This had come together almost perfectly.

"Wasn't blinding and disarming them your plan?" Saelli whispered.

Karl grinned. "That was the first part. Winning one fight is one thing. I'm about to win the next five before they start."

CHAPTER THIRTY-FOUR

"Isn't this too much magic?" Saelli whispered. "Don't we risk creating too much attention? I understand if we'd killed them, but they are all alive."

Karl kept his voice low. "They can't see crap, and this is one situation where I think believing in a little magic will help. Just not the elven kind."

Saelli's face scrunched in confusion. "I don't understand."

"Rumor can do a lot to keep a place safe," Karl explained. "That was something Mark Wong understood. Zaena kind of gets it, but she doesn't understand humans well enough to take advantage of it."

"You think we should imitate a corrupt elf gangster?" Saelli frowned. "I don't understand America well, but I find that odd, especially given your past profession."

"In some ways, yeah, we should imitate him. What works, works." Karl stood. "Just follow my lead. I'm not going to do anything that'll offend the elements or Zaena's sense of honor. This is just informational warfare and taking advantage of people's superstition."

He marched toward the men. They continued to struggle and wiggle, but their ice restraints held them firmly.

"What the hell did you do to us?" James asked. "It feels like ice."

"Stealing the blueprints or whatever you did isn't the same thing as knowing what to expect inside this place." Karl stopped a yard from James, then picked up a flashlight and put it beneath his chin. "Came in here in the dark, in the fog. Sounds like a good time for spooky stories. You like scary stories, asshole?"

"What's wrong with your head?" James yelped. He sucked in a breath. "You have night-vision goggles. You were ready for us."

"I already told you that, dumbass. Next time, listen. All those fancy toys, but you didn't bring night-vision goggles? You've got to think these things through." He tapped the side of his head. "Not that you had a chance since you thought you knew what was up. You were smart enough to know where to grab me but not smart enough to be ready for what you'd need to do to pull that stunt off."

"What are you wearing?" James asked, sounding amused.

"Night-vision goggles. Try to keep up."

"I'm not talking about that. Are you in your underwear?"

"Sorry, I don't sleep in a full suit for when people invade my place," Karl replied with a sneer. "And I'm not the one on the floor without his gun, am I, asshole? I'd watch the attitude."

"You going to kill us?" James asked. There was no fear in his voice. He sounded embarrassed. That was what Karl wanted to hear.

Karl kept the flashlight on his face. "Nah. You didn't even hit me. Plus, I need you alive to tell the police all about your annoying boss so he'll stop messing with me. My boss and I don't want to get all tangled up with a weird rich guy trying a land grab. That garbage about lawsuits doesn't mean much when he sends an armed team after me and invades my employers' building at the same time."

"It's not too late," James insisted. "He respects skill. He'd pay you much more than these people. You've just proven how skilled you are."

"It's not always about the money," Karl replied. "Let me make this clear. Next time he tries something like this, I'll shoot his ass, but I think he's going to spend some time in jail pretty soon. If he wants to play at being a gangster, he should have played for keeps." He backed away. "Dying might not even be the worst thing that could happen if he tries to take this property. That's what's going to be clear to you very soon."

James scoffed. "We've checked you out enough to know you're not working for violent criminals. Though Mr. Conroy suspects some financial tricks are being played with this building and the restaurant. Why put a young girl with no business experience in charge of the local company? Is it a roundabout way of getting around regulations? Are you laundering foreign money?"

Karl chuckled. It built in volume and deepness until a

thunderous, booming laugh shook the area. "You don't get it. You don't understand what we're doing here and why Conroy was stupid to ever come here. You've got it all wrong."

"Oh, spare me." James snorted. "You're not going to kill me; that much is clear. You had plenty of chances. You can't scare me now. That's the problem with interrogating someone who has done that kind of thing to other people."

Karl lowered the flashlight. "I'm not the one you should be afraid of. You don't understand that White Ruby didn't come here for business. They came here for something else entirely." He backed toward Saelli and whispered, "Float some ice back and forth over them. Do something flashy with it, but don't hurt them."

Saelli gave him a confused look. "As you wish."

Karl pointed the flashlight down the hall. Illuminated ice danced in the air. It traced different patterns one moment and broke into erratic and unpredictable paths the next. A piece shattered into dozens and reformed.

James' eyes widened. "What? Huh?'

"Don't you get it, asshole?" Karl asked. "You can't cause as much suffering and pain as the Demon Overlords did and not leave a mark on a place like this, a spiritual mark. You understand what that means?"

"A spiritual mark?"

Karl wasn't sure how well James could see him without the flashlight on his face, but he kept his expression serious. Conventional intimidation hadn't worked, so it was time for more radical tactics. Despite what he'd said, he wasn't ready to go gun down a billionaire. It'd require too many annoying explanations later.

"How many innocent people do you think the Demon Overlords tortured and killed?" Karl asked. "What about the triad men? A lot of them died when this place was taken out. Hell, did you guys even do a background check on it? Didn't you know about its rep long before the Overlords took over?"

"You can't be serious." James swallowed. "The rumors about it being haunted?"

Karl glanced at the other men. They all stared at him, eyes wide with fear. It was working.

"Yeah. It didn't surprise a lot of people that the Overlords picked this place. It's had an odd reputation for as long as people have lived near it."

He hadn't cared much about it before meeting Zaena, though he couldn't deny he'd felt something strange near it. Now he understood he had been feeling the nexus, but the rumors that had popped up around the land proved he wasn't the only person in San Francisco with distant elven blood.

James let out a nervous laugh. "There's no such thing as ghosts. This is a pathetic trick."

Karl waved his flashlight around to emphasize Saelli's ice show. "You think I'm psychic? Do you think I'm doing this with my mind? Does that make it better, asshole? Should I go all Carrie on your ass?"

"It's a trick," James stammered. "You knew we were coming. You had the equipment, you set something up, or it's a projector."

"A projector didn't knock your ass down and capture you." Karl pointed his flashlight at James' wrist. "Take a look."

"It doesn't just feel like ice. It *is* ice!" James gasped. "That's impossible."

"Ghosts are dead, right?" Karl shrugged. "They're all about cold and that kind of thing. That's why those ghost hunter guys are always looking for cold spots. It's common sense. The thing is, they're cold because they don't have life. That makes them empty, and that makes them hungry."

"Don't feed us to the ghosts!" screamed one of the other men.

James' face twisted in anger. "Shut up, you idiot. He's tricking us. There are no such things as ghosts. He just used liquid nitrogen and a sprayer. Something like that. Think about it. If there are ghosts here, how come Smith isn't getting attacked? Ghosts don't eat washed-up ex-cops?"

"They're not messing with me because my boss hired a Taoist priest to come in here and negotiate a deal," Karl lied. "He set up statues of the Four Symbols and did all this feng shui crap. I don't understand half of it, but the gist is, they only come out when there's not a lot of positive energy around. The restaurant customers keep them away most of the day, but when this place gets empty and filled with bad thoughts," he waved his gun around, "it calls them and looks for anyone not filled with positive energy."

"This is insane," James insisted. He strained against his ice restraints. "I'm not listening to this idiocy."

"Plus, it helps that I almost died, according to the priest." Karl slapped his chest. "It's kind of like they think I'm one of them. Maybe the victims don't care because I was an enemy of criminals, and the dead Overlords are afraid of me as a symbol of the police. All I know is I'm okay, but you're not going to be for long."

The men whimpered. He was proud of himself. This was the most creative he'd been in years. It helped that the truth was equally ridiculous.

No, that wasn't right. The ghost story made more sense.

"What are the Four Symbols?" James asked, the defiance gone from his voice.

"Come on. You come to Chinatown, and you don't know anything about Chinese culture? I had to learn a lot of this stuff when I was working this place as a cop. Learn the language. Learn the history. Learn the culture. I would have thought a rich bastard like your boss would have thought the same way, but it doesn't matter. The point is the ghosts aren't going to eat me, but they *are* going to eat you. It's not just about dying. See, there are worse things than dying, like getting your soul chewed up by a hungry, angry ghost. It's probably the single most painful way to die."

The other men cried out for mercy. One man sobbed.

"They even listen to me a little." Karl snapped his fingers. "It's not something I normally do, but special guests deserve special entertainment. Oh, ghosts of this place, show them your true power."

A pulse of magic washed over Karl's skin. Blue, white and green light bathed the hallway.

He'd never anticipated Saelli might use the Diamond of Protection as part of his scheme. He was impressed.

"Whoa," James shouted. "What the hell is that?"

"That's a mark of the ghosts' anger," Karl said. "Damn, I haven't heard about them being this angry since before the

Demon Overlords got taken out. I never thought I'd see this crap."

"Let us go, please!" yelled one of the other men. "I'll never work for Conroy again. I promise."

Karl tried not to laugh. He turned away to calm himself. "I'm going to go get some zip-ties to secure you bastards. Then I'll try to convince the ghosts to leave. It's pretty damned messy after they eat souls."

"Do you want me to kill them?" Saelli asked, her voice scratchier than usual. She stepped forward, her pale face and red eyes highlighted by the illumination from the artifact's forcefield.

"It's a ghost!" screamed one of the men. "Please don't eat my soul!"

"I don't know," Saelli replied, turning toward the man. "Is your soul delicious? It's been so long since I've had a good soul. He won't let me eat. I'm always hungry, so hungry."

"Yeah, I'm a real asshole that way." Karl pulled out his phone and waved it. "Now, this is the part where you all confess to everything you've done and who you're working for. It'll make it easier when I hand this over to the cops, and it means I spend a lot less time in interviews."

"I'll tell you everything," James shouted. "Anything, just keep that ghost away from me."

"Good. No soul-eating then, just good old-fashioned justice. Lucky you."

That was how a man pulled off an elf-assisted reverse-Scooby Doo plot.

CHAPTER THIRTY-FIVE

Karl groaned when his phone rang. At least this time, it wasn't an alarm. He rubbed his arms and grabbed the phone. The call was coming from Gary. The man wouldn't call without a good reason.

"Yeah?" Karl answered, still annoyed. "You couldn't have let me sleep in? You know what kind of night I've had."

Gary chuckled. "You've been keeping my guys busy. I was hoping we'd never have to go back to that place except to eat at the restaurant. Sometimes I think the building is cursed."

"Not my fault some assholes decided to break in," Karl replied. He laid his head on his pillow again. "Some people just don't learn their lessons any way but the hard way."

"I'm not going to keep you long, but I figured I'd give you the good news first. Trevor Conroy was just picked up."

"Really?"

"It wasn't hard with your recording and the confessions. His head guy clammed up at the station, but half the other guys spilled their guts right away." Gary whistled. "What the hell did you do to them? They were all acting scared, but some of them straight-up claimed you threatened them with a ghost. How did you pull that one off?"

Karl laughed. Fooling someone was more of a rush than he'd realized.

"I don't control any ghosts," Karl noted. "If I had that kind of thing going on, I would have had much better clearance rates as a detective. These assholes saw one of our albino employees and freaked out because they were dumbasses who were probably high."

"Uh-huh." Gary didn't sound convinced. "They also said they saw stuff moving without explanation. Last time I checked, being an albino didn't give you telekinesis."

"Did they mention the part where the lights were off, and they'd dropped their flashlights?" Karl asked. "I tripped them and told them a ghost story, yeah. I didn't think it'd work so well." He snickered. "Let's be real, Gary. These weren't elite mercenaries. They were a bunch of wannabes working for a guy who thought he was smarter and tougher than a mobster, but no one was brave enough to tell him he was an idiot. They paid the price."

"Maybe," Gary replied, "but this is San Francisco."

"Last time I checked."

"Which means we've got more interesting things going on than a lot of places," Gary offered. "I don't know of any other city on the planet that has the Crimson Wind. See what I'm saying?"

Karl frowned. He'd thought his ghost strategy would be

so different than Zaena that no one would make that kind of connection.

"She's not a ghost," he noted. "She's a chick in a powered suit. You told me you think she's working for the feds."

"Maybe, or at least contracted by them," Gary replied. "The point is, a year ago, if you said there'd be a woman who could fly around and knock foes out with invisible force, I'd say to put down the pipe, but she exists. That makes me wonder what would happen if someone shut off the lights and she started doing that kind of thing."

Karl grunted. "You think my ghost is the Crimson Wind?"

"I don't know. You've crossed paths with her more than a lot of people. She might have your back."

"Because she was interested in taking down the Demon Overlords at the same time I was. It's not like we are buddies and go golfing on the weekend."

Gary sighed. "Okay, I've got to put on my captain's hat here. This isn't an interrogation, and you know I've got your back, but I need you to be straight with me. Did this involve the Wind? Because it might come up. I think most of these guys are going to plead, but we don't want a creative lawyer getting away with anything."

Karl chuckled. "Put me under a polygraph if you want. I can testify with a hundred percent honesty under oath that the Crimson Wind wasn't involved in this incident, and neither were any ghosts. These dumbasses just can't tell a pale Scandinavian girl from a ghost."

"That sounds about right," Gary offered in a hesitant voice.

"Despite what everyone thinks, I don't have a Crimson Wind signal I can throw up and get her help." Karl snorted. "If the Wind had shown up, there'd be a lot more broken walls and bones, and probably a dead body or two."

Gary laughed hard. "That also sounds about right. She's not one to play subtly."

"So, what's the deal, then?" Karl asked. "Am I going to have to testify because of that James asshole?"

"Probably not," Gary offered. "Everyone but the head guy is admitting everything they've ever done back to middle school. He can play hardball, but he's got five other guys who are already rolling, so it's only a matter of time. One guy even admitted to shoplifting when he was in fourth grade, and he's begging us to charge him for it so the ghost doesn't eat his delicious soul.'"

"What about Conroy?"

Gary chuckled. "He's already trying to cut a deal, even though his top guy isn't throwing him under the bus."

"Really?" Karl didn't hide the surprise in his voice.

"Yeah. He's throwing his guy under the bus. Once James finds that out, I'm sure he'll turn. You know how it goes with rich bastards. This is going to bounce back and forth for a year, and he won't serve much time, but I'm sure he'll never mess with you or that building again."

Karl scoffed. "Next time somebody shows up at my place with a gun, I'm shooting."

"You do what you have to. I'll let you go. Just thought you should know what's happening."

"Thanks. Let's get together soon for a round."

"Sounds good, but I've got to go," Gary replied. "Talk to you soon." He ended the call.

Karl pinched the bridge of his nose before texting Zaena.

Jerks working for the rich jerk from before tried to break in. Saelli and I handled them. All under arrest, and their boss is too.

He wasn't sure if she was awake until her response came.

Excellent. Thank you both for handling things. We might be moving up the timetable on our task, so I might not be in contact for some time.

Karl stared at his phone. He wished he could be there, but he knew the best way he could help her was to continue protecting the building.

"I hope you find some jackasses you can scare, too."

CHAPTER THIRTY-SIX

Wrapped in camouflage, Zaena skimmed the surface of the English Channel. Moonlight reflected off the water. In other circumstances, she would have taken the time to soak in the beauty.

She'd made one complete circuit over the tunnels between France and England, trying to sense any magic. She moved away from the water and headed back toward the tunnel opening on the English side.

There was definite magic, even from the air, which pointed to a strong source below. The trip wasn't a waste of time.

The minutes passed, and she spotted the tall light towers, temporary fencing, and lines of troops and vehicles sealing the tunnels. She dropped behind the line and headed into the England-to-France tunnel, finding the two suited DIA agents and Vokasin and Lae'yul standing just inside.

Zaena landed and reappeared. The startled agents jumped back and went for their guns before sighing.

"Don't do that," Agent Lyle protested, "or at least say something first."

Zaena stared at him. "You said it was important to conceal ourselves when traveling to and from the tunnels."

"I did, but…" Agent Lyle scrubbed a hand down his face. "Sense anything?"

Zaena replied, "Yes. There's a strong source of magic in the tunnels."

Vokasin hadn't performed any recon because the flame and smoke accompanying his propulsion were easier to spot. Traveling in the city gave him plenty of places to hide, but the open water presented a difficulty.

She looked at Lae'yul. "Did you sense anything?"

Lae'yul nodded. "Yes, fairly strong."

Agent Lyle frowned. "You didn't mention that to us."

"I'm not required to answer your questions, human," Lae'yul responded.

"I don't know why people were ever into mermaids," complained Agent Lyle. "Shouldn't you be hanging out with a Jamaican crab?"

Zaena had tried to cut down on the discomfort after an initial meeting by having Lae'yul wear a one-piece swimsuit. It was like the agents had never seen a naked woman's body. Even now, the agents kept staring at the Sea Elf. Perhaps lust was preferable to hatred.

Zaena frowned and peered down the tunnel. It was narrower than it looked in the pictures. She understood there was no need for a vast cavern to hold a sleek train, but between the rails and the narrow spaces on the side, there wasn't a huge amount of room to maneuver. At least the accident hadn't taken out the lights.

"This isn't a wild duck hunt, then," Zaena mused. "That's good."

"I think that's wild goose chase," Agent Waves suggested with a sheepish look.

"I keep getting that one wrong. In any case, we know something is here."

Vokasin inclined his head down the tunnel. "Then we should stop wasting time talking about it."

"We have no guarantee we'll encounter everything we need to take out before the summer solstice," Zaena stated, "but I don't see any reason to wait for dawn. We could begin exploring the tunnels at midnight. We could walk them without a rush."

"It's over thirty miles," Agent Waves observed.

"We have all day. From what you've said, even longer if we need it." Zaena turned to Lae'yul. "Was the magic you felt steady?"

"Yes." Lae'yul pointed down the tunnel. "It also wasn't far from where they said there was an accident."

"I wonder if there is a nexus beneath the Chunnel?" Zaena mused. "That would explain it."

Agent Lyle grimaced. "Can those blow up?"

"Not normally," Zaena replied. "Humans can't even perceive them under normal circumstances."

"That means there's someone there," Agent Lyle concluded. "Someone like Mark Wong."

"Perhaps, but we don't want to jump to conclusions," Zaena replied.

Vokasin scoffed. "This isn't new construction. If there were a nexus here inhabited by an elf of murderous intent, why would he only care now?"

Agent Lyle replied, "You tell us. Our elven knowledge is summed up by what we've learned from you and the Mark Wong incidents."

"We won't know the answer without more exploration," Zaena noted. "It's pointless to theorize until then."

She still didn't want to talk about the prophecy. Bringing in the government might be inevitable given the threat of a great beast, but the situation remained tenuous.

"Fine," Agent Lyle muttered, then, "I want to re-emphasize that heavy damage to the Chunnel will create a serious international incident, even taking into account the previous damage associated with the accident. Let me remind you there have been shifts in the different tunnels and additional collapses. Everything's stable now, according to the engineers, but they were evaluating it based on how quickly they could repair it, not if a bunch of elves had a battle inside."

Zaena frowned. "Those shifts could have been caused by earth magic or an earthquake powered by a nexus."

Agent Lyle paled. "You can cause earthquakes?"

"Not the kind and scale you'd normally be worried about," Zaena told them quickly, regretting mentioning it. "This might only be a problem in a place like this. I can't see the average elf doing something like that since they'd be at risk."

Agent Lyle asked Lae'yul, "What about rogue mermaids?"

Lae'yul glared at him. "All of my people are accounted for."

"Hey," Agent Waves interjected and clapped once. "It's

like the princess said. It's all just us talking out of our butts until we get more information."

Zaena gave a firm nod. "Let's gather our tools and prepare for midnight. We will solve this mystery, and we won't let this human triumph be destroyed."

CHAPTER THIRTY-SEVEN

"Can you hear me?" Zaena asked in Elvish, pressing the transmit button on her radio.

"Once I change, this will be useless," Vokasin replied, also in Elvish.

"I can hear you, Princess," Lae'yul announced.

The agents weren't controlling the mission, but they were monitoring things. Zaena had made it clear she would be coordinating with her team without relying on English.

She didn't care right now. It wasn't as if the agents spoke Elvish. That alone would keep things secure.

Zaena stood at the entrance to the England-France rail tunnel in her armor, her sword on her hip. Midnight had come and gone seconds before.

"No one sensed a pulse of magic?" she asked. "I didn't, but I wanted to be sure a ritual hasn't started."

"Nothing," Vokasin confirmed.

"I feel the same magic as before," Lae'yul reported.

Vokasin was taking the France-England rail tunnel and

Lae'yul the service tunnel. She had a backpack with a few water bottles, though her tests had confirmed that water was running in the emergency lines. Her artifact shell necklace freed her from having to expend magic to breathe.

The more Zaena thought about what it would have been like to bring Min'tuk, the more logistical issues arose. She wanted every ally she could muster, but while the Night Elf enclave was under an island, it wasn't underwater.

"I'm initiating my patrol," Zaena announced. "From what Lae'yul found earlier, we have a couple of hours before we arrive at the most likely suspicious point."

"You don't want to fly there directly?" Vokasin asked.

Zaena understood his desire to have everything over with, but she didn't want to miss something in her haste. "We have plenty of time, and depending on what we encounter, we might regret using up magic. We need to make sure we don't miss any sigils."

"I suppose."

"This is also impressive," Zaena noted. "That the humans dug an underwater tunnel that goes so far. That's not something even we've done."

Vokasin scoffed. "Because we're not stupid enough to need something like this."

"Why would we Sea Elves build a tunnel like this?" Lae'yul asked.

"You can't deny it's impressive," Zaena countered. "We've always been fewer in number than humans, so we didn't need to spread out as they did. In that sense, and given our magic, such a project might have never been necessary, but they've not let a lack of magic stop them. They've turned a weakness into a strength by harnessing their minds to create machines that let them be as powerful as an elf."

Lae'yul let out a sound reminiscent of a growl. Zaena's heart rate kicked up.

"Have you encountered someone?" she asked.

"No, I was just thinking about your precious human technology," Lae'yul replied. "You show admiration for them rather than a more natural reaction."

Zaena looked around the tunnel. There was nothing but curved walls and rails.

"What's a more natural reaction?" she asked.

"Concern and fear," Lae'yul suggested.

"Why would you say that?" Zaena asked. "Your tribe were never cullers."

"The humans are different than they once were," Lae'yul complained. "The humans used to change slowly over the centuries, but it's faster now. When we were all born, the humans didn't even have trains, and now besides underwater tunnels for trains, they fly all over the sky in their machines and have even landed on the moon."

Zaena let out a wistful sigh. "That would be a wonderful experience."

Lae'yul snorted. "Don't you understand what this represents, Princess? My people chose the oceans because we believed humans could never get to us, but now they have submarines. There's nowhere that's safe left on this entire planet, from the ocean to the stars."

Vokasin chuckled. "Their technology is impressive, as are their numbers, but if we don't fight them for land, there will be no struggle. The enclaves haven't been discovered or breached. It's not as if we couldn't inflict pain. I won't fear them because of their toys."

"Our needs were met in different ways," Zaena noted. "We didn't feel the need to push forward and rely on their kind of tools, but that's not a bad thing, nor is their advanced technology. The lack of parity was what caused so much tension. Things are different now."

"Yes," Lae'yul replied. "Now they outnumber us like a vast, nuclear-armed horde."

Zaena shook her head. "We're here with the help of government agents. That provides proof that not everything must end in pain and violence. We're providing an example of coexistence, combining elven magic and human technology to solve a problem."

"You can't be so naïve as to think it'll go this easily in the future," Vokasin suggested.

Zaena snorted. "Why not? When I started this mission, I was fairly certain that many of my tutors thought it was nothing more than a way to dispose of an unplanned and unnecessary princess on an errand of dubious possibility."

"You're saying they were lying?" Vokasin sounded amused.

"No. The rituals are all the result of careful research and experimentation, but a single elf uniting the tribes and gaining their trust after all these centuries? It sounds absurd when you think about it."

"You lacked confidence in your mission?" Lae'yul asked, sounding disgusted.

Zaena laughed. "Of course not. I would have never set out if I believed I was destined for failure. It's only after my early success that I've come to realize how fortunate I've been. If either of you were different in your fundamental natures, I couldn't have recruited you. I was lucky that Vokasin was an artifact bearer. I begin to wonder how much of our success is the hand of fate."

"A convenient belief." Lae'yul snorted. "You sound like the priestess."

"Perhaps, but it's not as if everything has come easy," Zaena noted. "I had to deal with Mark Wong before meeting either of you. I'll admit several battles came closer than I would have liked. Less arrogance and more preparation could have led to his victory."

"You've given up on fate in seconds," Vokasin noted.

"No. I've learned that fate can give one a hand, but sometimes *it* needs a hand."

The sensation of warmth had grown in the past few minutes. Zaena couldn't attribute it to the others, given the direction.

"You feel it?" she asked.

"Yes," Lae'yul and Vokasin answered in unison.

"We're not that deep into the tunnels," Zaena replied. "We should have at least another thirty minutes by my estimate. We're also nowhere near dawn."

Vokasin laughed. "Finding our target early is hardly unwelcome, Fourth Born. Someone might have come out of a nexus."

"I don't see anything yet," Zaena replied.

"There's something ahead," Lae'yul reported.

Zaena frowned. "What's the last service access door you passed?"

Lae'yul offered the number. Zaena had fallen behind. There was another access door in about a hundred yards.

"What is it?" Zaena asked.

"I—"

Static swallowed the rest of Lae'yul reply. Strong magic pulsed ahead.

Zaena blasted toward the nearest access door. "The accident wasn't in the service tunnel."

Another wave of magic marked Vokasin's movement. "Things have shifted, Fourth Born. It's time to adjust the plan."

"I'll meet you there." Zaena poured power into her flight and screamed down the narrow tunnel.

CHAPTER THIRTY-EIGHT

Barreling through the tunnel at top speed brought Zaena to the next service tunnel access door in less than thirty seconds. She cushioned her turn with an air shield, saving her armor from scraping as she passed through the heavy metal door.

There were no rails in the service tunnel, just a road and the occasional stray cart or crate. When she turned to head toward Lae'yul's last position, she threw up her hands and stopped herself with a powerful burst of air.

Mud, rock, and cement blocked most of the tunnel. The top and sides were undamaged. A crack in the bottom appeared to be the source of the material.

The magic she'd sensed had grown stronger. Based on what she'd felt earlier, Lae'yul must have been behind the obstruction.

Zaena spun when she felt a magic source rapidly approaching from behind. She drew her blade before spotting the fluttering cloak and burning smoke of Vokasin. He turned his body and landed in a run before skidding to a halt.

She turned back around and pointed her blade at the blockage. "Lae'yul, can you hear us?"

There was no response from the comm. Zaena's heart thundered. Lae'yul was a strong warrior. She wouldn't be taken out so easily.

"Where is she?" Zaena asked. "She should be here."

Vokasin frowned, then pointed at a thin line of water droplets running along the road to the blockage. Zaena hadn't noticed them.

"She might have moved fast to avoid getting trapped," he suggested, nodding at the blockage.

Zaena looked around the tunnel. Scuffs and scratches were everywhere. It was hard to tell what was new and what wasn't.

Raising her blade, she fed magic into amplifying her voice. "Lae'yul," she thundered. "Can you hear us?"

A scratching noise sounded from the other side of the blockage, along with an odd clacking. Zaena didn't know what to make of it, but she couldn't ignore the powerful source of magic coming their way.

"That doesn't sound like Lae'yul," she observed.

Vokasin summoned fireballs in both palms and offered her a grin. "He will come, but not without pain. Our little priestess is proving far too accurate."

A chunk of debris blasted toward them. Zaena jumped back and lifted her blade. Another part collapsed, and a huge barbed, jointed leg poked through. A few yards in length, the red and dark-green limb was covered with a hard exoskeleton and fine hairs.

More hammering as the owner of legs collapsed the wall, revealing a giant spider that filled most of the diameter of the tunnel. It scuttled forward and clicked its mandibles before abruptly stopping. Three cloudy eyes, one red, one green, and one blue, were covered by intricate arcane sigils and glowed brightly. Bright white sigils also scribed the bottom of its body.

"An Eyed." Vokasin shook his head in disbelief. "I was always disappointed these had become extinct before I was born."

"Apparently, they didn't," Zaena noted, peering past the monster. "I don't see Lae'yul."

There was no sign of a body. More disturbing, there was no sign of a hole that would have accommodated the monster. She hoped that meant it'd collapsed back in, but another mass of mud, dirt, and rock sealed off the rest of the tunnel.

"Hearing about a legend isn't the same thing as seeing it," Vokasin noted, watching the monster and focusing on the eyes. "The legends say their bodies were far harder than steel."

"I wouldn't be surprised," Zaena replied. "It's giving off almost as much magic as a weak nexus. I wonder if we were sensing this thing the entire time. There were many tribes experimenting with such creatures during the wars. The Eyed were first created by Night Elves, but the Mountain Elves and the Ice Elves took to their use later."

The monster hadn't moved. It clacked its mandibles but stayed in the rubble of the destroyed blockage.

"Why isn't it attacking?" Zaena asked.

Vokasin shrugged but kept his arms in a position to

blast his fireballs into the beast. "Maybe it's no longer hungry."

"There would be signs if it had killed Lae'yul." Zaena crept away from Vokasin to make it harder for the spider to take them out with one attack. "We need to find her. She might be under attack by another. It's hard to tell with all the magic coming off this thing. It might have sealed her off so a comrade could attack her."

"We have only one choice," Vokasin stated.

"Indeed."

Zaena shot toward one of the spider's legs. It snapped forward and smacked her into a wall. It swung another, and she met it with her sword. The force of the blow sent her flying backward and left only a small scratch on the limb.

Vokasin launched his fireballs into the spider. When it reared, the spells exploded against its body but didn't seem to damage it.

Zaena hissed in frustration. "That thing is stronger than it looks."

"I wouldn't say that," Vokasin countered with a grin. "I think it's exactly as strong as it looks."

This level of battle-hardened and magic-infused monster pointed at a living creator. Zaena's hopes dimmed for a peaceful discussion with the Mountain Elf she suspected was responsible for releasing their attacker.

More magic pulsed from beyond the blockage. Heavier overlapping waves followed. Something worse than the Eyed lay deeper in the tunnel.

Zaena charged again, shooting herself to the side with an air gust to avoid the quick and powerful legs of her foe.

She swept her blade across its stomach, carving a thin line but not drawing any blood.

The spider reared back and tried to spear her with two legs. She launched backward, avoiding the blow.

"This thing shouldn't be active," she insisted. "Something sent it here."

Vokasin flung his arm up and conjured a circle of fireballs, which then surged forward and blasted the spider. It scuttled back a few yards.

"It might take more than a pretty speech to convince its owner to join you," Vokasin offered with a grim look. "I hope you're prepared for that, Fourth Born."

"I have no problem demonstrating might," Zaena said, "but there are two of us here, and Lae'yul is alone."

Vokasin's eyes turned reptilian. Scales shot over his body as his claws grew and his body contorted to his dinosaur form. "Go," he let out in a deep, growling voice. "I'll take care of it."

With a roar, he charged the massive spider. It battered into a wall, but he jumped off and ripped a deep gouge in its leg.

"Are you sure?" Zaena asked. "I'd rather not trade one ally in danger for another."

"I will not die from such a pathetic creation," Vokasin insisted. "She's not fighting in her preferred environment. She'll need more help than me."

He launched into an uppercut and smacked the spider's head. The spider reared back and let out a strangled hiss. Its mandible snapped in a resounding *crack*.

"Face me, monster," Vokasin growled. "Learn what a real beast is."

Zaena brought back her blade and channeled magic into it until it shimmered. She needed to get through the wall with one hit.

Vokasin growled and hissed as the spider slapped and prodded him, its spear-like legs gouging his thick scales. He clawed its arm, ripping chunks out and making the Eyed drip dull-orange blood onto the ground.

"I can win," Vokasin declared in a low, barely intelligible voice. "Go."

Zaena took the opportunity and flew past the spider. It spun and tried to pin her with a leg, but Vokasin charged its exposed abdomen and knocked it against the wall.

"I've got this handled, Fourth Born!" Vokasin shouted.

Zaena stabbed her sword into the dirt and mud wall, and it penetrated with a powerful roar. The wall blew inward. She could make out more glowing lights in the distance.

"Stay alive," she ordered and flew down the tunnel.

CHAPTER THIRTY-NINE

Zaena blasted forward at full speed and didn't look back. She had to trust Vokasin to defeat the Eyed. The vague glow she'd spotted from before resolved into a horde of smaller Eyed surging down the narrow tunnel. Her enemies were a yard in length, enough to be only bad dreams instead of chilling nightmares. They made up for it with their numbers.

A shudder passed through her and a distant possibility of what they represented threatened her stomach, but she refused to believe it. For now, it didn't matter where they had come from. She needed to kill them.

Lae'yul stood in front of the monsters, drawing streams of water from two ruptured pipes on either side of the service tunnel. They'd be easy to seal later, but for now, they were providing precious water for her defense.

Shards of ice lay scattered around the tunnel. It was obvious she'd attempted to block the spiders out, and they'd broken through her wall.

Blood stained her swimsuit. She raked the approaching monsters with a hateful gaze.

Zaena didn't stop flying, just created another air shell around her blade as she zoomed past Lae'yul and slammed into the horde. She twisted in the air and brought her blade down on the first of the new arrivals. It was blasted into mush, and the roaring shockwave sheared limbs off the others nearby.

Azure crystals spread across her victims within seconds. They glowed and then vaporized with a sizzle.

Zaena dropped to the ground and skidded to a halt, stunned by what she'd seen. She'd never heard of the Creeping Azure affecting anything but elves. Two spiders leaped for her.

Water tentacles snapped from behind Zaena and knocked the spiders back. The Creeping Azure disintegrated them as quickly.

She leaped back. Solving the magical mystery would have to wait until the end of the battle.

Even with all the magic emanating from the spider monsters, it was hard not to notice the background increase in magic. They were almost certainly close to a nexus.

Zaena slung an air blade with a wide swing of her blade. It carved into one of the smaller Eyed, knocking it back, but didn't kill it. Lae'yul launched a huge spear of ice that shattered over the surging horde. The deadly hail shredded their bodies and left them staggered. Air blades and ice spears downed a half-dozen in less than thirty seconds.

"Are you all right, Lae'yul?" Zaena asked.

"I'll live," Lae'yul replied, holding her arm out. A steady stream of tiny ice spears blasted from one of her water lines, whereas the other writhed like a tentacle that slapped and smacked any of the spiders that scuttled too close to their position.

One monster made it past Lae'yul's defenses. Zaena cut it in half.

"The legends of the Eyed spoke only of huge monsters, not these smaller ones," Zaena complained. "Did you see the larger one?"

"No. I was overwhelmed by these when I sensed something behind me," Lae'yul snarled. Her water tentacle whipped through the line. "Even you royals can't believe you have all knowledge of the hidden horrors of the past."

Air blades sliced and gouged the front line of spiders. A steady line of reinforcements continued to come from farther down the tunnel. They were surging into the service tunnel via the door to the France-to-England rail tunnel.

"You'd sensed something farther along before," Zaena noted. "We must be close to the source."

"So it seems," muttered Lae'yul. "It won't matter if they kill us first."

She dropped her icy machine gun to grow another water tentacle, then split her two larger ones into three smaller ones. They twisted and shot out, bashing and battering the advancing monsters. The blows didn't finish them, but the disrupted line was easy prey for Zaena's air blades.

"Are these monsters endless?" shouted Zaena before sliced two in half.

"I wouldn't doubt it," Lae'yul complained.

The Creeping Azure consumed and destroyed the remains of each monster, including their blood. At least they wouldn't have to worry about the humans having to clean up piles of horrors.

Three spiders rushed along the walls, making it past the water tentacles. Zaena shoved them into the air with a gust and sliced them apart.

The relentless glowing eyes, sharply pointed legs, and mandibles didn't give her enough time to think. All she could do was react. The only plan she could come up with was a pincer movement where she flew to the back of their formation and drew their attention, but Lae'yul might be overwhelmed in the meantime.

Distant explosions and the echo of a roar behind her proved Vokasin was still fighting. She didn't like that he was fighting alone.

A mass of spiders erupted from the doorway. She'd lost count of how many they'd killed, and there were no bodies left behind to help with estimates.

Lae'yul continued grabbing and tossing the spiders into their charging friends. Her efforts disrupted the front line, but it didn't slow them.

Zaena swung back and forth with furious speed, shoving out air blades as fast as she could manage. Not every attack finished an enemy, but she killed or wounded most.

Another loud boom echoed from ahead. She gritted her teeth.

"It must be another of the large ones," Zaena shouted.

Roars and explosions sounded from behind as well. Vokasin was still fighting his enemy.

"We should fall back," Lae'yul suggested, "or we should acknowledge this battle can't be won without extreme measures."

A spider jumped onto Zaena and bit her armor. She threw it off and sent it backward with a blast of air.

"Extreme measures?" she asked.

Lae'yul separated her water tentacles into a swaying hydra-like monster. She stared forward with her arms outstretched as spiders tried to surge past only to be snagged, whipped, or tossed. "We could flood the tunnel. I killed one early on by drowning it in a bubble. That's what happened; a single one leaped out and knocked off my radio. Many more came right after."

Two spiders stabbed Zaena. She hissed as one pierced her armor and her leg. She sliced through it before flinging the second back with a spell and then cutting through it.

"Angering three powerful human countries wouldn't be good," Zaena shouted, trying to ignore the throbbing in her leg, hoping it was a simple injury. She'd never heard of the Eyed being poisonous, but she'd never heard about having to face hordes of them, either.

The monsters of the past were supposed to have died with the past. It didn't help the details in legends and old books couldn't be trusted after so many centuries.

Lae'yul spun and avoided a spider before one of her water tentacles flung it in the air for Zaena to chop apart. "I'm not trading my life for us to be on better diplomatic terms with humans. They can build a new tunnel."

Another loud boom sounded. Something flashed blue

in the distance, farther down the tunnel past the door that kept spitting spiders. It was hard to make out, but some of the horde was moving in the opposite direction.

Had Vokasin defeated his enemy and flanked the rest?

No. It couldn't be. She could still make out the distant sounds and magic of his battle behind her.

"Keep them off me for a moment," Zaena ordered. "I need to see what's happening."

Lae'yul shouted in defiance and spread her arms out. Dozens of water tentacles filled the tunnel, pushing, yanking, and throwing monsters backward.

Zaena brought back her sword and moved the wrist of her free hand to produce a magnification spell. She refused to flood the tunnels, but a temporary strategic withdrawal might be necessary.

Peering deep into the tunnel, she gasped. She'd expected another large Eyed, maybe two, but instead, she saw a figure in blue armor riding a thin, flattened disc of gray rock. It had to be an elf.

The armored elf leaped off his platform. It reformed into a gray sword, and he grabbed it and cleaved through two spiders. His movements weren't as agile and elegant as Zaena's, but his powerful blows couldn't be dismissed.

"He's coming," Zaena declared, recalling the prophecy.

"What?" Lae'yul demanded.

"Another elf is attacking from the rear," Zaena noted. "We must press the attack."

"He might not be a friend."

Zaena dropped the spell and took a moment to charge an air shell on her blade. "He's friend enough for now."

CHAPTER FORTY

Vokasin roared and bit the leg of the huge spider hard. He punctured it and drew blood, but he couldn't rip it off. The spider whipped around the affected leg, slamming Vokasin against the roof. His thick scales blunted the impact, but pain reverberated through his body.

The monster tried to spear him with another leg. He dodged and raked the leg, gouging and carving into it with his claws. With a roar, he blasted fire from his mouth. It scorched the creature's eyes, forcing it to rear.

Vokasin let out a dark, deep chuckle, not that the monster could appreciate it. He'd left cuts all over its body. Blackened patches from fire breath had mottled its chitin.

Not that he'd escaped unscathed. Cracks in his scales and a puncture wound in his chest left him dripping blood. Despite that, this was the most fun he'd had since testing the princess.

No political considerations were holding him back, no deep concern about threats to the enclave or vengeful tribe members he needed to hunt. He was taking on a mindless monster that threatened both humans and elves. Removing it from the world would only help the cause of freedom.

The monster crouched. It'd gotten slower as a result of all the orange blood it'd leaked all over the ground. Strangely, that blood had crystallized and vaporized with increasing speed as the fight continued.

Vokasin needed to finish the creature and reinforce his allies. He had not brought the Sun Gem on the mission since he didn't trust the humans, so using it wasn't an option. That left him relying on magic and brute force.

A battle of attrition didn't favor him. His transformed body granted him strong damage resistance but not regeneration, other than by communing.

Keeping the creature busy until his allies returned would be an embarrassment. He needed to remind the other tribes of the power of a Desert Elf warrior.

Vokasin let out a loud, defiant roar. The giant monster scuttled back as if it were intimidated. Its mandibles twitched, and it didn't attack.

He ran toward the side of the tunnel. That snapped the monster out of its indecision. Its spear-tipped legs came down in rapid succession, leaving shallow holes and cracks in the concrete. The humans had more repairs ahead of them.

Flames erupted from Vokasin's feet, propelling him forward. It was hard to pull off nuanced spells in his transformed state, but he needed the speed. He skimmed the side of the tunnel, flew over a leg, and went for the monster's head.

The spider tried to smack him back, but he dropped, avoiding the blow. He twisted his body, letting his magic rocket him toward the eyes while he brought back his claws.

Vokasin pierced one of the eyes, releasing a shower of orange blood. He cared less about the wound and the rearing of the spider than the fact his claw was embedded deep in the head of the monster.

The spider stabbed him with two legs. He growled when the hits left scratches and peeled off scales, but he didn't let the blows dislodge him.

Instead, he flipped forward and wrapped his legs around the back of the monster's head, then lunged at the head. The first few glancing blows didn't do much except scratch the monster, but soon chunks of its carapace ripped away.

He found the soft tissue inside. The blows sliced deeper, with the giant spider thrashing and stabbing, trying to dislodge him.

Vokasin's claws ripped through the head to the other side. It didn't take him long to sever the rest. The monster collapsed, and he let go.

Blood dripped from several deep wounds on his body. Holding his breath, he moved a clawed finger toward the worst ones and conjured a thin flame. He roared at the white-hot pain from cauterizing his wounds.

Vokasin fell to one knee. Communing would help him later, but the battle wasn't over. Magic and shouts from the tunnel proved the princess and Lae'yul hadn't finished off whatever lay ahead.

Crystals spread over the defeated monster. They glowed and vaporized, taking the monster with it. He wasn't sure how much the humans were recording, but they'd have no specimen to examine.

"The Eyed are legendary," Vokasin growled. "So are we."

CHAPTER FORTY-ONE

The blue-armored elf continued his relentless advance with no sign of hesitation. Small spiders swarmed him, poking and biting his armor, but he threw them off and cut them apart with his blade.

Zaena and Lae'yul continued their advance, using much the same strategy. Now that the smaller Eyed had split their forces, they were having trouble overwhelming the elves.

After destroying several more, Zaena rushed toward Lae'yul's tentacle line. Wasting magic on air blades wasn't necessary as long as her Sea Elf partner could keep the creatures off her. She kept swinging, stabbing, and battering, leaving more creatures dead and disintegrating.

A familiar roar sounded from behind. Zaena smiled with triumph as the echoes of thudding footsteps preceded the appearance of the charging Dino Boy.

She'd worried about leaving Vokasin alone. The damage to his armor proved he'd had a good fight, but with four powerful elves converging on the monster horde, victory was all but assured.

Vokasin charged to the front line to rip through a leaping spider. Zaena matched him monster for monster.

Lae'yul shifted tactics. She pushed back the monsters with her tentacles before freezing thin ice javelins in groups of three to fling at them. She concentrated on piercing the monsters in the middle of the oncoming group, leaving Vokasin and Zaena to cut up the flankers.

Team Princess pushed on one side and the blue-armored elf on the other. The horde dwindled in number. The endless river had become a trickling stream from the rail tunnel.

Now that they were closer to the other elf, she worried that the blue-armored elf might try to fling an attack their way, but he paid no attention to Team Princess. He concentrated on cutting the spiders apart.

The trickle became a tiny group. Zaena and the blue-armored elf killed the final pair of small Eyed.

She took a deep breath and looked around. Scratches and gouges marred the tunnel, evidence of their battle, but the monsters had all vaporized.

Vokasin growled at the blue-armored elf. Lae'yul flowed water into a dozen ice javelins and floated them above her.

The blue-armored elf threw his sword to the side, where it hovered. His helmet retracted into nothingness to reveal a handsome dark-haired male with pale skin, almost certainly a Mountain Elf. Given the lines on his face, he probably had a few centuries on Zaena.

"The Armor of Tarilan," the Mountain Elf observed in Elvish with a huge smile. "I have one of the finest sets of artifact armor in the Mountain Elf Kingdom, and I doubt it lets me move as fast and grants as much strength and magical power as that legendary artifact."

"Is that an invitation to a challenge?" Zaena asked warily.

The Mountain Elf threw back his head and laughed. "What a feisty one you are, bearer of the Armor of Tarilan. A good battle is always appreciated, but I think we must save our strength for what might lie ahead."

He lifted his hand. His sword broke into tiny chunks that embedded in his armor.

Vokasin and Lae'yul stayed still. Neither relaxed their stance.

Zaena nodded slowly. "You claim no responsibility for these monsters? I'm willing to accept it if something got out of hand, but I need to know the truth so I can decide what to pass along to my human allies, who are concerned about the Chunnel."

The Mountain Elf's brow lifted. "You're dealing directly with humans? I didn't think a servant of the Tarilans would be willing to tolerate these sorts of monsters, so I didn't suspect you, but no, I came to hunt these creatures, not send them to harm people." He bowed his head with his fist over his heart. "I am Champion Darvane of the Granite Order of the Mountain Elf Kingdom."

Zaena resisted something unusual for her: snark. The Desert Elves and their obsession with freedom had made their breaking away from her people logical. The Sea Elves had sought a completely different environment. Even the Ice Elves' ancestors had tended different beliefs than the Forest Elves, but the Mountain Elves had broken away just to make a new monarchy. After everything that'd happened with Mark Wong, she couldn't help but wonder if the later culling had just been an excuse to support that.

The conversation reminded her about her equipment. She looked around for her radio, but it'd long since been ripped off her body. Vokasin and Lae'yul were also missing theirs.

Vokasin's cold, monstrous eyes flicked toward Zaena. "No battle is coming." When he shifted back into his elven form, he was paler than normal.

Lae'yul's spears melted into water before flowing into a giant bubble. She maneuvered it until it covered her head and the upper half of her body.

Zaena dismissed her helmet. "I am Princess Zaena vel Tarilan, First Princess and fourth in line for the throne of the Royal Elven Kingdom. These are my allies Vokasin of the Desert Elves and Lae'yul of the Sea Elves."

"Their tribes, and yours, are obvious," Darvane replied. He bowed his head again, this time deeper than before. "Though I offer my complete allegiance only to my king, I respect your position, Princess Zaena. I'm surprised to see a Tarilan royal out of their enclave battling creatures, but I suppose much has changed since our tribes regularly interacted. I'll admit I've been in and out of the enclave for centuries, and I've never run into another Forest Elf." He glanced at Vokasin. "The occasional Desert Elf, but no Sea Elves, either." He smiled. "You are all mighty warriors.

Excellent! That will make the rest of this hunt far less taxing."

Everything about Darvane was the opposite of the snide and hateful Mark Wong. Zaena was tempted to ask him about Mark Wong, but it wasn't the time or the place.

"I was wondering why the humans seemed to understand something unusual was happening, yet their soldiers weren't entering," The Mountain Elf said to Zaena. "You've forged alliances. Ah, you Tarilans never change."

"I have some contacts with human governments, yes," Zaena admitted. "They're aware of the tribes, though in a limited sense. Their help was necessary in case this situation got out of hand."

"Undoubtedly." Darvane frowned at a scratch on his armor. "I never expected so many Eyed to be here. This is my first time dealing with them. They were smaller than I'd been led to believe."

"Those were. There was a larger one farther back."

"Ah. You got to have all the fun."

Vokasin snickered. "Yes, I did."

Darvane's gaze flicked between the gathered elves. "This is far too amusing. A Tarilan princess leading a Desert Elf and a Sea Elf to aid humans. It's like a grand conclave of the tribes. We just need an Ice Elf."

"We have an Ice Elf priestess as an ally," Zaena offered, "but she's not part of this outing."

"Excellent!" Darvane let out a loud laugh. "There's so much I'd like to know, Princess Zaena, about how and why a Tarilan has gathered such rare immune allies in one place, but..." He looked uneasy. "You are all immune, aren't you?"

Vokasin and Lae'yul nodded. Zaena added her affirmation.

"Well, then," Darvane continued. He held out his arm to the side, and the stones flew out of his armor and reformed into a sword. "We've fought well, but this isn't over. This place didn't have a nexus I could sense the last time I traveled through here, and now it does."

"How long ago was your last trip?" Zaena asked.

"About ten years ago," Darvane explained. "This potential nexus caught my attention when I was involved in other duties. I'd assumed the Sea Elves were up to something, but I see now I was mistaken."

Lae'yul snorted. "Why would we create air-breathing monsters?"

"You can't kill air-breathers without air-breathing monsters," Darvane suggested with a shrug.

"Your tribes were cullers, not mine," Lae'yul noted. "We ceded the land to the humans and went on our way to avoid unnecessary bloodshed."

Darvane chuckled. "The distant past is simply that. I did worry that the humans had done something. I don't understand what, but that's the only explanation I have for the sudden appearance of this nexus and these monsters."

Zaena said, "Humans can create many things, but not magical monsters."

"They might have dug somewhere," suggested Darvane, "but I can't be sure."

"You mentioned duties," Zaena noted. "What are you talking about?"

"It's simple. As a Granite Order Champion, I hunt

monsters." Darvane offered the explanation like it should have been obvious.

"Are there that many monsters left?" Zaena asked. "The dangers I've encountered outside the enclave have been less than monstrous in nature until now."

Darvane rested his sword on his shoulder. "It's surprising how many there are, Princess. It's getting worse. It used to be I'd find a true monster only once every five or ten years, but these last forty or fifty years, I run across at least one a year."

"Is someone creating them?"

Darvane gave her a curious look. "I couldn't say. The monsters I've found are ones that I believe were sleeping for centuries, only to reawaken for unknown reasons. Humans have spread everywhere. They dig in the land and the sea and fly through the air. Ancient spells have a way of lasting. That might explain it."

"I know," Zaena replied. "I've found some strange and awful things in my short time on the surface, but you sound much more experienced. You're what, in your fifth century?"

"Yes." Darvane grinned, cupping his chin. "I'm glad my duties haven't aged me too much. Champion work can add a century to an elf's face, but I'm 504. I'd imagine immunity is no more common among your tribes than it is mine. I'm currently the only living champion immune to the Creeping Azure, so I must serve my given duty to travel outside the kingdom and hunt whatever strange beasts remain outside the enclaves and outside of whatever might be left in the enclave of the fallen tribe. Some things are just better left alone."

Zaena's stomach knotted. Every new elf she encountered on the surface reinforced that her tutors had massive gaps in their knowledge.

She looked at Vokasin. "You never encountered monsters in your time outside your enclave?"

"I wasn't looking for them," he offered with a shrug.

Lae'yul turned back to Darvane. "I don't understand. Why does your king care about monsters outside your enclave? What threat are they to the Mountain Elves?"

"He cares because our ancestors made mistakes, including creating monsters," explained Darvane. He gestured around. "I didn't get a close look at the sigils, but possibly this was an ancient stronghold of my people during the culling period. According to our records, Eyed were a favored monster of the ancient Mountain Elves. They liked to use them in combination with stone spiders, but it'd be hard to keep so many alive, even asleep, so I have my doubts."

"You're trying to redeem your ancestors' honor?" Zaena asked.

"Something like that," Darvane replied. "There's no reason to let monsters wander uncontrolled." He stared at her. "I'm proficient in human languages and blending in, but I've never formally dealt with human governments these few centuries. You're an interesting risk-taker, Princess."

"I have duties that necessitate it," Zaena replied. "We'll discuss them later."

Lae'yul's bubble lifted off her head. She scowled. "She's right. You said we didn't have time to stand around talking,

Mountain Elf. If this is a stronghold that has awakened, there might be more creatures coming."

"Oh, don't worry. You won't dry out, and you'll get your chance to kill more." Darvane motioned toward the door from which the monsters had emerged. "You all sense the nexus' magic, do you not?"

The others nodded in agreement. Zaena looked around for more sigils or hints of elven camouflage.

Heat scorched Zaena's skin. She gasped in surprise and dropped to her knees. Vokasin doubled over, and Lae'yul hissed. Darvane staggered as if struck.

It was magic—a massive amount of magic. That had been only the briefest pulse, but it was more powerful than any magic she'd felt in a long time. The sensation faded as quickly as it'd come, leaving the steady and powerful warmth of the nearby nexus. It felt weaker than the nexus controlled by Team Princess. The tunnel shook.

"What did you do, Mountain Elf?" demanded Lae'yul. She glared at him.

Darvane put his hand to his head and groaned. "I did nothing."

Vokasin shifted back into his reptilian form. "Someone else might be waiting for us."

"The polite thing to do is to greet them," Darvane suggested. His helmet reformed. "I'd only ask that if a Mountain Elf is behind this, you let me speak to them first, but I understand if this must end in bloodshed. There's one possible elf who might be behind it, but he preferred a different type of minion."

Zaena summoned her helmet, again thinking about

Mark Wong. "We will end the threat without violence if possible."

Lae'yul snorted. "Doubtful."

Darvane jogged toward the doorway, sword in hand. Zaena hurried after him, unsure about the whole thing,

She'd expected to find a Mountain Elf, but not one like Darvane. The pain part of the prophecy was arguably already over, but she suspected something much worse was coming.

CHAPTER FORTY-TWO

It didn't take long for the team to reach another suspicious pile of concrete, dirt, and rock. The intensity of the magic had increased, but it was coming from beneath them. Scattered construction equipment lay nearby, along with a small electric cart.

"This matches the reported location of the initial accident," Zaena noted, "but the information passed along didn't suggest a monster."

Darvane pointed his sword at the pile. "Our final enemy awaits."

"Are you reconsidering flooding the tunnels?" asked Lae'yul. "It's worth thinking about."

Zaena shook her head. "We can defeat Eyed, large and small, without flooding the tunnels."

Darvane lifted his sword. Rock and mud floated away from the pile and settled to the side. Zaena pointed her sword and started pushing debris to the side. Despite the impressive pile, they managed to clear it away quickly and reveal a jagged hole in the cement walkway against the service-side wall.

Zaena marched over to the hole and peered in. A soft blue glow emanated from below, highlighting a rough tunnel that had not been dug by magic or machinery. It'd be a tight fit, but the larger Eyed could have squeezed through.

"I don't understand how the humans could have the Chunnel here for years, and suddenly whatever's below became active," Zaena explained. "There's something we're not understanding."

"There's another elf," Vokasin concluded. "What's to understand?" He pointed a claw at Darvane. "I don't trust this one, but he had no reason to help us, which makes him less suspicious. The horde could have forced our retreat if that was his goal."

Darvane pointed toward the hole. "The only way to discover the truth is to go there. Fear is just another monster to slay." He jumped into the hole and landed in a crouch about five yards down. "It continues at an angle," he called up. "I see no enemies, but it's cramped. Should I widen the tunnel?"

A narrowing tunnel argued against the larger monster having emerged from it. The more they discovered, the more questions she had.

"No," Zaena suggested. "We don't want to trip any alarms." She turned to Lae'yul. "I'd feel better if I knew our rear was secure, and we can't be assured you'll have easy access to water down there."

Lae'yul agreed. "I will remain, Princess, but be wary of the Mountain Elf champion."

"I will."

Zaena floated into the hole. Vokasin shifted back to his elven form and leaped.

Darvane, Vokasin, and Zaena continued down the tunnel until it widened out and stopped. A metal wall densely inscribed with glowing sigils blocked further movement.

Zaena peered at the sigils and scoffed. "A four-element lock?" She concentrated on changing the direction of the air carrying her voice. "Lae'yul, come here. We need you."

The Sea Elf descended into the hole, carried by a tentacle of water wrapped around her waist. She wrinkled her nose and proceeded toward them, her scowl deepening. It must have been uncomfortable to be trapped in dirt and rock while moving farther from water.

Darvane tapped on the door. It sounded hollow.

"There is no elf who wields three elements, let alone four," he noted. "I'm now far less concerned about one of my brethren being behind this." He traced one of the sigils. "Princess Zaena, do you recognize the elements of the design?"

She stepped forward to inspect the fine details. Bile rose in the back of her throat. "It can't be."

Darvane stepped away from the door. "This isn't Mountain Elf; it's Night Elf. It's as I suspected. This must be a war hive."

"No!" Zaena shouted. "After they wiped themselves out with their cursed ritual, you know the history. The Desert Elves went their separate way, but my ancestors continued to look for war hives. Even if this was one of their monster factories, it couldn't maintain itself for centuries without Night Elves controlling it."

Vokasin gave a light shake of his head. "We both know that's not true, Princess. The memory gems and soul-binding proved it in the Mojave."

He was right. The isolation of the Royal Elven Kingdom hadn't only made them ignorant about humans. The Mountain Elves had been sending people like Darvane to explore the world with far more freedom than her tribe. Mark Wong's ability to fit in made more sense now.

The Night Elves should have been extinct, along with their influence. She was tired of them returning to rub her nose in the hateful past.

Darvane shook his head. "This is the first war hive I've encountered, but it's not the first champions have found throughout the centuries. You should know I was one of two immune champions charged to defeat monsters outside the enclave by our king. The other champion was killed twenty years ago, taking on a war hive."

"Near here?" Vokasin asked.

"No. It was in Siberia. She managed to destroy it, but it cost her her life. Word of what she'd done was passed along to human allies in a nearby village. I later talked to them and learned what had happened."

Vokasin snickered. "I thought you were impressed with Zaena for seeking human aid."

"A small village of respectful humans is far different than a greedy government," Darvane countered, "and I did admit to blending in."

Zaena punched the tunnel wall. "Will this world never be free of Night Elf wickedness?"

Darvane looked at Zaena and Vokasin. "I don't understand how soul-binding could make this place active, but you two have clearly encountered something I haven't."

"I recently had to deal with the soul of an insane and murderous Mountain Elf," Zaena admitted. "Bound into a village and feeding off the souls of others of his tribe. He'd lived far longer than our natural span."

She watched Darvane, curious about his reaction. His respect for her surprised him, but she was going beyond hunting monsters and pointing to evil in his tribe.

"I see." Darvane gave a curt nod. "I trust you've already handled this monster?"

"He's been handled," Zaena replied. "We might be dealing with something similar. I've been worried about it ever since that encounter, that there might be a Night Elf sleeping without a body, but if this is a war hive, it explains everything other than why it decided to wake now."

"Does it matter?" Darvane asked. "Find the monsters. Kill them. It's easy. Then find the heart of the war hive and disable it."

Zaena took a deep breath. "This goes beyond monster hunting. Are you willing to turn on your old allies?"

Darvane grasped his blade with both hands and held it in front of him. "My king ordered me to hunt and destroy monsters. Anyone creating them has the choice to stop or die." He pointed his sword at the door. "We're accomplishing nothing by standing here."

"Wait." Zaena looked around. "There's not enough space in the tunnel for the horde we killed, yet this door is closed."

"That magic we felt must have been this place shutting down," Darvane suggested.

"I'm not sure about that," Zaena admitted.

"Let's open it back up," Darvane replied. "We'll need to ensure the monsters are no longer a threat."

Zaena looked at Lae'yul. "Once we open it, my earlier request stands. We might need to retreat to the upper tunnels, depending on what we find."

Lae'yul raised her palm. "Are you certain, Princess? What if this is part of the other prophecy?"

"What prophecy?" Darvane turned toward her. "Sea Elves have mastered the art of prophecy? Things have changed among the other tribes."

Zaena would have preferred Darvane didn't have that information yet, but she was trusting him enough to walk into a war hive and fight at her side. "She's not the one with the power of prophecy. Our other ally is."

Darvane laughed. "Oh, I see. Princess, you've let some Ice Elf convince you of nonsense. I've not run into one myself, but I see they haven't changed their strange ways."

"It's not that simple," Zaena insisted. "That prophecy led us to this place on this day, and another prophecy spoke of unearthing past sins and the awakening of great beasts." Her head bowed. "In particular, the last of the great beasts will awaken, and the world will be forever changed as the ghosts of a dead race try to rise again." She ground her teeth. "What is this war hive but a past sin birthed by a dead race?"

"You're here," Darvane replied. "I can't question that. Eyed are dangerous monsters, but no one would call them great beasts."

Lae'yul snorted. "There could be one on the other side of this door."

Zaena raised her head and squared her shoulders. "Then we *must* open it. Better to face it while it's contained than after it's escaped and killed hundreds if not thousands of humans."

Darvane pointed his blade at the door. Dirt from the ground swirled around the tip and shot toward an earth-marked sigil. "We have a fine and brave team. Let's test your Ice Elf's prophecy."

Zaena channeled air into the air sigil. Vokasin produced a stream of flame. Lae'yul's backpack had long since been lost, so she brought a small stream of water from above and shot it toward the lock.

With a shudder, the door slid open. Bright blue light spilled out.

Zaena walked forward, flanked by Darvane and Vokasin. She was expecting something elaborately carved, not the oblong chamber covered with throbbing blue vines covering the floor, walls, and roof. Wide but rough tunnels ran in all directions from every portion of the chamber. Every few seconds, the vines flashed, and ghostly sigils blinked in and out of existence.

Despite the intense magic washing over them, the nexus pulled them in one direction. She no longer had any doubts. Darvane was right; this was a reactivated Night Elf war hive.

"Your fellow champion," Zaena began. "You said she brought down the war hive. How?"

"From what she told the villagers before she died, she had to fight off the monsters there," Darvane explained.

"She also explained something they passed onto me. We don't have to use overwhelming power to destroy this place. I know how to shut it down." He sucked in a breath. "There's one problem, Princess," Darvane noted. "The method might cause these tunnels to collapse in on themselves. We'll have to be fast in our retreat."

"It's time for our past sins to sink back into history," Zaena muttered.

Darvane laughed. "I'm beginning to like you, Tarilan."

CHAPTER FORTY-THREE

Zaena didn't like that all the tunnels were so wide. She didn't want to carve her way through the war hive, but the facility seemed like it'd been dug for creatures much bigger than the horde of spiders they'd fought. She now understood how the larger monster had gotten to the tunnels above.

The only saving grace was that they ran into nothing over the next few minutes. Surprisingly, they reached the heart of the nexus without any trouble.

The crimson sphere was in the center of the room, resting in a nest of overlapping blue vines piled in an irregular shape. Unlike the nexuses she'd seen before, there were no sparks, but translucent and ghostly sigils swirled around in a dense, overlapping mass.

Zaena moved closer and her breath caught. Bits of shriveled flesh and smooth bone peeked through the vines. The roots grew out the mummified remains of an elf. Whatever clothes they'd worn had long since been lost to the hungry centuries.

"What is this abomination?" she spat. She looked at Darvane.

"I've never seen anything like it. The villagers didn't mention anything about this, but they might not have been told about it."

"This is true commitment to their cause," Vokasin suggested. "Assuming this is the body of an immune Night Elf."

"I've never heard of war hives having anything like this at the heart. Did this elf die with the rest of their power when the ritual failed?"

"Most likely," Darvane suggested. "From what I was told by the villagers, my fellow champion disrupted the control sigils with a combination of fire and air magic. Fortunately, she wielded both."

Zaena sighed. "The war hives destroyed during the war relied on huge armies of elves. That might be our only chance to stop it without unnecessary deaths."

"It won't be a quick process," Darvane noted. "Once it's finished, we'll need to flee quickly if we don't want to get trapped here."

Zaena pointed her sword at the sigils. "I'm ready when you are, Vokasin."

He raised his palms. "What an unfortunate resting place."

Her air magic mixed with fire to create a swirling fire devil over the nexus. It scorched the vines and set them alight. Tremors struck the chamber. Clicking and scuttling noises echoed from all around.

"I think I know what we felt earlier," Zaena suggested. "A new batch being created."

Darvane gripped his sword tightly. "Bring it down, Princess," he offered in a cheerful tone. "I'll kill anything that comes close to us."

Smaller Eyed poured out of tunnels in the ceiling and the sides of the room. Zaena continued fueling the fire devil with Vokasin but shot air blades with her free hand at approaching monsters. Vokasin raked the wall with small fire blasts while fueling the tornado.

Darvane threw his sword into the air. It broke into three pieces and shot toward different parts of the room. Each portion sliced through a spider and ripped out its innards. He moved his arms like he was conducting. His three stone blades danced through the air, slicing up the monsters surging into the room.

Zaena presumed he hadn't done it before for the same reason she hadn't fired two streams of spells in the tunnel; it was incredibly draining. She wasn't sure how long she could maintain this.

The room continued shaking. Sigils winked out of existence around the nexus. This wasn't a proper attunement disruption, but this investigation had provided one unexpected revelation after another.

Orange blood splattered the chamber. It didn't last long before the Creeping Azure, if that was what it was, destroyed the dead spiders and removed the evidence of their existence.

The vines in the room began to dim and shrivel. More of the sigils faded out. The tremors intensified. Spiders surrounded them.

Darvane split his blades apart again. Six blades sliced through the room, doing their deadly work. He spun, screaming in defiance. Two of the blades stayed near the tunnel they'd entered through. No monsters were coming in, but he was cutting up any spiders close to it.

Half the sigils had vanished. Zaena lifted off the ground to avoid getting knocked over by the intense shaking. They'd lost so much light from the dying vines that they were now relying on the uneven illumination of the fire devil and Vokasin's blasts.

Time blurred. The Eyed horde seemed endless. Fatigue sapped Zaena. A couple of legs from a dead spider bounced off her, but she ignored them. They needed to take down this horror show. Only a quarter of the sigils now remained.

A spider bit Zaena's shoulder, then two of Darvane's blades decapitated it. She ignored the pain of the injury and didn't bother to dislodge the head. The Creeping Azure would take care of it.

The last of the sigils disappeared. There was no light left in the vines. Vokasin summoned a dancing ball of flame near the exit tunnel.

They didn't need it. Spiders fell out of the tunnels, twitching and covered in crystal. They flashed and shattered, vaporizing and filling the room with glowing blue dust.

"Retreat!" Zaena shouted.

Vokasin rocketed toward their entrance tunnel. Darvane's sword fragments flew together and flattened into a disc. He hopped on top of it and flew over Vokasin. Once the others hit the tunnel, Zaena zoomed after them.

The shriveled vines blew apart with a loud pop. The

tunnels started caving in. They burst out of their entrance as it collapsed and headed toward the open exit doors.

A huge chunk of the roof dropped toward Zaena, then jerked to the side and knocked another piece out of the way. She spotted Darvane pointing his sword in her direction.

They flew through the entrance in seconds, and the rest of the roof collapsed. The door sealing it slammed close and shimmered. Dirt and rock flowed over it.

Vokasin didn't stop. He charged through the final tunnel and back up to the rail line tunnel. Darvane followed him up. Zaena leaped into the top-level tunnel just ahead of a massive plume of dust. The whole area continued to shake for a half-minute before stopping.

She waved dust out of her face. "That was both far easier and far harder than I expected."

CHAPTER FORTY-FOUR

Zaena sat down beside the hole and willed her helmet away. "Your aid proved invaluable, Darvane."

"You're welcome, Princess." He bowed with his fist over his heart.

Vokasin stared at the hole. "What do you intend to tell the humans?"

"Enough to satisfy them," Zaena suggested. She looked around for cameras. "They've undoubtedly been watching this, but it remains unclear to me how much of the tunnels are under direct video surveillance. I can't guarantee they haven't seen Darvane."

His helmet shrank. "From what you've told me, they know about the tribes. My king has not authorized me to deal directly with any human government, but if your human allies already know about elves, I see no problem with informing them a Mountain Elf helped to solve a problem. It's not as if you know where the Mountain Elf enclave is."

"That's true." Zaena smiled. "I am thankful for your aid.

We've all taken wounds today, but none we can't recover from."

"Before we part ways, tell me, Princess. Why are there so many tribes working with you?"

"Because I carry the hope of our entire race," Zaena offered. "My mission isn't to hunt monsters. My mission is to cure the Creeping Azure."

She gave him the concise version of her mission, including explaining that she'd need a Mountain Elf to bring their Thunder Opal for their ritual.

"You have the other artifacts already?" Darvane asked.

"I have commitments from the other tribes or their artifact bearers," she explained. "I've yet to raid the Night Elf enclave. We were saving that until we earned the agreement of the Mountain Elves. I didn't know how you might react, and I was worried you would be hostile."

"Because of the soul-binding incident you mentioned?" Darvane asked.

Zaena stated, "I've already encountered another Mountain Elf. I don't know his true name, but he had an artifact mask that let him control memories and minds. He was in control of the nexus in San Francisco, but he chose to use the power to lead a human gang. I tried to reason with him, but he was power-hungry and murderous."

Darvane's brow lifted. "You killed him?"

She agreed. Lying wouldn't serve any purpose. The only chance of gaining the cooperation of the tribes was behaving honorably.

He scoffed. "I know the elf, and I briefly suspected him of being behind this incident." He frowned. "I *knew* the elf you encountered. I'm not surprised to hear he reached such an end. We always suspected he stole the Mask of Intention, but there was no one near the enclave when he left it who could follow him. I and the other champion spent some time looking for him, but it was not our primary duty." He smiled and clapped her on the shoulder. "If you worry that you've offended our people, don't. I've not known you long, but I've seen you in battle, and it's told me what I need to know about you."

Zaena smiled. "Then you'll cooperate? You'll join us with the Thunder Opal?"

He gave her an apologetic look. "I am not the custodian of the Thunder Opal, and I can't give you my commitment. The king must make that decision. I must travel back to my enclave and consult him."

"I see. Can you give me any idea when you might return?"

"There are other places I must investigate, but I will come to your White Ruby Building when I have time."

"Shouldn't you hurry, Mountain Elf?" Lae'yul suggested. "We are close to curing the Creeping Azure."

"My king decides my life and course," Darvane insisted. He offered her a bright smile. "I can pledge to bring news within three months."

Zaena nodded. "It's not my place to ask for more. Thank you for your assistance."

Vokasin stepped forward. "The tremors might have worried the humans. We lost our communications toys.

We should return to the agents, so they know what happened."

"That's true. Again, thank you, Champion Darvane."

He waved. His form shimmered and disappeared. "It was an excellent battle, Princess. Take no offense, but I will not meet with your human allies."

"Do as you must and come back soon."

Sitting comfortably in a sedan with tinted windows, Agent Lyle pinched the bridge of his nose while his partner stared at Zaena slack-jawed. "Let me get this straight. You're telling me there was a damned monster nest under the Chunnel?"

Zaena agreed, "Yes. That's an accurate summary."

"It's destroyed? We're still coming up with a cover story, but we do appreciate that you didn't trash the place. It's not going to be as nice if we have to go and do pest control."

"The creatures and the mechanism of their creation have been destroyed." Zaena smiled. "There's a nexus there, but the control magic for the nest has been disrupted. It can't be easily reconstituted without incredible effort by many elves, and the tunnel system beneath your tunnels has been destroyed."

"Okay. That's good to hear, I guess." Agent Lyle swallowed. "I think I liked it better when it was just mind-control gangsters we were dealing with."

CHAPTER FORTY-FIVE

Zaena reminded herself to talk to Saelli about redesigning the chairs in the nexus chamber. She sat in one and offered a satisfied smile to Saelli, Vokasin, Lae'yul, Grace, and Karl. They'd only been back in San Francisco for a couple of hours, but it was as good a time as any to discuss everything that had happened that week.

Karl finished explaining his ghost incident with Conroy's men. "Yeah, Conroy is already talking about pleas, so I'm not worried about him."

"You should just kill him," suggested Vokasin. "Dead men pose no threat."

"Leaving a trail of bodies can be annoying," Karl replied with a shrug. "It took me a while to get to the point where the cops weren't looking at me, and don't worry—everyone's rolling on everyone. We should circle back to what Zaena said. I'm not an elf, but I can't be the only one worrying why a monster factory turned back on all of a sudden."

Zaena furrowed her brow. "It continues to trouble me, and I don't have a good explanation or even a decent theory."

"You're sure this Darvane isn't playing you?" Karl gave her a stern look.

"He had many chances to betray us," Zaena noted. "He didn't take them. He could easily have buried me in that place as it collapsed. I don't know what it all means, just as I don't know why the Creeping Azure was killing those monsters."

Karl frowned. "It doesn't automatically kill anything magical?"

Zaena shook her head. "It didn't do that in the past. I don't understand much of what I saw in that place, but the Night Elves always practiced dark and twisted magics."

"Wait." Karl gestured around the room. "I get how archaeologists haven't found tons of elf skeletons because the Creeping Azure eats them, and there's not enough of you immune types otherwise, but what about monsters? If they weren't destroyed in the past, why weren't we finding them?"

"You have, in some cases," Zaena noted. "Why do you think so many of your cultures have legends about dragons, giants, and horrific sea creatures? You haven't always done a good job of preserving the remains. Occasionally humans have pulled up a monster skeleton, but they always assume it's something else. Your species has a remarkable ability to ignore obvious evidence."

Lae'yul folded her arms. "The element lock needed four elements, but the monsters came out. Was it open before?"

"We'll never know," Zaena stated. "There's no way Darvane could have done it."

Grace cleared her throat. "It could be like a human security system, a failsafe to make sure elves didn't get trapped inside. When it was inactive, it was open, and the monsters didn't dig out until something woke them up."

"That's what bothers me," Zaena continued. "I don't believe those monsters were asleep for thousands of years. I believe the war hive was asleep, and that's the only reason we weren't overwhelmed by an army. I think it created batches of new monsters, but only recently."

Karl scoffed. "From what you told me, it was an army, complete with tank-sized spiders."

"A fully active war hive is far more terrible," Zaena noted. "A handful of elves wouldn't have been able to handle it. We would have been killed."

Vokasin said, "It doesn't matter. It's destroyed. Why worry about what it wasn't?"

"Because we can expect similar horrors in the Night Elf enclave," Zaena explained with a grim expression.

"Your ancestors have been there more than once," Vokasin replied.

"That doesn't guarantee they disabled every war hive, and I know they left behind some monsters because it was more trouble than it was worth—in their estimation— to hunt them." Zaena went on, "We have time to wait for Darvane, but the next step is going to the Night Elf enclave. What we fought in the Chunnel wasn't a great beast, which means it'll be there."

Saelli offered a nod. "You fully believe now, Princess?"

"Yes, I do, which means I think we'll need human help." Zaena frowned. "However, the location poses an issue, given my existing relationships."

"Why is that?" Grace asked.

Zaena sighed. "Because my human allies are all American, and although I'm far from an expert on human geopolitics, I doubt if the government of Vietnam is prepared to allow a large American military force into their territory."

Karl grimaced. "The Night Elf nexus is in Vietnam?"

"More specifically, it's underneath an island that Vietnam controls," Zaena explained. "You see my dilemma."

"Well, the US is on decent terms with them nowadays," Grace commented. "Yeah, I see what you're talking about. I doubt a diplomat could show up and say, 'By the way, some elves want to poke around in a dead ancient magical city in your territory. Can we park an aircraft carrier by them to be safe?'"

"Huh." Karl snorted. "Should we let the agents know?"

Zaena answered, "I think it's necessary, but not right away. We'll pass it along and see what they can come up with, but perhaps we should wait until Darvane returns. That way, we won't create any unnecessary friction with the American government."

"There's nothing to do here for now." Vokasin stood. "I will come back in the future."

"You could help us strengthen the defenses," Zaena suggested.

Vokasin inclined his head toward Saelli. "Her magic is better suited to that than mine." He walked out of the chamber and stopped at the entrance. "What if the Mountain Elf king says no?"

"I refuse to believe he'll ignore the obvious advantage of working together to free ourselves of the Creeping Azure," Zaena insisted.

"I see. Let's hope your faith is justified."

CHAPTER FORTY-SIX

Zaena flew up the basement stairs, threw open the door, and sprinted toward a side door. She was grateful she'd spent much of the last month working on defenses, including alarm wards. They were mostly limited to the nexus area, but any unexpected magic used on the grounds now caught her attention.

She didn't summon her armor. Although she knew it wasn't Lae'yul, Saelli, or Vokasin because of their nexus attunement, it might have been Min'tuk. Threatening an ally didn't make sense.

Zaena slowed and approached the side door. Someone magical stood on the other side. She flexed her fingers, heart thundering, ready for everything.

The intruder knocked.

It turns out she was ready for almost everything. She'd never anticipated he'd knock.

Zaena raised her hand and flicked her finger. She stayed down the hall and opened the door to the outside. A gorgeous dark-haired man in a bright orange Hawaiian shirt and cargo shorts stood on the other side. He was licking the stump of a vanilla ice cream cone.

She let out a sigh of relief. His ears were disguised, but that didn't make it harder to recognize Darvane.

He stepped into the building and closed the door behind him. Zaena brought up a sound curtain.

"You said you'd be back in three months, not one," she observed with a smile.

Darvane grinned. "I believe I suggested it'd take up to three months, Princess, not that it must." He took another lick of his ice cream cone. "Be aware that things have become complicated."

"What does that mean?" Zaena frowned. "Has your king refused to aid our mission?"

Darvane shook his head. "No, not yet." He finished the ice cream and munched on the waffle cone beneath. "His Highness is presenting you an impressive offer, Princess. He wishes you to visit the Mountain Elf enclave to negotiate with him face to face. You'll be our first guest in centuries."

Zaena's eyes widened. "You're going to show me where the Mountain Elf nexus is?"

"It's not as if you're in a position to invade by yourself," Darvane explained. He kept a happy smile on his face. "The only real threat is humans, and if for some reason they find out, they might also happen to find out the locations of the Desert Elf and Forest Elf enclaves."

"You know where they are?" Zaena asked, doubt in her voice.

"Your people have always been less secretive than others, and the Desert Elves are more devoted to freedom than security, despite what they think." Darvane sighed. "I apologize, Princess. I've been ordered to deliver that message, but I don't believe you will engage in that kind of behavior. We're all talking now for the first time in centuries, and it makes no sense for us to fall back into the petty patterns of the past when we can free ourselves of the Creeping Azure." He finished the cone and swallowed. "The truth is, Princess—and I choose to share this with you—we've known where your kingdom is for a long time, but we saw no reason to contact you. When our most recent king ascended, he became reform-minded, but these things move slowly. We might have reached out to you in a few decades, but this provides a good opportunity. If you swear on your honor not to tell the humans, we can make the trip soon but not immediately."

"What about the others?" Zaena asked. "If this is about establishing open relationships, it makes sense to bring Lae'yul and Vokasin. Saelli's a more complicated case." She averted her eyes. "There's instability among the Ice Elves. She's partially at the center of it."

Darvane agreed. "Politics are the bane of warriors like us, Princess. For now, the others can come if they wish, but only your elven allies. No humans, even the ones here." He reached into a pocket and pulled out a slip of paper. "I'll be staying in town for a few weeks, enjoying it. It's been a while since I've been in America. Call me if you need help with monsters, but otherwise, I'd like to be left alone. I have another hunt soon."

Zaena shook her head, trying to clear it of all the competing thoughts. "When can we go to your kingdom?"

"November," Darvane explained. "I think after thousands of years, waiting for a few more months won't hurt."

"Thank you," Zaena offered. "I know you didn't have to advocate for this plan."

He waved and opened the door. "We all benefit in the end from your success, but thank you, Princess, for not being what I feared."

"What did you fear?" she asked."

"That you'd be an arrogant, delusional princess with an impossible dream."

Zaena laughed. "I think that's an accurate description. Incidentally, the same offer extends to you. Not to visit the kingdom, not yet, at least, but if you need an ally to slay monsters, you have my sword."

Darvane stepped outside. "I might take you up on that."

She stood there for a while, soaking in the news. A visit to the Mountain Elf enclave was so important that she might need to risk a trip back to her enclave to report the news.

"I might not have their commitment, but it's coming," Zaena whispered. "Freedom is coming."

AUTHOR NOTES

SEPTEMBER 10, 2011

First, thank you for not only reading this story but these notes in the back as well.

Michael Anderle, who would normally write these notes, is on a four-state road trip with our own Craig Martelle. Since his psyche is being abused enough during this period, I offered to write these in lieu of his trying to find his scattered wits across four states and put something coherent together.

Ever wonder what it's like to work with Michael Anderle? Well, I can give you some hints, at least from my perspective.

First, you have to understand that he runs an international organization, so almost everything is done on Slack, a team collaboration platform. This allows Michael to run in, drop some sort of bomb ("What do you think about...") and then scuttle back to his safe writer/publisher's garret.

Leaving you scrambling to come up with a reasonable

answer to his latest madness. That man is nothing if not creative!

He does the same thing in Zoom meetings, where Bethany Anne looms large behind in cardboard to reinforce his every whim (He really does. It's one of those statues). "What do you think about us changing the whole direction of the company? We could...hang on..." Then he has to take some call and leaves you with that thought, expecting an answer the next time you talk to him. Or he has forgotten all about it. You never know, which keeps you on your toes.

The long-suffering Stephen Campbell, aka ZenMaster Walking™, has had to put up with this much longer than I have, since he came in almost at the beginning. Apparently, Steve used to be a ginger, but those who know him understand that every one of his white hairs was caused by Michael.

OK, that's not true. Maybe only three-quarters of them.

Time to get serious. Michael has assembled the most amazing team and process at LMBPN, which you, the readers benefit from. It all starts with him. He sincerely wants to put out the best entertainment he can, and it reflects through his management/admin team, his JIT and beta teams, his art team, and all his other teams. Everyone who works with Michael is here because they love what they do, which is as scarce as hen's teeth in today's world.

I'm proud of what we've accomplished, and I'm glad to say I'm part of it.

Hope you enjoy it too! Michael will be back for Zaena's next adventure.

Ad Aeternitatem,
Lynne Stiegler

BOOKS BY MICHAEL ANDERLE

Sign up for the LMBPN email list to be notified of new releases and special deals!

https://lmbpn.com/email/

For a complete list of books by Michael Anderle, please visit:

www.lmbpn.com/ma-books/

CONNECT WITH MICHAEL

Website: http://lmbpn.com

Email List: http://lmbpn.com/email/

https://www.facebook.com/LMBPNPublishing

https://twitter.com/MichaelAnderle

https://www.instagram.com/lmbpn_publishing/

https://www.bookbub.com/authors/michael-anderle

Printed in Great Britain
by Amazon